PRAISE FOR
UNHOOKED

"This dark, violent, gripping, and twisty retelling of Pan
is so good, there's no going back to the original!"

—Ellen Oh,
author of the Prophecy series

"Lisa Maxwell's [Unhooked] spins the classic Peter Pan *tale
into a tempting, spine-chilling adventure. Maxwell transports
readers into the haunting, and yet breathlessly romantic,
world of Neverland that will spellbind readers into
making them wish they could stay forever."*

—Christina Farley,
author of the bestselling Gilded series

"Perfect for fans of A.G. Howard's Splintered *trilogy and
ABC's* Once Upon A Time, *this twisted* Peter Pan *retelling
isn't the Neverland of your dreams—it's the
Neverland of your nightmares."*

—Sara Raasch,
author of the Snow Like Ashes trilogy

Also by Lisa Maxwell

Gathering Deep

Sweet Unrest

UNHOOKED

By Lisa Maxwell

SIMON PULSE

New York London Toronto Sydney New Delhi

SIMON PULSE

An imprint of Simon & Schuster Children's Publishing Division

1230 Avenue of the Americas, New York, New York 10020

First Simon Pulse hardcover edition February 2016

Text copyright © 2016 by Lisa Maxwell

Jacket photo-illustration copyright © 2016 by Steve Gardner

Jacket photograph of ship copyright © 2016 by Getty Images/John Lund

Jacket photograph of clouds copyright © 2016 by Thinkstock

For information about special discounts for bulk purchases, please contact
Simon & Schuster Special Sales at 1-866-506-1949 or business@simonandschuster.com.

The Simon & Schuster Speakers Bureau can bring authors to your live event.

For more information or to book an event, contact the Simon & Schuster Speakers Bureau
at 1-866-248-3049 or visit our website at www.simonspeakers.com.

Jacket designed by Karina Granda

Interior designed by Steve Scott

The text of this book was set in Bodoni Book.

Manufactured in the United States of America 0116 FFG

2 4 6 8 10 9 7 5 3 1

Library of Congress Cataloging-in-Publication Data

Names: Maxwell, Lisa, 1979-

Title: Unhooked / by Lisa Maxwell.

Description: New York : Simon Pulse, [2016] | Summary: "Gwen is kidnapped to an island
inhabited by fairies, a roguish ship captain, and bloodthirsty beasts—and she must save their
Queen before it's too late" —Provided by publisher.

Identifiers: LCCN 2015013296 | ISBN 9781481432047 (hardback) | ISBN 9781481432061 (eBook)

Subjects: | CYAC: Fantasy.

Classification: LCC PZ7.M44656 St 2016 | DDC [Fic]—dc23

LC record available at http://lccn.loc.gov/2015013296

FOR KATHLEEN,
WHO BELIEVED IN
THIS STORY FROM
THE BEGINNING.
THANKS FOR SAYING
YES TWICE.

Whatever the stories may say, not all
children grow up.
Some lose their lives before their milk teeth.
Some run away.
Others are taken.
Many leap headlong, tempted by a tale
of who they might be . . .
Never to find that other shore.

Once upon a time, there was a boy not so very far from being a man. He crossed a sea to venture to London, for he wanted to find his brother, who was the bravest of soldiers. He carried with him only a light pack, for he had every intention of returning. . . .

CHAPTER 1

OUTSIDE THE RAIN-SPLATTERED WINDOW of the taxi, London looks like it's dressed for a funeral. The streets are a blur of monotone gray, and the sidewalks are filled with commuters scurrying home under dark, faceless umbrellas. When the car turns away from the main road, we find ourselves in a neighborhood of empty streets that shine darkly in the rain, the quiet houses still waiting for their owners to return.

The driver makes one more turn before stopping at a corner and glancing over his shoulder at the three of us in the backseat. "One-Thirty-Three Gloucester Road," he barks as he stops the meter.

My mom doesn't make any move to get out of the cab. She's sitting in the seat across from me, chewing absently on her thumb. Her eyes are wide as she stares out the window, but I'm not sure she's actually seeing anything.

1

"I think we're here," I tell her gently, and she blinks over at me, like she's startled to find me there.

My best friend, Olivia, looks up from her phone and peers out the window of the cab to see where we've stopped. Her brows bunch together as she stares out through the rain. "Are you sure this is it, Gwen?" she asks, not even bothering to disguise her disappointment.

I'm not really surprised the house doesn't meet Olivia's expectations. She grew up in the sort of place that can only be called an estate. Before my mom decided to move us to London, we actually lived in her family's gatehouse, while my mom worked on commissioned art for Olivia's parents—pretty much anything would be a disappointment by comparison. But when I lean over to see the building Olivia's looking at, my stomach sinks.

One-Thirty-Three Gloucester Road stands apart from the other brick and stone buildings that crowd the street. Narrow alleys flank either side of its redbrick walls, almost like the other houses don't want to get too close. Its peaked roofline soars at least one story above its flat-roofed neighbors, and its chimneys claw toward the gray sky. A wrought-iron balcony on the third story looks like it's barely holding on to the ivy-covered brick, and one of the windows on the second floor has been boarded up.

"Are you sure this is the address you were given?" I ask my mom, who by now has also noticed where we've stopped.

"I . . . think so." Her face betrays only the slightest bit of uncertainty, but her hands shake as she searches through her lumpy oversize bag. It seems like her hands always shake unless she's holding a paintbrush, especially lately.

Finally she retrieves a worn envelope and pulls out the contents. A deep crease forms between her brows as she looks over the papers.

"Let me see," I say, taking the rumpled sheets when it's clear she's having trouble finding the information she wants. Which is just another sign of how overwhelmed and anxious she's been recently—she's looked at those papers so many times in the last few days that they're creased almost to tearing.

Ignoring the way she's picking nervously at the hem of her coat, I scan through the narrow script to find the address that's been arranged for us by her newest commission. Then I lean forward and check it with the driver. He gives me a gruff confirmation before opening his door to start helping us with the bags.

In the seat next to me, Olivia has gone very still. I think she's suddenly realized her hastily conceived decision to invite herself along to help us move might not turn out quite the way she'd expected.

"I guess this is it," I say, breaking the silence that has overtaken the cab. I hand the envelope back to my mom.

Her eyes meet mine as she takes the papers, and her mouth presses into what might be the start of a smile. Her expression is so expectant, and I know she's waiting for me to say something. Because, usually, this is where I'd paste on a smile of my own and make the best of things. This time, I just stare back at her.

Her expression falters, and she looks away before I do.

Without another word, she steps out of the stuffy warmth of the car, pulling the hood of her jacket up against the rain.

But I don't follow her. Not right away.

I'm used to ending up in all sorts of odd places—a trailer park in Sedona, a shacklike cottage near a beach in Costa Rica infested by tiny lizards (which, thankfully, ate the not-so-tiny bugs), a gorgeous jewel box of a studio apartment in Prague. My life has been a series of poorly timed moves for as long as I can remember. But something about this place has me pausing.

"You know my parents would let you live with us back in Westport," Olivia whispers when I don't get out of the car. "We have plenty of room, and they're never around enough for you to even bother them. You don't have to move. Or live here. I mean, it's less than a year until you're eighteen, and I *know* we could convince your mom—"

I shake my head before she can say anything more. It's not that her offer isn't tempting. It is—*too* tempting. For the last week I've been hoping Olivia would offer this exact thing, but now that she's holding out a different future like a lifeline, I can't seem to grab hold. I see the way my mom's slight shoulders are swallowed up by her coat, the way her hands clench nervously as she supervises the driver unloading our bags, and I know I need to stay.

"You really want to spend our senior year here?" Olivia asks, surprise clear in her expression.

"No." I shake my head. *Of course I don't.* But I'd been stupid to think our life in Westport could last. For the first time since I could remember, I'd felt almost at home some-

4

where. With Olivia's friendship as a shield, I never had to prove myself like I had in so many other places. I'd almost felt like I finally belonged.

But even if I could convince my mom to let me go back with Olivia—which is more than doubtful—I can't just leave her.

"She doesn't have anyone else," I explain to Olivia for the thousandth time. And neither do I.

"You can't give up your life for her, Gwen." Olivia's voice is gentle, like it always is when she makes this argument.

And I get it, but . . . "I know. I won't," I say, trying to convince myself as much as her. "But I need to make sure she's settled here. I have to know she's okay before I leave."

Olivia stares at me with those bottle-green eyes that see more than most give her credit for. "Your mom might never be okay," she says gently. "What about college?"

I have no idea. "I have a year to figure that out," I tell her, which is what I've also been trying to tell myself. "A year to get her ready."

Olivia frowns, like she wants to say something more, but she doesn't. She knows me well enough to know when not to push.

There's nothing else I can say, so I give Olivia a shrug and get out of the taxi. The air is thick, and the rain feels cool against my cheeks. Even though the driver has already started to take our bags to the front porch, my mom hasn't moved to follow him. She's staring up at the dark facade of the house, like she doesn't even notice the heavy drops falling from the gray sky.

"Why don't you go wait on the porch, and I'll help with the

bags?" I say, nudging her gently in the direction of the house. Her eyes are tight with worry when they meet mine, and for a moment I think she'll argue. But she doesn't. Instead, she fishes some crumpled pound notes out of her purse and offers them to me before she shuffles toward the house.

As the driver returns from depositing the last load of our luggage, Olivia still doesn't look like she's going to get out of the car. With her dad's credit card in her wallet, she could be at the airport and on a first-class flight back to her own life before I even unpack. Our whole friendship could be nothing more than a story about this girl I once knew, and I wouldn't blame her at all. It's what people do, isn't it? They move on. They forget.

But a second later, Olivia surprises me by climbing out of the car's dry interior. She hitches up her hood and gives me an impish grin before running for the rusted gate. Even with the rain soaking me, I can't help but laugh.

By the time I've paid the driver and I'm ready to follow them up the wide steps to the arching front porch, my jacket is completely soaked and my short hair is plastered to my head. But with Olivia waiting, somehow I don't feel quite as cold.

"Ready?" my mom asks once the taxi disappears around the corner. Her hands tremble at her sides, like she's having second thoughts about knocking. Or maybe she's just waiting for my approval. Usually, we'd be in this together, but this time I haven't been able to fake it. This time I don't want to.

"It'll be fine," my mom says as she knocks on the heavy door. Her voice sounds like she's swallowed something bitter and hard that hasn't quite worked its way down her throat.

And I can't tell who the words are meant for. "We're safe," she whispers to herself.

As we wait for someone to answer, I pretend I didn't hear her.

My mom knocks again, this time harder, but it seems like no one is home. Olivia shoots me a doubtful look as we stand huddled in the entry, and I adjust my worn duffel bag on my shoulder and try to look confident. But the truth is, I'm not sure what my mom will do if no one answers. She's not exactly good with the unexpected.

Then, just as I'm about to suggest that we call another taxi, a shuffling comes from within, followed by the mechanical *swish-click* of locks receding. After the third lock releases, the door lurches open to reveal a small, wizened man with glasses so thick, they make his cloudy eyes appear three times larger than anyone's should be. I'm barely five feet, and the man isn't any taller than I am. I can't help but think that if goblins were real, he could almost pass for one.

"Yes?" His voice grates across my skin as he looks us over. I can only imagine what he's seeing. We make quite a trio with my mother's wild red hair and even wilder, paint-marred clothes; Olivia's classic beauty; and me, in my exhausted and rumpled glory. His eyes rest on me last, and his nose gives an odd twitch. His stare is a little too intense to be comfortable, and from the scowl on his face, I can tell he finds something about me lacking.

I glance away and resist the urge to smooth down my soaked jacket.

"Arrangements have been made for us to lease your flat," my mom says, thrusting the creased papers toward him.

The man stares at her for a long, awkward moment before he finally takes them from her outstretched hand. He reads one sheet and then the other, and when he's finished, he glances up at us. With another questioning look at my mom, he jerks his head toward the interior and disappears into the house.

My mom follows him without too much hesitation, but Olivia grabs my arm. "Are you sure about this?"

Of course I'm not sure. I give her a halfhearted shrug. "I guess we should go in," I say instead, avoiding her eyes as I follow my mom into the house.

*Inside the smoke-darkened barroom, the boy could scarcely believe that the soldier who sat across from him was the apple-cheeked brother he'd once known. His brother sat stiff and straight, his eyes like flint even as he smiled. "I'm not frightened," the solider assured the boy. **Neither am I frightened**, the boy thought to himself. . . .*

CHAPTER 2

INSIDE, THE ONLY LIGHT COMES FROM A DIMLY burning chandelier fitted with what look to be gaslights. My mom is already speaking in hushed tones with the goblin-shaped man, so I let my bag slump to the floor and dump my jacket on top of it as I take a look around. I'm not surprised to find the rest of the house is as gloomy as the sky outside.

Everything about the place feels old and worn-out. The air has the thick mustiness found in closed-up attics or forgotten parts of old libraries. Which, actually, isn't a bad description for what I'm seeing, because everywhere I look the walls are covered with all sorts of junk. Ornate mirrors, decorative plates of all shapes and colors, ancient-looking portraits of stern men and unsmiling women. The carpets are worn dull and smooth from age, and the woodwork has lost any bit of shine it might have once had.

Olivia's shoes scuff into the hallway behind me, and despite my misgivings about the house, I relax a bit. She didn't leave. Not yet, at least.

But she will, I remind myself. In two weeks she'll be gone. And I'll still be here. At least until my mom decides it's time to move again.

"Is this place for real?" she whispers over my shoulder.

"Unfortunately," I say.

She takes a few steps to examine one of the oil paintings on the wall. Its surface is barely visible from a combination of age, soot, and dust. She swipes at the surface and then rubs her finger and thumb together to smudge away the grime.

"It could be worse," I offer, trying to keep my voice light, but my throat is too tight even to pretend optimism.

"Gwen—" Olivia starts, but thankfully, my mom's voice interrupts us.

"We're all set," my mom tells me, and I realize with some relief that her voice—her whole demeanor, really—has changed. It's finally started to take on the usual steel each of our moves normally begin with. Sometimes that calm, focused determination will last months before it starts to crack. It can last longer if she's working on a project or one of her commissions—in Westport it lasted for more than two years.

"My rooms are back there," the small man is explaining as he jerks his head toward a hallway behind the large central staircase. "If you need anything . . ."

"Thank you," my mom murmurs, but I know she'll never take him up on his offer. Once her supplies arrive, she'll keep to herself and her art, like she always does. Until something sets her off and she decides we need to run.

"Come on, then." Assuming we'll follow, the old man turns to the stairs and starts up. When we reach the second floor, he pulls out a large ring of skeleton keys and uses one to unlock the first door we come to. "This 'ere's the flat."

The door swings open, and he steps inside a room that smells like it hasn't been aired out in at least a decade.

With a wet snort, he looks around the sparsely furnished apartment as though approving of what he sees. I can't imagine why—the apartment looks like it was last lived in about fifty years ago. "The other bedroom is this way," he says. Without bothering to make sure we're following, he heads farther into the darkened flat.

We follow him back through a narrow hallway lit by the strange and ghostly glow of more gas lamps and up another staircase so narrow, we have to climb single file. At the top, though, we find a room that is surprisingly airy. Here, the ceiling follows the sharp point of the roofline, and windows line the far wall, helping to make the space feel more open. Even with the overcast skies outside, this room is by far the brightest place in the house.

A studio, I realize. Because my mom will need the light to work.

The lower level of the apartment had been decorated by someone who had a thing for avocado green, but the décor in this room might be original—it looks Victorian and seems to have been untouched by any previous tenants. The walls are washed in a soft blue, and a large bed stands against the back

11

wall. A massive carved fireplace that now houses a small heating unit takes up most of the wall to the right.

On the wall opposite the fireplace is a large and intricate mural. Time has faded its colors, so the design is barely an impression of its former beauty, but even so, it's striking. Wispy figures that look like they might have once been beautifully rendered fairies dance beneath flowered trees as bright, starlike orbs swirl around them.

"What is *that*?" my mom asks. I've heard her sound less horrified with the lizards we lived with a few years back. There's a strangled quality to her voice, like her panic is already wrapping its fingers around her throat, even as she tries to pretend she's calm.

It hasn't even been an hour. Our boxes haven't even arrived yet.

She turns on the landlord, her eyes fierce. "Is this some sort of joke? Because it's not—"

"It's just a painting," I tell her gently, touching her shoulder before she can finish.

She flinches away, her words forgotten. She never wants me to touch her when she's like this—I should know that by now. Still, her rejection stings.

"This room used to be a nursery." I can feel the old man lurking too close behind me. "Course, it's been a lot more since, but no one never could bring themselves to get rid of the wee folk."

My mom turns back to the mural. "I can't stay here," she whispers in a ragged voice. Her unease feels like a living thing snaking through the room, but I don't understand her reaction. The mural is beautiful, charming even. "And I can't work here. Not with them watching and—"

"Mom," I say gently, before she can work herself up too much more. "It's okay."

She turns on me, her eyes wide and wild, and I sense Olivia stiffen beside me. She knows my mom can be eccentric, but I've managed to hide most of this from her. Two years, and Olivia has only ever seen the aftermath. She's been there when I turn up exhausted and at the end of my rope, and she's never asked the questions I know she wants to ask when she lets me stay the night at her house.

"You see them, don't you?" my mom asks me in a strangled whisper.

"I see them just fine," I assure her. "We all see them. It's a painting. That's all it is."

She shakes her head, her mouth set tight as her eyes dart between the mural and me. "I can't work here," she says again. "Not until they're gone. I won't stay here."

"You don't have to." I try to reach out for her again. "We can go back to Westport. It's not too late."

"No." Her eyes are hard and almost accusing as she takes another step back, jerking away from me again. "It *has* to be here. It's been arranged. But this room . . ." She's no longer looking at me. She has eyes only for the wall, and I know what she's thinking—she needs to work. Hers might never be calm or easy paintings, but those canvases are the way she keeps herself centered. She needs to create, or she will lose herself bit by bit to her fears and delusions.

"I can't," she whispers over and over as she shakes her head, and I know that if I don't stop this, things are going to get bad, fast.

"We'll get some paint to cover it, then," I say, trying to calm her down. I look to the old man for assurance. He gives a halfhearted shrug, which is close enough to permission for me. "Olivia and I will stay up here tonight, okay? Tomorrow we can talk about painting it or going somewhere else."

I hold my breath and wait as my mom stares at the mural for a long unsettled minute. Part of me hopes she won't agree, that she'll decide this place is all wrong, but then she gives a small nod.

"We can paint over them." She finally looks at me again, and I see her slowly coming back to herself. "We *need* to stay here," she says, her blue-gray eyes serious.

"We'll deal with it tomorrow. Tonight Olivia and I will sleep up here. It'll be fine. Right, Liv?"

"Sure, Mrs. Allister. We'll be great," Olivia says, stepping forward and giving my mom a quick hug. My mom doesn't pull away from her.

"See? All settled." I touch my mom's shoulder again, feeling her muscles quiver as she forces herself to not jerk away from me like I'm one of the monsters she imagines. I pull my hand back and give her the space I know she needs as I try to ignore the bone-deep loneliness I feel in a room filled with people.

"Is there a way to turn this thing off?" Olivia asks as she walks over to get a better look at an antique sconce hanging over the bed. The lamp is an elegant twist of glass that reminds me of a fluted flower. As she examines it, the orange-red flame throws a strange glow across Olivia's upturned face. Like the lamps downstairs, it's burning even though there's plenty of daylight left.

"It ain't safe to turn it off—" the old man starts with a growl, but then he stops short, like he's just said something he shouldn't have. "Old lines and all. Never can tell what would happen," he finishes, his voice only a bit softer. "Besides, it's tradition to keep it burnin'."

"Leave the lamp be," my mom says softly, her voice still filled with worry.

I look over to find her staring at the fairy wall again, one hand slightly outstretched. I can't tell if she's reaching for it or pushing it away.

"I assume everything's in order, then?" the old man says.

When my mom doesn't answer, he eyes me.

"Yes," I say, trying to smile. "Thank you."

"Right." The old man seems satisfied enough as he leaves us alone in the attic room.

"He's not serious about the light, is he?" Olivia asks, her brows bunched.

"I think he was," I tell her. Because I don't know how I'm supposed to explain that there's always *something* in each of the places we've moved to. Rows of stones carved with protective runes. Lines of salt or iron nails buried at the four corners of the property. Crystals hanging from the windows or, this time, lights that must always remain burning.

"I guess we should start bringing up the bags," I say, glancing at Olivia.

"He's not going to get them for us?" she asks, and her confused expression is almost enough to lighten my mood.

I shake my head. "It shouldn't take us too long. The rest won't be here until tomorrow anyway."

"Right," Olivia says, shooting me a concerned look. I give her a subtle nod to let her know I want a second to talk to my mom before I follow. "I'll just get started then," she tells me, heading toward the stairs.

I hesitate, waiting to see what my mom will do. But she only seems to have eyes for the fairy wall. It's like I'm not even there.

"We could still go back, you know," I say, taking a step toward her. "We could get you some help. I'm sure Olivia's mom knows someone at the hospital who could—"

My mom glances at me, and the look on her face makes the words die in my throat. "We're safe now," she whispers. "Everything will be fine."

"We were safe in Westport," I say with more bitterness than I mean to let slip. "I was happy there."

My mom frowns, like she doesn't really understand why I'm pushing her on this. "I know you were, but . . ." She doesn't finish her thought, but her brows pinch together. "This is the right thing to do," she says finally. "You'll just have to trust me."

This is where I'm supposed to say, *Of course I trust you.* But I can't. Maybe in a few weeks, after the rawness of being torn away from the life I'd dared to make for myself has eased, but not yet. "This won't be the last time, will it?" I ask instead.

My mom has never said any of our moves would be the last. She's never even pretended, and I've never asked—

16

only hoped. But this move is different. This move doesn't feel like me and my mom against the world. This move feels like me and my mom against each other. This time, I need to know.

She gives me a wobbly sort of smile, and in that moment I understand Olivia was right. If I stay with my mom, my future is destined to be a series of never-ending moves. It will be a life without any true home or any lasting friendships. And if I leave? If, once I'm eighteen and legally free to go, I walk away? I'll lose the only family I have. Because my mother will never stop moving. Not as long as she believes there are monsters chasing us.

When I start to turn away, she catches my hand. "Gwen," she says, turning my name into a plea, like she understands where my thoughts have gone. She lets go of my hand long enough to take a bracelet from her own wrist and slip it onto mine. "You're nearly grown, you know," she says, brushing my damp hair back from my face. "It's time you have this."

I pull my arm away from her and examine the bracelet. It's one I've never seen her go without—blue-gray stones almost the exact color of her eyes. They aren't quite round, like pearls, but they are smooth and almost translucent. When I was little, I used to love running my fingers over the cool, wobbly stones as I counted them.

"You don't have to," I say, because I'm not sure I want this. It feels too much like a bribe. *Here, have this bit of glass and forget all the things I'm pulling you away from. All the things you're leaving behind.*

"Take it," she insists. "Your father gave it to me, and now I'm giving it to you."

"My father?" I glance up at her, surprised. She's never told me that about the bracelet.

"He wanted me to keep you safe, Gwen," she says, which is the only explanation she has ever given me for anything when it comes to my father. As far as explanations go, it stopped being enough a long time ago.

"If he wanted me safe, he shouldn't have left," I toss back.

My mom's face pinches into a scowl, and her whole body goes rigid. "He didn't want to leave," she says. "He did it to protect us. To protect *you*."

Of course. Because it's always been my fault that the love of her life left.

I start to pull off the bracelet, but she stops me by putting her hand over mine. "No, it's yours now. Don't ever take it off. Promise me."

Not a gift, then—a shackle. Another burden I'm supposed to carry for her. I frown but don't argue. There's no point in it.

Olivia finds us locked in uneasy silence when she returns with one of her carry-ons and my duffel. "Everything okay?" She glances at me for the answer.

"Fine," my mom replies. "Everything is going to be fine."

"I brought up your bag," Liv tells me.

"Thanks," I tell her, glad for the excuse to turn away from my mom. The bracelet feels so much heavier on my wrist than the small stones should feel.

"I suppose I should help with the rest," my mom says to no one in particular.

When my mom's finally gone, Olivia glances at me. In her expression I can see the questions she wants to ask, but she hands me the bag instead. "Rain stopped," she tells me. "Want to go for a run?"

When the others had gone home from the pub and it was just the two brothers, the boy leaned forward eager to know more. "Do you kill many?" he asked. His brother smiled, his crooked tooth winking in the dim light. "Tons," the soldier said. Perhaps, if the boy had been paying attention, he would have noticed his brother's eyes weren't laughing. Perhaps he might have realized it was like they no longer knew how. . . .

CHAPTER 3

BY THE TIME WE CHANGE AND MAKE OUR way down the front steps, the evening air is still damp, and a light mist has settled over the streets. Neither of us says much as we work through a few stretches on the sidewalk in front of the house.

When she feels like she's ready, Olivia glances over to me. "The map I looked at said there's a park not far from here," she says. "Want to check it out?"

"Lead the way," I say, glad she hasn't brought up anything about my mom's behavior.

She gives me a sure nod and takes off.

I follow without a word, and with the first few steps, I start to feel the tension draining out of my muscles. For the past week, ever since my mom announced we were moving, I've felt like I was holding my breath and waiting for something even worse to happen. But as my shoes connect with the uneven sidewalk in a steady tempo and my arms swing at my side, I feel like I can breathe again.

Running is how Olivia and I met. When I first moved to Westport, we'd see each other on our separate routes, and then somehow we started leaving together and following the same route. Eventually we started talking and discovered we had more in common than the running. Her parents might be rich, but they aren't there for her any more than my mom is for me.

We never really talk while we run, though. She runs with a focus I don't have—a better mile time or more calories burned—I'm not exactly sure what drives her. But I run because when I'm pushing myself, when I'm only worried about the next mile or if I can make it back without stopping, I don't have to think about anything else.

At one point I glance over at her, and she gives me an almost smug smile. She'd known I needed this, and she'd been right.

By the time we're both breathless and exhausted, the sky has gone darker, and a wet fog has settled over the park. "Which way do you think the house is?" I ask when we come to a place where a couple of paths intersect.

Olivia considers the options. "I don't know. I'm all turned around," she says, just as we hear the soft rumble of thunder off in the distance. "But if we don't hurry, we're going to get caught in that. Come on." She loops her arm through mine, and we pick a direction.

Her steps are brisk, and my tired legs struggle to keep up with her long strides. We haven't gone very far when she stops. "I think I see someone," she says. "I'll go ask."

"Olivia, wait—" I start to call, but she's already off, jogging toward the person she thinks she's seen.

There's not much else I can do but follow her. But when I see who she's found, I slow my steps.

With her long tangle of white-blond hair and the jewelry cluttering her wrists and fingers, the girl Olivia's found reminds me of a very pale gypsy. She's wearing a long skirt and a purple velvet turtleneck that seems strange for June, even on such a cool day. And I can't shake the feeling that there's something off about her. Maybe it's her eyes—it looks like she's wearing deep, glossy black contacts that give her an almost alien appearance. Or maybe it's that the way she's looking at Olivia seems too intense—it reminds me of the way a hungry animal would watch its dinner.

I barely catch myself as I stumble at the abruptness of that thought. That's *exactly* the crazy sort of thing my mom would think. The girl's kind of odd-looking, sure. But she doesn't *really* look dangerous.

Taking a deep breath, I force myself to catch up with Olivia, but when I'm only a couple of feet away, I stop short again. It's such a small thing—the flick of dark eyes as the girl glances at me, and then the flash of teeth as she smiles knowingly. Certain.

It's not the obvious fakeness of her brittle excuse for a smile that stops me from taking another step. No, that would be understandable. Explainable. What stops me cold and makes the skin on the back of my neck prickle in warning is that the gleaming white teeth peeking from behind the girl's lips look like they've been filed down to jagged points.

I force myself to blink the image away. I *have* to be seeing things. It must be a trick of the light or the fog, because it's not possible for a beautiful girl to have a grin as sharp and wicked as a shark's. But if I'm starting to see things . . .

I open my eyes, and the girl's teeth are once again hidden behind her plump lips. She looks normal . . . mostly. Strangely dressed, but normal. I must have imagined it.

Just like your mom, a small voice deep inside me whispers.

No, I think, silencing that voice. I am *not* like my mom. I wouldn't *be* like my mom. I would get help. I would get better. And, besides, this is all perfectly explainable. What I saw is just the effects of too little sleep. Or maybe I'm just keyed up from a good run.

But I can't shake the feeling that the air suddenly feels more dangerous than it did a few minutes ago. Real or imagined, I feel so uneasy that I don't want to stay anywhere near the girl. Even though my legs feel like jelly, I want to turn around and run, and I want to keep on running until I've put days between us. The feeling is so strong, so sure, it takes everything I have to force myself to walk the final few steps to where Olivia is standing, still talking to the blonde.

Olivia's not acting like there's anything at all strange about the girl. She's not staring at the girl's teeth or backing away from those predatory eyes. And she doesn't seem to notice that the air around us feels suddenly alive with dangerous electricity.

You are overreacting, I tell myself. Not that it helps.

I can't make myself pretend that everything is fine. I want to get away from the girl. I *need* to get away from her. Now.

"Come on, Liv," I say, tugging at her sleeve. "We need to go."

Even as I speak, I can feel the eyes of the blonde on me, sharp as needles digging into my skin.

Olivia pulls away. "But she was just telling me—"

"We'll figure it out on our own," I say, tugging at Liv again. The prickling across my skin is suddenly sharper, more painful, and when I look up, the blond girl is staring at me openly now. Her eyes are such an unnatural black that panic spikes in me, and my heart feels like a winged thing trapped in my chest. It's enough to spur me on, and with another sure tug, I finally get Olivia to follow me toward the main path.

"What's gotten into you?" Olivia asks, pulling her arm away.

Now that I'm away from the blonde, the panic I'd felt in the girl's presence has eased some. "I don't know," I say honestly, glancing back to make sure we haven't been followed. "I just had a feeling about her." I know it's weak as explanations go.

"A feeling?" she says doubtfully.

"I can't explain it. I just—" I falter, unsure of how to explain what I felt without sounding like I've lost it completely. I'm still not sure whether what I saw or felt was even real. I settle on an apology instead of an explanation, but before I can even get the words out, the pricking sense of danger I felt near the blonde returns.

All at once, the air smells of ozone, that almost electric scent that signals a storm is near. But it isn't rain I'm sensing. There's something more dangerous sifting through the air around me, brushing its cool fingers against my skin and ruffling the hair at the nape of my neck.

Then I hear something.

If I wasn't already on edge, I might have missed it completely. The sound is faint at first, like the rustling of dry leaves kicked up by the wind. But there is no wind. The fog hangs undisturbed in the air around us, even as the sound grows.

"Do you hear that?" I ask instead of giving Olivia the explanation she was expecting.

Though she looks confused at the abrupt change in subject, she doesn't question me. She listens for a moment before shaking her head. "I don't hear anything. What does it sound like?"

I stare at her, willing her to hear it too. Because the sound is so loud now, I can practically *feel* it vibrating against my skin.

But it's clear Olivia doesn't hear anything. Just like she didn't see the girl's teeth.

"Are you okay?" She steps closer, examining me with a concerned expression. "You look even more pale than usual."

I swallow hard. All around me, the sound has taken on a metallic edge and grown louder, like whatever is making it has surrounded us. "It was probably just the wind," I force myself to say, but the words come out stiff and an octave higher than I intend. "Can we just get back to the house?"

She cocks her head and narrows her eyes at me. "What's going on, Gwen?"

"Nothing," I say, trying to pull myself together. "It's been a long day, and I just got a little spooked or something." I try to laugh it off, but I can't force out anything but a dry cough. Not with the danger I still feel filling the air around us, not with the steady thrum of the metallic buzz surrounding me. I take a deep breath and make myself meet her eyes. "It's probably just jet lag. Can we go?"

She studies me for a minute longer, but she doesn't push. "Sure," she says, giving me space. Because she knows I'll tell her when I'm ready, like I always do.

Except this time I know I won't.

What could I possibly say? That I think I might be starting to see things and hear things, just like my mom? *No way.* I'll get some sleep and enjoy the two weeks we have before Olivia goes back to her life in Westport. If I'm starting to lose my mind, Olivia never has to know.

I force myself to follow Olivia down another block and then over one, the sound buzzing in my ears as I walk. It's all I can do to keep moving. When we get to the house, she takes the stairs two at a time, but when I go to follow her, the sound goes completely silent, and my steps falter.

Olivia turns back in time to see me catch myself. Her brows draw together. "Are you sure you're okay?"

No. "I'm just tired," I say, but I can tell Olivia's not buying it. My whole life, I've seen people look at my mom the way Olivia is looking at me right now—like she doesn't quite know what to do with me. "I'm fine," I lie, glancing away.

Olivia's not stupid, though. She gives me a pointed look before she opens the door.

As I follow her up the crooked steps to the porch, I look once more at the darkening streets for some sign of movement, for some indication of the danger that felt so real. Nothing is there, but that doesn't make me feel any better somehow.

Stepping into the heavy warmth of the old house, I try to leave the cold panic and all my stupid worry outside, but it doesn't work. Unease still clings to me like a cobweb, sticky and thick. It follows me inside and trails behind me as I take the flight of steps up to our flat. As I climb, the memory of that sound scratches in a dark corner of my mind, like it's trying to unearth something.

I lock the door of the flat behind me, a second barrier against the night, but that isn't enough to help me relax, either. There was something about that sound—something that scraped at my nerves, leaving them feeling raw and exposed.

I'm almost all the way to our attic room when it hits me. It wasn't just that the sound felt unnatural or imaginary. It was that it felt *familiar*.

Dawn broke a familiar gray when his brother, the soldier, put the boy back on a train pointed toward home. With deep regret, the boy thought that his small adventure had come to an end. But as he waited for the train to depart, a soft voice startled him. He turned to find an old woman in a dark cloak looming over him, like a crone from the fairy stories of old. Her eyes were sharp, her expression damning. "A gift for a brave soldier," she said, her scorn twisting her voice as she held out the challenge of a single white plume. . . .

CHAPTER 4

OLIVIA DOESN'T SAY MUCH TO ME FOR THE rest of the night. She's giving me space and waiting for me to be ready to talk, but I know she's also irritated because I haven't told her what's bothering me. I can tell by the way she spends the rest of the night with the fancy new international phone her parents bought her, checking in with people back home. Back in Westport, I mean.

I don't know how to make things right between us without explaining more than I want to though. I can only hope it'll be easier to fix in the morning.

She turns in before me and is dead to the world in a matter of minutes. But even though we've been traveling for more than a whole day, I have trouble getting to sleep. The notion that the sound I heard in the streets could somehow be familiar has taken ahold of me. Try as I might, I can't place where I could have possibly heard something like that. And if I did actually hear it somewhere, I doubt I could have forgotten it. Still, it feels like the memory is there, waiting.

I force myself to let go of the idea, because I know I'm obsessing, and there is nothing healthy about that.

After changing into my pajamas, I check on my mom and find her asleep on the couch in the living room downstairs. Despite the lines that have started to etch themselves into her face, she's still beautiful. I've always wished I had her fiery hair and fine porcelain skin instead of the wheat-colored hair and dull complexion my absent father must have given me.

When I was little, I thought she was the most magical and courageous person I knew. All I wanted was to be as strong as she was. I'm not sure exactly when the way I thought about her changed. Maybe about the time I realized the monsters she was protecting me from couldn't be real. Maybe when I started to grow up, and she wasn't enough to be my whole world anymore.

I let out a sigh. There are days when I almost wish I could go back. It was easier then, before I realized I wanted more. Before I understood there was something more to want. I pull a throw up over her shoulders, and she murmurs in her sleep but doesn't wake.

Back upstairs, Olivia's snoring softly, her arms and legs all splayed out with a kind of awkward clumsiness she never lets the rest of the world see. I have to admit, I'm still a little surprised she didn't run when she had the chance. Part of me wishes she would have, though. It's not like it's going to be any easier to say good-bye to her in two weeks, and now that she's here, I'm always going to think of what London was like with her in it.

The fairies in the mural seem to agree. The whites of their

eyes glint as the gaslight's glow flickers across them, like they're mocking my regret with a ruthless glee.

Which is, of course, an insane thing to think. I can't—*won't*—let my thoughts go down that path. I have to focus on what's real—the rain that has started up again, drumming softly against the windows. The wind whistling past the house.

Even if it does sound like something is trying to get in every time the wind rattles the ancient windowpanes.

I climb into the bed, grateful that Olivia insisted on bringing her own linens. The sheets smell like the lavender detergent the Peels' maid used back in Westport. If I close my eyes, I can almost imagine I'm back there. If I let myself forget. I can almost feel like I'm home. But the feeling doesn't last long, and sleep does not come as quickly as I hoped.

After a while, the room feels too close and too warm, so I get up and try to pry open one of the windows. It takes some effort, but finally I manage to jar it loose. Outside, London is quiet. Faintly I can hear the sound of the traffic in the distance over the soft patter of the rain that has started up again, but the neighborhood we're in sleeps peacefully. The night doesn't seem as threatening now.

With a regretful sigh, I go back to the bed, but even with the cool night air drifting into the room, I can't sleep. The glow of the stupid lamp isn't helping any either.

I try to tell myself that the strange shadows thrown across the walls by its ornate bowl aren't anything to worry about, but when I turn over, my eyes find the fairy wall. The shadows there look deeper, more menacing as they mask the fairies laughing faces.

My mom was right about one thing—that mural has to go.

The longer I toss and turn, the more frustrated I become. The angrier my thoughts turn. Because I wouldn't be dealing with any of this if my mom didn't believe we're being chased by monsters no one else can see.

And now I'm stuck in this stupid room, with these stupid fairies, because she can't handle them. My anger lurches dark and sharp inside me.

My eyes go to the gaslight. *What could it really hurt?* I wonder.

Nothing. The answer comes as quickly as my panic did in the street. *It won't hurt anything at all.* Because my mom's fears are unfounded. Because the monsters aren't real. Her superstitions have always been just that. None of her little rituals actually do anything. They definitely don't protect us.

And she doesn't even have to know. I can wake up early and fix the lamp before anyone even realizes I've touched it.

A strange sureness settles in me. This is a good plan. A *sane* plan.

I stand on my bed and examine the lamp. There's a small wheel on the side, which I figure must control the flow of gas. Maybe I'll just turn it down a bit. I only need to dim the room so I don't have to contend with the shadows and the damn dancing fairies with their too-knowing eyes.

I just want to find some sleep. Tomorrow I can wake up refreshed and be back to my old self again. Tonight doesn't have to be anything more than a random blip, a bad dream.

But the tiny wheel is hot when I touch it, and when I jump at the unexpected bite of heat, it moves too far and the flame goes out.

The feather was still heavy in the boy's pocket when he found his brother at the station later that day. "I'm not going back," the boy said, showing his brother the papers freshly signed and stamped. The other soldiers had not questioned the small lie he'd told about his age. No, they had seen him as one of their own—as brave and ready. "I'm coming with you," he told his brother, and he could not stop the joy of it. Only when his brother's hands began to shake did the boy begin to think something was wrong. . . .

CHAPTER 5

THE SOUND COMES SOFTLY AT FIRST. IT STARTS as a whispering scrape that scuttles dry leaves across the pavement of my dreams. But then it builds to a throbbing buzz until it finally tears me from my hard-won sleep.

When I open my eyes, our bedroom is still clad in night. The only light comes from the soft glow of the city beyond the smudged and cracked windows, but there's enough light for me to see that nothing in the room could be making that sound.

It was just a dream, I tell myself as I nuzzle under the covers and close my eyes against the noise. If I can just slide back into the warmth of sleep, maybe it will go away.

I've almost drifted off again when I hear something else—a rustling that almost sounds like words in a language I don't understand. This sound is closer, more immediate than the humming buzz. Like it *is* coming from inside our room.

My eyes fly open, and I realize that somehow the room has turned darker. In the corners, the shadows seem to gather and creep as though they are alive. Their dark shapes crawl up from the corners and out from under the bed, cloaking the room in darkness. In a few moments, all the light is gone, and the room is so dark, I can't see anything. But the buzzing sound hasn't stopped. It is still ringing in my ears, unmistakable in its warning, like the wind picking up velocity as it rustles through a forest before a storm.

I cover my ears to block out the sound, but the memory of it remains, teasing at me. Taunting me. The thought I had earlier rises again—the noise is strangely familiar. Slowly, I pull my hands from my ears, and the sound rushes in again, brushing against something deep inside me. It sets off a slow-burning fuse in my mind that throws light across the dark corners of my memories.

Something is waiting there. Something I'd forgotten.

And then, all at once, I'm overwhelmed by an image so startlingly clear, it feels as though the room has dropped away and I've found myself in another place. . . .

Only a thin shaft of moonlight penetrating through the trees. All around me, the forest smelling damp, half rotten. And my heart pounding in time with my running feet. Slipping on the slime of the forest undergrowth, the cadence of my heartbeats slipping as well.

I sit up in bed, shocked by the intensity of the images. It's like I am there again, in that forest, running from—or maybe toward—someone. Or some*thing*? But I don't know where *there* is. And I don't know where that image is coming

33

from, because I don't remember living anywhere so cold or so damp.

A cold night. The scent of winter in the air.

I shut my eyes again and force myself to focus on what is real—the soft brush of cotton sheets, the comforting scent of lavender, the soft snores of Olivia. I focus and concentrate and—

A broad, cold hand covers my mouth before I can scream, and the weight of an intruder's enormous body presses me into the mattress. The roughness of his damp clothing scrapes against my exposed skin.

I am not imagining this.

I know I *couldn't* have imagined this, just as I know with unerring certainty that for as long as I live—however short that time may be—I will never forget how this moment feels. Like I am being pinned down by night itself.

I thrash wildly, trying to get away, but the intruder holds me easily, and then, pressing his face into the curve of my neck, he inhales—a sharp intake of breath—like an animal scenting its prey. When he exhales, his hot, fetid breath crawls against my skin.

Instinctively I jerk back, but his body cages me in, and his scent overwhelms me—he smells like the damp underside of old leaves, earthy and a little sour from decay. Like hunger and wanting. But as close as he is to my face, I can't make him out. The room has grown so dark, there isn't enough light for me to see him.

Without warning, something warm and wet traces the length of my exposed neck with excruciating thoroughness.

He's licking me. *Tasting* me. Bile rises hot and acidic in my throat, and I understand I am not going to make it out of this untouched. I don't know if I'm going to make it out at all.

Olivia whimpers nearby as another rasp in the same unfamiliar language comes from across the room—there must be at least two of them. But the darkness refracts the sound, and her panicked cries surround me, teasing me with my own helplessness.

And I *am* helpless. Even as I struggle to get away, my legs are being secured, and then my arms. In just a few seconds I'm trussed up. That hot breath crawls against my neck again, and I flinch, trying to pull away. But he doesn't lick me this time. With a voice like cracked parchment, he lets out a low growl.

When his hand eases away from my mouth, I take a breath to scream for help, but he lets out another rattling growl that makes me swallow my scream. I don't want to die. Not yet.

The dry rasp of another string of unfamiliar words grates along my skin as he says something to his partner, and then he hoists me up as easily as a rag doll, flopping me over his large, broad forearm.

When cool, damp air rushes against my bare legs, I know he's climbing out the window and onto the rickety balcony, three stories up. A guttural moan sounds from somewhere close-by. But it's not Olivia, and it's not the intruder making that noise. The sound, desolate and defeated, is coming from *me*.

I force myself to take a breath, to calm down, but instead I inhale the musty scent of him, and my fear spikes again. I have to force myself to focus—I need to think. I will *never* get out of this alive if I can't think, but for a long and terrifying moment, it's all I can do to breathe.

Outside, the night isn't as dark as the inky blackness that saturated the room. I can almost make out my attacker. He's huge, which I already knew, and dressed all in black, but I still can't quite see him. There's something wrong with him, or maybe he's drugged me somehow, because no matter how hard I try to focus on him, he remains fuzzy and indistinct.

Once we're outside, the steady London drizzle begins to soak through my pajamas, and it's not long before more than fear causes me to shake. But I force myself to hold perfectly still, to think. To plan.

It takes everything I have not to struggle too soon. I want to writhe, to try to get away, but I know I need to wait. Because I know that if he drops me now, I'll fall three stories to the cracked and uneven sidewalk below.

As soon as he climbs down, I *will* fight.

No. As soon as we're close enough to the ground that the fall won't kill me, I'll fight. I'll do anything I can to get myself free. I will *not* let him take me.

The buzzing suddenly starts again—the same low, metallic scraping I heard earlier in the streets. The same sound that woke me from my dreams with strange memories of a place I don't recall ever being. Then the wind kicks up, making my skin go colder and my hair whip at my face. And then, without any warning at all, and before I can do anything else, my attacker leaps, and the air rushes around me as we fall to the ground below.

Of course his brother demanded the boy return and tell the other soldiers the truth—that he was not yet of age. He must return home. But the boy refused, for he was sure that his brother was not the only one who was brave. Not the only one capable of a great adventure. And besides, the challenge of the feather was still heavy in his pocket. He would not be seen as a coward again. . . .

CHAPTER 6

I CLOSE MY EYES AS WE PLUMMET, PREPARING for the moment when we will hit the ground. But that moment never comes. All at once a strange heaviness surrounds me, like the air is pressing inward, squeezing me into an impossibly small lump of barely alive flesh. Until the pressure becomes so strong that I *want* to die. But still I don't.

Then almost as quickly as the pressure started, it's gone, leaving me breathless and shaking from the force of it. Little by little, the darkness eases, and as my eyes adjust, I realize this is not the same unnatural darkness that flooded the bedroom. Instead, it's simply night. A night so brilliant with stars, I can't stop myself from gasping at their unexpected beauty.

Though we are no longer falling, the air continues to stream past at a dizzying speed. It takes a minute for me to understand why—I'm *flying*. Or rather, whoever or *whatever* it is that has me slung over its shoulder is flying.

My head feels muddled, and pain pounds behind my eyes, and I'm still not exactly sure what happened. But the sharp bite of the claw-tipped fingers holding me steady tells me that I'm not dreaming. And if I can feel pain like this, I know I'm not dead.

That single thought bubbles up, dangerously hopeful in its promise. If I'm not dead, I still have a chance.

I've barely started to figure out how to use that chance, when light begins to break over the horizon. It starts soft, a glow just barely illuminating the edge of the night, but as it grows and the sky begins to ease into a dawn, I realize I'm surrounded by a swarm of dark beings, each one like the intruder that has me. They are so dense, I cannot see the ground below us, and though they are shaped like men, that's where the similarities end.

Each of the beings has inky skin covering their well-muscled limbs. Some have wild manes of ebony hair that whip about like small whirlwinds, and each has a pair of massive wings that move like liquid against the rushing wind. They look like dark angels or, maybe, like nightmares come to life.

But they are faceless nightmares. Where eyes and noses should be, there is nothing but a gaping black emptiness on each of their faces. They don't have mouths—at least not that I can see—but I can sense their hunger as they fly on, determined, toward some unknown destination.

A thought slices through me: maybe I'm dreaming and can't wake up. Or maybe I've been drugged, and this is just one horrifying hallucination. But if not—if I'm really seeing what I *think* I am seeing—I was wrong. I've *always* been wrong.

All those times I told my mom that the monsters weren't real. All those times I thought she was crazy—the times I *treated* her like she was crazy—for believing something was after us. For trying to protect me. I'd been wrong.

The danger *was* out there.

The monsters *are* real.

I think of the window I opened, the lamp I put out, and I know that this is all my fault.

I don't know how long we have been flying when chaos erupts. Out of nowhere, a ball of flame bursts up from below, and the dark creatures begin darting around in a disordered panic. The next burst comes so close, I can feel the flash of heat on my skin. My attacker dodges sharply left to avoid it, and my heart races as I realize what's happening—they're under attack.

We're under attack.

The once-rhythmic flapping of the creatures' wings becomes a confusion of frantic, uneven bursts. The fireballs continue to come quickly, with hardly a break. One hits a creature nearby. It tears through the broad, dark chest and leaves a gaping hole that doesn't close. The creature wails a rusted, inhuman screech of pain before its wings jerk with a body-shaking convulsion and fold, leaving the heavy body to plummet gracelessly to whatever waits below.

But even with the chaos around us, the creature that has me never falters. He—*it*—tightens its hold as we dart through the confused swarm, deftly maneuvering around falling bodies and the panic that surrounds us.

The farther it flies, the thinner the swarm around us

becomes. The creature's huge wings pump powerfully, and for a moment I think we might actually make it. For a moment, I'm almost happy that we'll escape. But just as I see the blue of the sky beyond the edge of the swarm, my attacker jerks like a top that's gone off course. A thick, heady stench like the smell of burning leaves overwhelms me, and we both begin to fall, plummeting through the sky, past the other dark bodies to whatever waits below.

The monster clings to me at first, its claws digging into my leg in a desperate hold, but then the pain stops. And it's gone.

And then I'm falling, tumbling into the bright blue of daybreak. I'm weightless. Boneless. And for a moment I think *I'm* flying too. For the space of a heartbeat, I imagine the impossible.

But mortal hearts aren't meant for flight, and human bodies are made to break. In one breath I'm falling through the night, and in the next I'm in the blinding brightness of the day. And when my body shatters the icy surface of the water below with a skin-splitting crash, it knocks every last bit of breath from my chest.

At first the boy did not realize his mistake. At first there was only the safety of training for what lay ahead. His brother was already at the front, but the boy found in the company of other lads a new sort of comfort. When it rained, they sat in their tents, listening to the pitter-patter of the drops and made up curses so devilish, that the boy struggled to keep from turning red. Because innocence was a weakness, and he refused to be weak. . . .

CHAPTER 7

IS IT ALIVE?" THE VOICE IS YOUNG, MALE, AND only a prelude to the sharp poke at my side.

"I fink so," another voice answers when I moan at the ache.

"Hey," says the first voice. *Poke. Poke.* "Wake up, you."

My brain feels impossibly thick, and my arms impossibly heavy.

I'm not sure what's happened to me, but even before I'm completely conscious, I know that it was awful and unbelievable.

They are still talking about me, poking at my tender skin, but I keep silent and still, my eyes closed tight, and I try to remember what happened.

It comes to me slowly. The terror in that dark room. The icy cut of the water. The peacefulness of floating free as I watched the brightness of the world recede above. My last burning breath as the water rushed into my lungs.

From the ache in my back and the incessant poking that continues to shoot sharp pains through my side, I know I'm not dead. My leg screams from the wounds made by the dark creature's claws, and my skin feels as taut and fragile as an overripe berry. *But I am not dead.* And for a moment, that is enough.

I take stock of what I can without moving or letting them know I'm awake—I'm still soaking wet, so I haven't been out of the water for long. My arms have been freed, but something heavy is cutting into my ankle, weighing me down and pinning me in place.

Not rescued, then. Still a prisoner. But the voices around me now sound human, not like the buzzing, accented voices of the monsters that took me. Still, I don't know who those voices belong to, or what they want from me.

"Leave it alone, Phin. We don't know iffen it's dangerous, now do we?"

The poking stops, but they're still in the room—whoever they are—close enough that I can smell the sour sweat in their clothes. I'm not sure what they're waiting for, but if I play dead just a bit longer, maybe they'll go away.

"Come on, then." It's the second voice again—male, too, and a bit older than the first, but also clearly human. His rough cockney accent is also nothing like the guttural, accented words growled by the monsters. "We best tell the Cap'n it's waking."

I listen to their footsteps retreat and, instinctively, I reach for the cold stones around my wrist, breathing a sigh of relief when I find them intact. I'm wearing little else—only my pajamas—but at least I haven't lost my mom's bracelet. The fact that I still have it makes me feel better for some reason. Like I'm not so alone.

When I'm sure they're gone, I sit up and take in my surroundings. I rub at my swollen, tear-crusted eyes, but they are so tender, it hurts too much to clean them. I can almost make out the room, anyway. Not that there's all that much to see— it's more of a closet than anything else. The floor is wood, darkened and worn smooth with age, and the only light comes from a narrow slit in the sloping wooden walls.

There is a heavy metal cuff around my ankle, as I'd suspected, and it's attached by a chain to a ring on the floor. I give it a good tug to see if I can loosen it. I'm not sure when my new captors will be back, and I'd rather not be tied down when they get here. So I make another effort to free myself by pulling hard at the chain, but it doesn't even budge.

It's only when I finally stop struggling with the chain that I notice something that makes my stomach drop. The room is *moving*. I didn't notice it at first, but now the motion—a constant, gentle rocking—is unmistakable. This is not just any room, I realize. I'm on a boat of some sort. Which means, even if I could get free from the chain, there might not be anywhere to run.

Refusing to believe that, I start jerking the chain around my ankle again, to try and loosen it from its bolt on the floor. I don't stop, not when my ankle is numb from pain or when my fingers start to ache with the effort. I don't stop until I hear footsteps just outside the door.

Just before the door opens, spilling light into the dark

space, I turn away and curl up into a ball to protect my tender stomach from the poking and prodding I'm sure will follow. Forcing myself to breathe slowly and steadily, forcing myself to ignore the way my pulse thunders in my ears, I wait. At first nothing happens. But then sure, heavy footsteps enter the room, stopping just beyond me.

"Come now," a new voice says. "I know well enough that you're awake." This voice too is male and human, but compared to the others it's lower, older. It's also tinged with the hint of an accent I can't place. Maybe Irish? But it's an accent that sounds like it's been softened by years in other lands.

"Get some water, Will," the new voice says. The command is soft, but it holds such a thread of authority, even I flinch.

After a flurry of movement and scuttling footfalls, rough hands flip me awkwardly onto my back, and before I know what's happening, water slops over my face. The second it hits my mouth and nose, the terror of the sea floods back to me in a sudden flash. I struggle to gasp for air and to get away from the wet that's threatening to drown me again, but my muscles are so tired that all I can do is cough and sputter, flailing as uselessly as a fish in the bottom of a boat.

"Christ! You're going to drown her," the newest voice snaps.

The water is gone, and unseen hands thump me roughly on my back. Panic laces through me as I struggle to pull away again, but the hands have my arms in a sure and steady grip.

"Make sure that she's ready, aye?" He gives me another rough pat, and I cough up the last of the water. "I don't need you drowning her again."

I try to pull away when I feel the brush of something wet

against my swollen eyes, but firm arms hold me fast. Gently, so much more gently than I would have expected from the steel in that voice, someone washes away the crust of seawater and tears until I can open my eyes almost completely.

"There now," he says. "Come have yerself a drink." The voice has gentled, but its words are still a command. Whomever the voice belongs to is clearly accustomed to giving orders. And having them obeyed.

I look up to refuse—the last thing I want is any more water—but the rejection dies in my throat.

They're just boys.

I'm not sure what I was expecting, but the youngest can't be much older than ten or eleven—there's a worn-looking Batman T-shirt peaking out from under his too-large coat. The other of the two boys is older—more my own age. His reddish-brown hair is short and unevenly chopped, and he's wearing jeans that are ripped on both knees and a dark long-sleeve shirt that's pushed up to his elbows. Down one shoulder is a row of what look like rusted safety pins, and his left wrist is wrapped in a thick stack of bracelets made from strips of leather or twine. He's scowling down at me as he holds the bucket of water, like I'm the one who's done something wrong.

I assume the third is their leader. He's not as tall as the one with the reddish hair holding the bucket, but he seems older—maybe a year or two older than I am—and the way he holds himself makes him seem even more mature, even more commanding.

He has a long lean face with a straight nose, and his sharp chin is tipped with the barest shadow of a beard. His hair—a black so dark and shiny, it's almost blue—is longer on top and brushed straight back from his face in an old-fashioned style. It looks like it might fall lazily over his forehead if he ever let it. Somehow, he doesn't look like the type who ever would.

From the tightness of his eyes to the grim set of his mouth, everything about him reminds me of flint. Still, he might have almost been beautiful if an icy-white scar didn't run a jagged course over the length of his left cheek and across the outer edge of his lips.

His sooty black eyes are narrowed at me, and for an instant, I have a disjointed memory of those eyes hovering over me as the brightness of the day pulled me back into this world. But if he was the one who saved me, he definitely doesn't look ready to save me now. Not with the blade he has pointed at me. It's longer than a dagger, but not quite a sword, and its burnished blade is triangular, rather than flat. I don't doubt it's wickedly sharp.

Without lowering the knife, he has the other boy offer the water again. This time I don't even consider refusing. I take the ladle with shaking hands and sip carefully. I don't intend to drink that much, but when the liquid hits my tongue, I shut my eyes and let the coolness slide down my throat. I can't believe how parched I am or how sweet the water tastes. It's gone before I'm even close to satisfied.

Frowning, I hand the dipper back to him. He motions for the taller boy to offer me another ladleful. Then another, until the uncomfortable tightness in my stomach makes me force myself to stop.

"Now then," he says, when I refuse another drink. "Let's start by you tellin' us just who it is that you are and why you came to be here."

I can't help but stare—his voice has an almost musical quality with the way he rounds some of his vowels but clips the end of *you* so it comes out *ye.* In any other time, in any other place, an accent like that would have had my stomach flipping in anticipation. Still, even through the shock and the fear, my face has gone warm.

With his face just inches from mine, I can smell the warm spiciness of cloves on his breath and the scent of the wind and salt water that hangs about him. This close, I realize his eyes are actually a deep chestnut brown flecked with gold. Until now, though, I'd never realized gold can be just as cold and unyielding as steel.

As if to underscore just how dangerous he is, he presses the sharp tip of his strange knife against the soft underside of my chin and forces me to look up at him. I struggle not to tremble, because I can already feel the bite of it and I'm afraid even the smallest movement on my part will draw blood.

"Not much for conversation, are you, lass?" He lowers the knife, and I collapse back as I take shuddering gulps of much-needed air.

"Please . . ." I hate the breathy whine of my trembling voice, but I can't seem to stop it. My throat is still too raw to do anything more than whisper, and I am so close to giving in to the tears that it hurts. "Please," I tell him, "just take me back. I'll give you anything you want."

His brows rise a bit, and genuine surprise—perhaps even

amusement—flashes across his face as he cocks his head. "And what is it you think I'd be wanting from you?"

After what I've been through, I can imagine any number of things he might want from me—some more awful than others. The memory of the warm wetness of a tongue tracing the line of my neck rises up in my mind, dark and chilling, and then I'm shaking again.

He scowls at my pathetic quaking before turning to the other two with a flash of violence that shocks me into stillness. "Can no one use the ounce of sense the good Lord gave you? Get the girl something dry to wear before she catches her death." He glances back at me once more. "I'm not sure I'll be wanting her to die quite yet."

The boy with the Batman shirt looks completely confused for a moment, and in that moment, he finally looks like the small boy he is. "What should we get it, Captain?"

"*It* is a her, Phin," he says with some impatience. "Get *her* something more appropriate than the bit of nothing she's wearing now." The one they called the Captain appraises me once more, his cold eyes calculating. "She looks about the same size as Wren. Take some clothing from him."

Neither of them moves.

"Go on!" he snaps, his voice still soft but unmistakably threatening.

The younger boy jumps then, but the scowling one sends the Captain a questioning look before going to fetch what's been asked for.

I flinch away when the Captain raises his hand.

"Easy, lass," he says softly, making his voice almost soothing

48

as he sets his blade on the floor next to him and reaches slowly toward me. I have the oddest sense that he's done this very thing a hundred times before.

I still again and wait, my jaw tense and aching from my attempt not to show just how scared I am. He's still reaching for me, slowly, like he's afraid to spook me. I meet his eyes and tilt up my chin with a courage I don't really feel, but he ignores my pretended bravery and touches me so softly that, at first, I barely feel the smooth leather of his gloved hand on my arm.

He probes one arm, lifting it and maneuvering the joints, like he's checking for injuries or broken bones. Satisfied with what he finds, he moves to my other arm and starts the same process. When he comes to my left shoulder, his hand stills over an old scar I have. He presses gently on its raised surface, but I wince all the same at the pressure. He glances up to meet my eyes once more, a question clear on his face.

I know what he's seeing—a small raised welt about the size of a quarter. The ugly, puckered mass of skin hasn't faded white, like his scar. It's still an angry pink that makes it look new, even though the mark is so old, I don't remember getting it. It's why I rarely wear sleeveless shirts, even when I'm running.

"Vaccination," I whisper, but his brows bunch in confusion, so I explain. "My mom and I travel a lot." I try to pull away, but his grip on my arm tightens, and the question in his expression grows more intense. "I had an allergic reaction or something. When I was little." I can feel my face heating again, and I can't meet his dark stare any longer.

He finally lets go of my arm. "We all have our scars, lass," he says softly. But then his expression gets dark and I think maybe I only imagined the words.

I try to pull away as his gloved fingers trace the skin around the raw, angry wound on my upper thigh, the one left by the creatures, but the chain holds me in place. He frowns as he examines the torn skin. To my surprise, he dips the rag he used on my eyes into the bucket and gently touches it to my sore leg.

I hiss at the unexpected pain, but he doesn't pay me any attention. He continues rinsing the wound. Then he picks up his blade. I think I see his mouth twitch when I jump, though I can't be sure whether it's from annoyance or amusement.

"Still now," he murmurs.

But he doesn't use the blade on me. Instead, he untucks the shirt he's wearing and cuts a strip of material from the bottom hem. With movements so deft that I know for sure he's done this before, he ties the strip of white linen around my leg, firmly binding the wound. He surveys his work for a second or two, and then, to my surprise, he unlocks the heavy chain from around my ankle and frees me.

I watch him warily, trying to figure out what he wants from me. Trying to figure out if I might actually be able to make it to the door. But the Captain seems to sense my intent, and without a word, he stands and lazily leans against the doorframe. His eyes meet mine, his brows rising in a silent challenge, and I know I'm stuck.

When the boys come back with the clothes, the Captain thanks them, and I notice the younger boy practically glows under his approval. Then the Captain places the clothes in front of me like a peace offering.

But I don't reach for them right away. As cold as I am, I don't do anything more than eye the pile of fabric warily.

Looming above me, the Captain's face doesn't give away any emotion as he nudges the clothes toward me with the toe of his polished boot. There is no longer any trace of the gentleness he's just shown me in his expression. "Be quick about it, aye?" The volume of his voice hasn't changed, but the steel is back. "I'm thinking that we've much to discuss, and it remains to be seen just how long you'll be with us."

Soon enough, the day came when the boy's training was at an end. As he stood with his newfound brothers, waiting to board the train that would take them to the battle, he was given a small slip of paper on which was written, In the event of my death . . .

Thus sharply did he learn the difference between the dream of make-believe and the same dream come true. . . .

CHAPTER 8

T HE CAPTAIN'S WORDS HANG IN THE AIR LONG after the door closes behind him.

I'm not sure what he meant by them, but I have a sinking feeling he wasn't talking about taking me back to London. No matter how gentle he might have been when the other boys were gone, the heavy chain, the blade at his side, and the locked door tell me that I'm no guest here.

All at once, the enormity of what has happened crashes down on me. My swollen eyes burn with the tears I've been holding back, but I swipe at them and force myself to stop. Then I pick up the first piece of clothing on the pile and rub the soft fabric between my fingers as I consider my situation. And my options.

I take a couple of deep breaths before I discard the damp tank top I'm wearing and replace it with the soft shirt. It's an old concert T-shirt that must really be vintage—it's worn so thin, it's almost transparent. Thankfully, they've also given me a heavy knit sweater, so I pull that on and button it up to my chin. The pants have an awkward buttoned fly, and they're a little too long—I have to roll the cuffs to keep them from dragging—but they're warm. There are also some thick woolen socks and lace-up boots made from soft leather.

I've barely finished securing the laces of the boots when the door to my prison opens and the boy called Will appears. I scuttle back into the corner of the room before I notice that he's brought another boy with him, a large, rangy boy with a dark tattoo snaking up his neck and cold, emotionless eyes.

"Hold out yer arms," he says, motioning with his knife. "Cross them in front of you, like."

When I don't move immediately, he demonstrates crossing his wrists. I know what he wants, but I don't want to be trussed up again, helpless.

"Go on now," Will says, clearly growing impatient. "Or Sam here'll have to help you."

I glance up at the other boy. His eyes narrow as he cocks his head, waiting to see what I will do.

If I let them tie me up, I'll be helpless again. I don't want to be in that position, but as I'm about to refuse, Sam takes the rope from Will and stalks forward into the room, his cold eyes glittering with anticipation.

All the air seems to go out of the small space. *He wants me to resist.* I have the strangest sense the boy wants me to struggle so he'll have an excuse to force me—to kill me? Suddenly, the prospect of being tied up again suddenly doesn't seem quite so bad. I take a breath and hold my arms out, trying not to let them shake.

I'm somehow not surprised to see the flash of disappointment in the boy's expression.

After Sam finishes securing me, he leaves. Will studies me, a scowl on his face, but he doesn't step into the room. "Come on, then. The Cap'n is waiting," he says. "And don't even fink of trying nuffin', else I'll be calling back Sam there."

I don't want that cold-eyed boy anywhere near me again, so I step carefully through the door and allow Will to herd me down a narrow hallway and up a short flight of steps. My legs are wobbly, and when I stumble on the last step, I barely have time to catch myself with my bound hands before my chin smashes into the deck.

Will hoists me up roughly and sets me to my feet, grumbling all the while. Like I've fallen on purpose. I think about telling him I wouldn't have fallen so easily if he hadn't tied me up, but as my eyes adjust to what remains of the daylight, all I can do is stand, stunned, all words forgotten.

I knew I was on some sort of boat, but my cell had been so dark and cramped that I didn't have any sense I was on a *ship*. It is huge. And it's *beautiful*—all gleaming, polished wood, with three soaring masts that tower above me, their arms outspread against the clear blue of the sky. The white sails are tied up so tightly, they don't even flutter in the gentle breeze, but in the soft evening air, a scarlet flag flutters from the topmost mast.

Then my heart twists with another, more devastating sight—nothing but water surrounds us. No land breaks the level line of the horizon. No other ships are in view. We are securely at sea, far from any means of escape.

How long was I unconscious? I wonder as I take in the endless water. How far have I been taken?

"Come on, then," Will barks, puffing his chest a bit as he gives me a not-so-gentle shove to get me moving. "Unless you want them to help you along."

The ship around me is not empty, I realize then. The decks are filled with people who have gone unnaturally still and silent, and every one of them is staring at me, weapons in hand.

Not just people. *Boys.*

There isn't a single person in view any older than I am, and most of the boys on the deck look much, *much* younger. They're just kids, but the way they're watching me, the way they're holding themselves stiff and ready for some unseen threat, makes them seem older. More dangerous.

I follow Will without argument after that.

As we make our way across the main deck, I can practically feel the wary eyes of the boys follow our procession. Most stand very still, but a few of the smaller ones shift uneasily and adjust their holds on their weapons when we come closer.

And *all* of them have weapons. Some have knives sheathed in leather slings secured to their thighs, while others have primitive-looking slingshots tucked into their pants. A couple of the older boys have long swords hanging from their belts, like Will does.

Each and every one of them is watching me warily, like I'm the most fascinating—and possibly the most dangerous—

creature they've ever seen. The absurdity of it causes a nervous laugh to bubble up in my chest. I swallow it down, but Will notices.

"Problem?" Will asks, pausing only long enough to regard me with narrowed eyes.

I want to point out to him that I'm not armed and not a threat, but I just shake my head and keep my eyes down as I let him lead me on.

With the entire ship still watching, Will directs me up a short flight of steps to the raised deck at the rear of the ship and knocks briskly on a heavy wooden door. When a muffled voice comes through, he pushes the door open and, without warning, thrusts me through.

As the boy filled in the lines and bequeathed to his mother all the things he'd never had a chance to accumulate, he wondered what his brother had felt doing the same. He wondered if his brother's hands had shaken as his were shaking. But then he threw off those dark thoughts and laughed with the rest—for they still saw death as an impossible horizon that, certainly, they would never reach. Though, if they did, what a right and fitting end it would be for brave lads such as they. . . .

CHAPTER 9

I BARELY CATCH MYSELF AS I STUMBLE THROUGH the door and into a large, dimly lit cabin. Most of the light comes from a wall of windows that provides a seemingly endless view of the sun setting over the surrounding sea. Beneath the windows is a large bed that looks as severe as the rest of the cabin, with its drab woolen blankets, flat pillows, and tightly tucked sheets. Everything about the space is sparse, organized, and downright tidy. Everything speaks only of usefulness.

In the far corner, a single lamp burns, swaying softly with the motion of the ship. Its glow is just enough to illuminate the dark form of the Captain. His bare back is turned to me, but the bunching and flexing of lean muscle barely registers. I can't quite see past the roughened skin that covers his entire left shoulder and most of his back.

We all have our scars, he'd told me. I thought I understood what he'd meant when I looked at the icy white line down the side of his face, but his back is more than simply scarred. The skin there is pocked with angry welts that look like he was shot with burning buckshot at close range or sprinkled with acid. And his arm—

"William, I—" he growls as he looks up, red-faced with frustration, but his words fall silent when he realizes I'm not the person he expected.

Grabbing his shirt, he quickly throws it around his shoulders, but he's not fast enough to hide what he's been struggling with. Not fast enough to hide the fact that his left arm ends just above his elbow in a gnarled mass of scar tissue. Where his arm should be is a prosthetic unlike any I've seen before—an intricate steel skeleton of a hand attached to what's left of his arm by a leather harness.

And his face . . .

In the dim glow of the lamplight, it is more than anger I see in his expression. For less than the length of a heartbeat, I see something vulnerable there as well. Something like embarrassment or guilt, but thicker than either of those things and more severe. Something, maybe, like shame.

"I'm sorry, I . . . ," But an apology doesn't seem to be enough of an offering for the emotion I've just witnessed. "They brought me . . . ," I start again, trying to shift the blame, but this is the wrong thing to say as well. When his expression goes thunderous, I stutter another half-formed apology and turn to flee.

The Captain is faster. In two or three long strides, he's across the room, his false arm reaching beyond me to slam the door shut before I can escape, sealing me in. The cuff of his shirt is still unbuttoned, and the sleeve falls back to reveal the steel rods that form his wrist and hand. They're so close to my cheek, I can smell the faint odor of metal and motors. The steel fist whirs and clicks like the gears of a clock as the Captain adjusts his stance and leans in. I understand implicitly in that moment that the arm is not a weakness. It is solid and strong, and somehow it has become a part of him. I'm pinned in place by steel and boy, and I'm not sure which is more dangerous.

"Leaving so soon, lass?" he croons into my right ear, all confidence and rough masculine charm. The warmth of his breath brushes across my neck, and the scent of him surrounds me as completely as his arms. I have the uneasy feeling that he knows exactly what his proximity is doing to me. That he's completely aware of the way my traitorous heart has kicked into a gallop and my skin has gone hot and cold all at once.

I'm too nervous and taken off guard by my reaction to him to resist when he turns me gently, until my back is to the door and his face is mere inches above mine.

He is just a boy, I tell myself. *He's not a monster.*

But he seems set to prove me wrong.

"Why, you've only just arrived, lass," he says softly, his lips inches from mine. "And you've gone to such pains to interrupt my solitude."

When I try to speak, the only thing that comes out is a sputtering sound.

His mouth betrays the tiniest curve of a smile at my inability to put together a coherent thought, and I know at once that my discomfort is nothing more than a joke to him. He *does* know exactly what effect he's having on me. He's using my reaction to him against me, and he's finding it amusing.

This time when my face goes warm, it's not because of any unwanted attraction I might feel. I square my shoulders and keep my eyes steady and—ignoring the thundering hoofbeats of my heart—I say, as clearly and calmly as I can, "You ordered them to bring me here. It's not like I had much choice."

His grim mouth twitches, and his eyes flash with admiration.

Or maybe I'm misreading him. Maybe it's impatience.

He eases away, so I no longer feel the warmth from his body. But he doesn't give me room to escape. "That's true enough, isn't it?" He backs up a bit more then, so he's no longer pressing the door shut behind me. "My apologies," he says, inclining his head in a small bow. Then he looks up at me, and after a moment he speaks. "I'd take it as a great favor if you'd not be mentioning what you've seen to anyone, aye?"

"They don't know?" It's so unexpected that the question comes before I think better of asking it.

He raises a single dark brow in my direction, as if to question my impertinence. "They don't," he says simply. "Well, Will does, but I'd trust him with my life."

I wonder why he doesn't trust the others, but I remember the wary look in the boys' eyes and I think maybe I already know.

Anyway, I'm not stupid enough to ask. I've pushed him enough as it is.

With an almost elegant sweep of his gleaming steel hand, he gestures toward a pair of barrel-shaped chairs, inviting me to sit down. I hesitate, because I want to keep what little ground I've managed to gain in the last minute. Ultimately, I know I'm stuck. There's nowhere to go but where he's directed me. Not that I go easily—I make my way as slowly as I can across the cabin.

Once he's satisfied I'm seated and stationary, he turns and, in an amazing flurry of motion, buttons his shirt quickly, using the steel hand as dexterously as the other. As a final touch, he pulls on the pair of dark gloves he was wearing earlier, hiding the mechanical fist beneath the supple leather. In a matter of seconds, he's back to being the boy I first met—the formal buttoned-up Captain.

Propping himself on the edge of his desk, he picks up a small jeweled knife, examining it as he speaks with a casualness that does not hide the threat. "Now then, I'm thinking it's time for you to be telling me just who you are and why it is you came to be here."

All I can do is watch him twirl the glittering knife effortlessly between the fingers of the mechanical hand. Not even the most sophisticated computers can make anything move as fluidly and naturally as that hand is moving.

He clears his throat and gives me a pointed look.

"Gwen," I choke out, answering his question in a heated rush of embarrassment. "My name is Gwen."

His mouth turns down. "Would that be short for something?"

"Gwendolyn," I say, but my voice breaks, so I try again. "Gwendolyn Allister."

He repeats my name, dragging out the syllables as he

studies me, and I force myself to ignore the fluttering warmth I feel in my stomach as his voice makes my name sound almost musical. Then he gives a dismissive shrug, and all the warmth that had been threatening cools as quickly as if it had been doused with a bucket of ice. "I suppose it suits you well enough, though it doesn't answer my question. *Who* are you and *why* have you come?"

"I told you, I'm just Gwen. I'm no one. I don't know what I'm doing here. I don't even know where here is."

But his expression never wavers as he take two menacing steps toward me, the glittering knife still in his hand. "I doubt very much that you are no one, Gwendolyn, else you'd not be here."

"Please . . ." My voice breaks at the sight of the knife so close, and I have to start again. "I was taken by . . ." But I can't make myself say it. Just thinking about the creatures, and I feel like it's happening all over again.

The Captain regards me with narrowed eyes. "Well?" he asks expectantly.

"They were monsters," I say, hating the way my voice falters.

His face doesn't betray any emotion. "Great, dark, creatures with enormous black wings, aye?"

I nod, refusing to look away from his steady gaze. "You rescued me," I realize, remembering more clearly now the dark eyes hovering over me as I floated back up toward the light. The firm hands that pressed the life back into me.

He quirks that annoying eyebrow of his again and gives a small nod in my direction. "In a manner of speaking, though I wouldn't be getting too far ahead of yourself, lass."

"But the fire, and . . . You pulled me from the water," I push, remembering now the strong hands that grabbed me from the depths, the steel-like arms that hoisted me up to the air.

"Aye. The Dark Ones came flying over us from the west, as they often do, but when we fired upon them, it was you who fell from the sky. It seemed the least I could do."

"You've seen them too," I whisper, relief and dread warring within me. "I didn't imagine it."

"No, lass. You didn't."

Something shifts in his eyes, and suddenly he closes the distance between us and raises the knife. I jerk away to fend off the cut, but the pain never comes. Instead, with a quick slip of his knife, I'm free from my binding.

I rub my sore wrists as the Captain settles himself on the table in front of me. There is a wary amusement in his eyes. "As the Dark Ones were those that brought you, I'd say you've more to worry about than me, lass."

"Please . . ." But I'm not even sure what I'm asking for— an explanation? An ally? A way to wake from this nightmare? "I need to get home," I say finally, settling on the one thing that matters.

From the way his expression goes grim, I know before he speaks what his answer will be. "Were there a way to get back to where you've come from, none of us would be in this fine mess, now would we?"

"I don't know," I whisper, as dread settles in my stomach.

"Don't you, then?" His gloved hand reaches for me, and I think he will touch my cheek, but he stops short. Instead he grabs one of my hands and pulls me, not so gently, to my feet. "Come." It is not a request, and I don't have any choice but to follow him out of the cabin, out into the cool night air.

The sun has gone down by now. All around the ship, the sea has turned a dark sapphire-blue in the dimming twilight, and the sky has taken on the purple-red of an angry bruise.

"It's best for all that you understand this now," he says softly, dropping my hand and gesturing to the sea beyond. "As you can see, lass, the place you came from is very, very far away."

I step closer to the bulwark, closer to the Captain. Far off in the distance, so far off and so small that I missed it earlier, a bit of land that's too small to be England disturbs the level line of the horizon. I stare out across the darkened waves, trying to gauge the distance between the ship and the island. If I could get there, maybe I could find someone to help. If I could make it that far, maybe I could find a way home.

"If you're thinking of visiting," the Captain murmurs close to my ear, "I'd advise against it. The island is a difficult place to survive, you see. It's constantly changing, and an unaware traveler might find herself quite lost. Or dinner for one of the beasts that roam there." He hands me a spyglass and gestures that I should use it.

Its leather-covered body is solid and heavy in my hands, and when I raise it to my eye, the island comes into sharp focus. At first glance it looks like any island might, though its topography *is* extreme for such a small place. Most of the shoreline is nothing but sheer cliffs rising out of the sea. Here and there, tufts of vegetation cling to the craggy bluffs like daredevil climbers, but most of the rock face is flinty and bare. Above the rocky shoreline, the sharp hills and mountainous terrain reaches high toward the ever-darkening sky, and most is covered with a wild green that speaks the hidden dangers of jungles.

Which can't be right. I know I was unconscious for a while, but we couldn't possibly be far enough away from England to find jungles. Still, there they are, plain as day.

Then I notice something that makes my stomach feel like I've swallowed a ball of lead—the island is moving. It's not moving in the water or like a ship. Instead, it's the land itself that is shifting and changing before my eyes. The mountainous terrain ripples in the evening light, the rocks slowly shifting and rearranging themselves moment by moment. One peak steadily shrinks while another grows.

The lush green of the jungle, too, looks unbearably alive. It shakes and shifts with a constant, steady movement. Trees melt into the earth only to be replaced by different types of vegetation as the jungle ruffles and shakes itself into a new tangle of overgrowth. The whole island continually changes, like a great sleeping beast breathing on the horizon.

"What—" My brain isn't even close to catching up to what my eyes are seeing. I lower the heavy glass and look to the Captain. "Please tell me you see that." I hesitate. "The way it's moving, I mean."

He raises his brows quizzically. "And why wouldn't I see what's right in front of me?"

But his words don't make me feel any better. "Things like that—they don't . . . It's not possible," I tell him.

"Maybe not in the world you were taken from. In this one, though"—he gives a shrug that looks more tired than careless—"I've seen more than most would care to, and I learned well enough that nothing's impossible."

Unease trickles down my spine. He spoke so casually, that I know I can't be hearing him right. I take a deep breath, trying to steady myself for the question I can't believe I'm about to ask.

"What, exactly, is that supposed to mean?" I say slowly.

"I thought I spoke clearly enough." He glances at me, his eyes dark and unreadable. "Have you seen or heard of many islands, then, that move and dance to their own heartbeat in your world?" He takes a step closer, and I resist the urge to back away. "Have you seen a forest rise and fall with its own will and of its own wanting?"

I swallow hard and, unable to form the words, shake my head. Of course I haven't, because such things do not exist. They *cannot* exist.

"And having seen such wonders, is it so hard to believe that you are no longer in the human world? Is it so impossible, after what you've seen through that glass, to believe you've found yourself somewhere else entirely?" His mouth goes grim once again. "It may look on the surface like the world you know, lass, but don't let that be fooling you. Though the sky is broad, there is nothing to this world but the sea and that," he says, pointing to the island. "And there are dangers on those shores you cannot have imagined."

"There has to be something else," I said, thinking about how impossible what he's saying sounds.

"You'd think it, wouldn't you? But I've tried myself to escape. I've sailed this ship for weeks on end, until my crew was near starvation, and I thought for sure we'd all die from the icy cold that coats the sea beyond. After weeks of sailing, what do you think appeared on the horizon?" He points toward the island again. "It's as though this entire world is centered on that one heartless piece of land. All directions lead there."

"That's impossible," I say, wondering how bad of a Captain you have to be to sail in circles like that without realizing it.

"Perhaps in the world you're from," he tells me, and his voice is so rough and worn, I almost believe he's telling me the truth.

"But even if I believe you, even if I accept we are in another world, it can't just be the sea and that island," I tell him. "There has to be a way out."

"There are boundaries between your world and this one, to be sure, but I've no idea where they're hidden. And I've no power to breach them." His dark eyes are serious and steady on mine. "Think of how you came to be here, lass. It wasn't a ship that brought you, now was it?"

"The monsters," I whisper, remembering the strange pressure, the dizzying flight.

"Aye," he said darkly.

I grip the railing so tightly, my fingertips ache, and I close my eyes against the sea and the island and a truth too terrible to accept. "What is this place?" I ask, my voice shaking. When he doesn't immediately answer, I open my eyes again to find him watching me. "Where am I?"

He studies me for a moment longer, and when he does

finally speak, his voice sounds haunted and very, very far away. "That bit of land is known now by only one name, lass. You've no doubt heard of it," he says, his serious eyes turning again to the sea, to the tiny speck of land in the distance. "In the world you came from, they tell tales of this place."

His voice has gone so grave that I'm almost afraid to ask, but I force myself to release the railing. "They do?"

"Aye, they do." His dark eyes glitter as he leans in close. "Let me be the first to welcome you to Neverland."

The ship rolled, angry, on the unsettled sea, bearing them onward toward those fabled shores. The boy knew death was a possibility there, yet he could not help but be tempted. For that land held the promise of living only for the present moment—without care for past or future, for who he might have once been.

There, he could become anything.

CHAPTER 10

I PULL BACK, MY HEARTBEAT THUNDERING IN my ears, and wait for the mocking curve of his mouth to break into a laugh. Because this has to be a joke. A hugely unfunny and terrible one . . . But the Captain's expression remains impassive, not playful.

A nervous laugh bubbles up in my throat, and I cannot stop it from escaping. The Captain sighs then, a weary exhalation of breath that has me choking back another nervous, completely panicked giggle as he draws away from me.

"They never do believe at first," he says. As he watches me with those hard eyes of his, what's left of my laughter dies in my throat. "And what you saw through the glass? That wasn't enough to be convincing you?"

"Even if I believe we're in some sort of magical other-world," I say, "even if I accept that much, you expect me to believe I'm stuck in some kind of fairy tale?"

His mouth turns down. "I never said this was a fairy tale, lass."

"You said we're in *Neverland*!" Saying it out loud only makes it sound more ridiculous. "As in the story? As in Tinker Bell and the Lost Boys and Peter Pan?"

The Captain stiffens, and when he responds, his voice has turned cold and dangerous. "He doesn't usually call himself Peter. Finds it a bit too *human* for his tastes."

I go still at the bitterness in his voice. At the absurdity of what he's saying. "Right," I say. Because what else is there to say? Rubbing at my eyes, I will away the headache that's started to throb. "What's next?" I ask doubtfully. "Fairies?"

"Well"—he turns and leans his hip on the bulwark so he can face me—"they have been a large part of the mess you're finding yourself in."

The sincerity of his tone makes me blink. He didn't miss a beat. He's either completely delusional or . . .

"I don't believe in fairies," I say firmly, smiling defiantly as I remember the story. "There. One less of them for me to worry about."

He shakes his head, but the ghost of a grin is teasing at his lips. "If it were as easy as that to kill the bastards, don't you think I'd have accomplished the task ages ago?" He fixes those dark eyes on me, and the grin falls away. "Besides, I'd think it would be difficult to refuse what your own eyes have seen."

"I've already seen a fairy?" I can't stop myself from asking.

"Aye. You met the Dark Ones, did you not?"

My mother told me all sorts of wild things about the monsters she thought were chasing us, but nothing she ever said could have prepared me for the dark creatures that took me from London. Still, as I touch the bracelet at my wrist, I think about the iron nails and the runes she was so obsessed with, and I wonder. . . .

I hesitate before speaking again, and when I do, my words are slow, careful: "You expect me to believe those things that took me are fairies?"

"They're not exactly wee things, are they? But then again, they're not exactly fairies in the sense that most usually think of them." His mouth turns down thoughtfully. "And I don't think they'd particularly enjoy being described as such."

"Of course they wouldn't," I murmur numbly.

His brows draw together, and his expression almost softens. "I understand, lass. After all, I grew up with all sorts of tales of the wee folk, but even they didn't prepare me for what I found in this world. Nothing about this world or the creatures that inhabit it is quite what the stories of our world would have us believe."

All I can do is stare at him. We are really having this conversation.

"The Dark Ones that brought you here, for instance," he continues. "Me mother used to tell me horrible tales of the *Slua*—the restless souls of the unrepentant dead that flew through the night, without heaven or hell to call their home, looking for children to take with them on their journey. I suppose her stories had to come from somewhere, did they not? Just as Mr. Barrie's stories must have come from somewhere as well." He pauses, and again I am struck by how completely serious he seems. "So, yes, the Dark Ones are Fey, just as all the creatures of this world are."

I take a shaking breath. "So, what are you—some kind of Lost Boy?" I ask doubtfully. He's maybe a year or two older than I am, but already there is nothing boyish about him.

"Perhaps, once," he replies without an ounce of irony. "But I decided there was a more apt part for me to be playing." With a mirthless smile, he holds up the gloved hand.

I realize then what I maybe should have seen from the minute he said we were in Neverland. The ship, the missing arm—it all makes a sick sort of sense.

I take a step back. "You're Hook?" I say, my voice faltering.

He gives me a dark and dangerous smile that has something equally dark and dangerous curling in my belly. "The role quite suits me, no?" The mechanism beneath his glove ticks softly as he opens and closes his fist.

"Looks more like Luke Skywalker than Hook to me," I say, a feeble attempt to disarm the moment.

"Aye?" he says finally, and the word carries with it more weariness than any single word should be able to. "Will said as much when he learned of it as well. Though I've not been able to discern his meaning, exactly," he tells me, his expression faltering. And in that moment the Captain *does* look like a boy—and a lost one at that.

But I barely blink, and that impression is gone. Wherever we are, whatever is happening to me, the Captain *believes* every word he's saying. This isn't a game for him. This isn't a joke.

"But if you're Hook . . ." I hesitate.

"Yes?" He turns his attention to me fully then, his body

held as stiff and alert as a soldier's. His eyes are locked on mine, expectant. Mocking me again. "*If* I'm Hook?" he drawls.

It's been years since I've seen the movie, but even I remember Captain Hook, with his scarlet coat and his villainous mustache. And his insistence on killing the Lost Boys.

"I can almost hear you thinking, Gwendolyn." The Captain's clockwork hand balls itself into a fist. "Out with it now, lass."

"Out with what?" I hedge. I'm suddenly feeling very unprotected, standing with him alone in the moonlight, surrounded by a ship full of dangerous boys and the endless sea.

He gives me a sour look. "You know well enough what I'm speaking of. You're thinking of the story, aren't you? I can see it on your face, clear as the sea on a calm day." He leans forward a bit, challenging me. "Say what you mean to say, so we can be done with it."

I'd rather not, but he's not going to let this go. I lick my lips and collect what courage I can find. "If you're Hook . . . ," I start again.

"Yes?" he says, mocking me yet again. Amusement dances in his eyes.

"That would make you the bad guy," I say softly.

He doesn't react immediately, but after a long, silent moment, he inclines his head slightly in what might have been agreement. "So it would."

He backs away then, giving me enough space so I finally feel like I can breathe again. "And there are many who would agree, Gwendolyn. In time, perhaps you'll count yourself among them." He turns then to signal to his crew. "Though some would say there are many sides to a story."

Two boys notice his call and begin to make their way up to the top deck where we're standing. One is Will, the glaring, russet-haired boy who doesn't seem to like me much. The other is taller and looks just as angry and severe. His face is marred by a dark tattoo—a jagged black line that crosses the bridge of his nose, bisecting his face top from bottom. Another dark tattoo winds itself around his bare bicep.

I don't have much time, and I don't understand nearly enough yet. Not thinking of the danger, I snag the Captain's arm. Beneath my hand, the hard rods that make up his forearm feel as solid and unyielding as the metal they are. Whatever words I was going to say die in my throat.

"Yes?" The Captain glares down at me, his lip curled in irritation at my insolence, and something dark, something cold and dangerous, moves behind his eyes. In that moment, I do not doubt him. In that moment, I believe wholeheartedly that he is who he claims to be. "Well?"

"Why me?" I choke out. "Why did those creatures bring me here? What can they possibly want?" *And what do you want with me?* I'm too afraid to ask.

"I haven't the slightest idea, lass," he says as he shakes off my hand.

But I won't be dismissed just yet. Not until I've asked the one question that matters: "Are you going to kill me?"

His eyes are shadowed, but I can feel his gaze moving slowly down my body, taking in the too-large sweater, the cuffed legs of my pants, and then up again before he finally meets my eyes. "It's not I who will kill you, lass," he says softly. "Neverland will do that well enough on its own."

He steps back abruptly then and turns to face the sea. I'm surprisingly aware of the loss. His attention was like a flame, warming me, even as it threatened to burn. His dismissal makes the night feel that much colder, that much more dangerously empty.

"But in the story—"

"Were I you," he says, turning back almost viciously, cutting off my words, "I'd not put my trust in stories. They tend to pass off lies as the truth and hide the truth in their lies."

The two boys—William and the one with the tattooed face—are waiting a few feet from us now. They're here for me, but I'm not ready to be taken belowdecks again.

"And Peter Pan," I whisper, a spark of hope flaring in my chest at the thought of a possible hero. "Is he a lie too?"

The Captain's face goes tight, and I know I've hit a nerve. "Aye. He's the biggest lie of all." He turns away from me then, dismissing me with a wave. "Enjoy your stay with us, Gwendolyn. While it lasts."

"But—"

The Captain's no longer listening. He gives the waiting boys a terse nod.

"Come on, then," the boy with the tattoos says, taking me so roughly by the arm, I yelp. He's stockier than Will, with hair that is the definition of the color brown and eyes that don't seem to see me.

"Gently, Devin," the Captain scolds. "There's no need to be rough."

The large boy's shoulders slump at the reprimand, but he doesn't loosen his hold on my arm. As he and Will escort me back down to the main deck and across to the stairway leading below, I don't meet the eyes of any of the boys who have again gone silent and still to watch our procession.

By now the sky has darkened from the bruised purple. The island is getting more difficult to make out. It's visible only as an empty space in the swath of diamond stars scattered across the velvet night. As Devin pushes me toward the stairs that lead belowdecks, I take one last look at the open sky and notice the double moons hanging overhead.

I understand then just how far I've come, and I wonder if I'll ever be able to find a way back.

After the sea, there was the march. And when they arrived, finally, through a maze of mud and unsteady planks, they found a land coated in mud. The boy soon grew to hate his new home under the ground—the trenches carved into the land like veins. He wondered where his brother was, whether they shared the same mud or slept under the same sky. But still he was not afraid. That would come later, when there was nothing that could be done. . . .

CHAPTER 11

THEY DEPOSIT ME INTO A TINY CABIN WITH a narrow bunk built right into the wall, but I don't have any intention of sleeping. I lie there instead, listening to the ship, until far into the night. At some point, long after the footfalls have gone silent, a wailing cry breaks the stillness of the night. I sit up, trying to figure out where the sound is coming from and what could be causing it, but in the end, I can't tell if it's a man or a monster that makes those terrible screams.

Eventually exhaustion takes over, and the next thing I know, I'm surfacing from a dreamless sleep. At first I'm completely disoriented. The room is unfamiliar, and when I try the door, it's locked. Through the slit that serves as a window, I can barely make out the sea, and from the slant of the light, I can tell it's already afternoon.

Tentatively, I take stock of my situation. My body still aches from the ordeal I've been through, but my eyes aren't so swollen, and my headache is nearly gone. The wound on my leg looks better too. It's red and angry, but at least it's starting to heal.

I'm still checking the wound when I hear a rustling in the corridor. Curious, I test the handle and discover that the door's unlocked. I ease it open and find a squat toad of a boy with hair as ruddy as the freckles across his cheeks.

He hands me a plate of lumpy biscuits as he blocks the door with his body. "Sorry, mum, but you're to stay in the cabin," he proclaims with a bashfulness that doesn't match the responsibility of his post. "Captain's orders," he says before he gently closes the door in my face.

I spend the next four days trapped in that cabin while an odd parade of boys brings me food. Most of the boys sport the same dark tattoos as Devin. I can't tell exactly what they're for, though—some sort of loyalty to the Captain? Some mark of rank?

Each night, I lie awake for as long as I can, listening to the sounds of the sleeping ship, and each evening, long after the ship has gone silent, the same wailing cry breaks the stillness of the night.

By the fourth morning, I'm at my breaking point. The muscles in my legs twitch with the need to move more than the four paces that make up the length of my quarters. So when the soft-looking, freckle-faced boy is the one who brings me my breakfast of lumpy biscuits, I know he's my best chance to escape.

"Breakfast, mum." He doesn't meet my eyes as he waits for me to take the plate.

I hesitate, wanting to hold him off while I consider my options. "What's your name?"

His eyes widen a bit, as though I've surprised him by speaking. Slowly he raises them to meet mine. They're soft eyes. Young eyes. "Owen, mum," he says, pushing the plate toward me again.

"Owen," I say, repeating his name as I stand. He shifts nervously when I don't immediately take his offering. "Where are your parents, Owen?" I ask, finally inching closer to take a biscuit from the plate.

Confusion flashes across his face as he backs toward the door. "I have other duties, mum." His eyes dart away from me as he speaks. "I best be getting back to them," he says with a curt nod before he eases himself out of the cabin. But he's so nervous and flustered, he doesn't notice the door hitting my toe instead of latching securely.

I wait a few minutes, and when I'm sure no one's around, I ease myself into the narrow corridor. The ship creaks and hums with the normal noise of the day, and once I know the way is clear, I don't hesitate to make my way up the short flight of steps to the deck above.

The sun is low on the horizon, and all around me, the ship is bustling with activity. No one seems to notice that I've managed to escape. The few boys who glance at me look away just as quickly, as though they don't care. Or maybe as though they don't even recognize me from the day before.

"Well, that was easy enough," I say to myself, trying not to worry that it was maybe *too* easy. I'll take what I can get. Not that I have any idea what to do next—I'm still on a ship. I'm still far out to sea, and they're all still armed.

So maybe I should find myself a weapon.

I find a cap sitting on a barrel and pull the hat over my short hair. Trying to blend in, I scour the deck for some boy careless enough to have left his weapon unwatched. But before I find one, I catch a glimpse of the Captain's dark head near the center of the ship. Hiding behind one of the crates, I watch for a moment as he shows one of the younger sailors how to properly lunge at someone with a dagger.

He looks so at ease helping the child. Considering how violent the lesson is, the Captain's face is strangely relaxed, happy even. When the small boy lunges correctly and manages not to tumble over, the Captain's face splits into a wide and sincere grin. "Well done, Davey." He laughs as he ruffles the boy's shaggy hair before sending him off to practice on his own.

But before the next boy can step forward for his turn, a hushed murmur falls across the deck. Thinking someone has seen me, I duck lower. After a moment, though, I understand it's not me that has drawn their attention. No one is even looking my way, because every one of the boys has turned toward the back of the ship. The deck quickly fills with their uneasy whispers.

When I turn to look in the direction the crew is all watching, I see that a girl with long blond hair is standing as regal as a queen on the upper deck directly above me. Her flesh-colored pants sit low on her hips and fit her like a second skin. They look like they're made of poorly cured leather, and they're covered in ragged seams that crisscross her narrow thighs like a spider web. She's also wearing a shaggy fur vest dyed the color of blood. It's not the color of fresh, bright blood, but the rusty red of blood that's gone thick and dark.

As I study her, I realize why the boys are so unsettled by her presence: beneath the vest, her bare skin is a pale alabaster and is covered in a weave of opalescent scales. The scales look like an intricate tattoo, only they have the iridescent shine of a dragonfly's wings. Even stranger, the scales seem to be shifting, moving. The individual scales melt into themselves and re-form into new shapes with an undulating rhythm that makes the very surface of her skin look alive. It reminds me of the island and the way the jungles shivered with life.

One thing is excruciatingly clear—there is no way the blonde can be human, and I can't help but wonder if she, too, is Fey.

But there is something else about her . . . something familiar.

I duck again as the Captain stalks toward the stairs. "Bloody hell," he mutters as he passes a few inches from my hiding spot, up to where the strange girl waits for him. Will is right behind him.

"Fiona," he calls to her as he mounts the steps. "What am I owing to the pleasure of this unexpected visit?" He doesn't sound at all happy to see her.

I glance up at the blonde. *Fiona.* The name strangely enough suits her—beautiful and exotic, just like she is. *Not just beautiful,* I think as my skin prickles in warning. *Dangerous.*

Her voice is low, but the ship is so silent, it's easy to hear her response. "Save your charm for your crew, Rowan. Come. We must speak." She doesn't wait for him to follow her to his cabin.

The Captain's jaw goes tight. He hesitates only a moment before he turns around and eyes the ship full of still and silent boys. "As you were!" he roars, and the boys snap back to their previous activities. Then he follows Fiona through the heavy door.

Quietly, I emerge from my hiding spot, bracing myself for an attack, but not a single one of the boys bothers with me. I make my way as quickly as I can toward the rear of the ship and hurry up the steps.

The Captain's door isn't completely closed, and as I edge closer to the opening, I can hear tense voices coming from inside.

"I must be absolutely sure. If I'm to do what you're suggesting, I need proof," the Captain says in his soft, lilting voice.

"You *do* want to end Him, don't you?" a female voice that must be Fiona's buzzes in reply.

"Of course. As do you. In fact, I think you may be wanting it a bit more, which is why I'll require some assurance that this isn't a fool's mission."

"You've wasted too much time already, boy," Fiona says, her voice like an angry hornet's nest. "If he takes the girl's life, he may well be unbeatable. Think on that as you hesitate." I hear a long, threatening hiss, and then a flash of light comes from within, followed quickly by a bark of surprise from Will.

"Bleeding hell," the Captain growls. "I hate when she does that."

"The flashing or the demanding?" Will asks.

"Both," the Captain says simply.

After a moment of silence, Will speaks again. "Do you trust her?"

There's a hesitation before the Captain speaks. "No. But we've not much choice. I've seen your arm, Will. I know well enough how you've been trying to hide the mark there, and I know as well that your time is running out far too quickly. For many of the others, too."

"But iffen she's wrong . . . Iffen we attack Himself and it doesn't work, or if the girl's not what she thinks, it could be the end of us."

"I'll not disagree, but if we're to hesitate and Fiona's right, death might be the best we can hope for," the Captain tells him.

A moment's pause settles over the conversation before Will speaks again. "Your mind's made up, then?"

Another long, tense silence follows, and I'm not sure what's happening. I'm about to retreat, when the door suddenly clatters open, surprising me enough that I fall back onto the deck. I look up to see the two standing over me, looking every bit as surly and irritated as the pirates they are.

"How much do you think she heard?" Will asks.

The Captain's face is impassive. "She'll have heard enough, I'm sure." He pins me again with his sharp glare. "Gwendolyn," he says pleasantly. "Perhaps you'd like to join me inside for a bit of a chat?"

It is pretty much the last thing I want, but he already is hoisting me up from the ground with that steel grip of his. "And, Will?" he calls over his shoulder as he pushes me through the door.

"Yes, Cap'n?"

"We're not to be disturbed."

When the call to "Stand To!" was passed like a grenade through their lines, the boy stood with the rest, as a good soldier does. They stood and stood and, eventually, began a verse to pass the time. But they never finished it, for another sound broke in and stilled them. . . .

CHAPTER 12

THE CAPTAIN DRAGS ME INTO HIS QUARTERS, and the sounds of the ship beyond disappear when he slams the door shut behind us. "Me mother taught me it's rude to lend your ears where they've not been asked for. I'm surprised yours didn't teach you the same," he says, pulling me across the cabin.

"I didn't mean—"

"Of course you did," he snaps as he deposits me into one of the barrel-shaped chairs to punctuate his point. "I would think that after I pulled your scrawny arse out of the sea, you'd at least owe me a bit of honesty."

A wild laugh escapes from my chest. I'm not sure if it's because I'm still in shock from being discovered or from the absurdity of what the Captain's just said, but his demand has shaken loose something wild and reckless inside me. "Honesty?" I huff, my voice cracking with a kind of hysterical disbelief. "You think I owe you *honesty*?"

The Captain's voice is low, almost pleasant when he speaks. "Have I not fed you and protected you? Have any of mine raised a hand to harm you?" He shakes his head. "No. And that is by my order alone." His voice has gone darker now, and the once-spacious quarters feel suddenly smaller, the air suddenly ten degrees warmer. "Are you not still on my ship? Are you not still *alive* despite your seeming incapacity for self-preservation?"

I suppose I should be intimidated. I probably should be shrinking back in the chair, begging for my life, but I am too crazed from being locked up, alone for days in a tiny cell, with nothing but my wild thoughts for company. I'm too angry about once again feeling cornered and helpless. "Am I the girl?" I ask instead.

"What?" Confusion lights his eyes at my unexpected change in topic. His face is so close to mine that I can see the fine down at his temples and the smattering of tiny freckles tossed across his sharp nose. For a moment, he seems almost vulnerable.

I swallow hard and ignore the fluttering in my stomach. I won't be distracted. "You were talking about a girl," I say. "You and Will, and— Wait." I stop abruptly and scan the room. The strange blonde never left. "Where did she go?"

His mouth twitches as he backs away from me. The tension that crackled just moments before eases with every inch he puts between us. "Fiona has a way of popping in and out when you neither expect nor want her."

"She just disappeared?" I ask, searching the room for some sign of her.

"She *is* Fey," he drawls. "They have all manner of tricks at their disposal."

When I meet the Captain's bemused expression, I know I've gotten distracted. Again. "The girl you were discussing," I say, focusing on what is really important here. "Were you talking about me?"

"It's none of your concern, lass," he says darkly. "But what I would very much like to discuss is how you came to be out of your quarters when I gave specific instructions that you remain within them." His mouth goes tight, and his eyes narrow at me.

I don't reply. There's no sense in getting Owen in trouble.

"Ah, then. Not one for conversation? Then I think perhaps it's far past the time for you to be returning to your quarters."

There's no way I'm going back to that coffin-size cabin without a fight, so I sit back in the worn velvet chair and cross my arms. "No, thanks."

He blinks at me, and I can't help but wonder if anyone has ever so blatantly disobeyed him before. I steady myself for the tirade that's sure to come, but all at once, he's *laughing*. And it's not the mocking, derisive sound I've heard come out of him before. It's a real laugh, one filled with the unexpected wonder of amusement.

When he's finally caught his breath, he wipes at his eyes and then rearranges his face to the stiff, formal expression I've come to expect from him. "You never cease to surprise me, lass, but wee thing that you are, you should stay in the quarters I gave you," he says, his voice growing more serious. "Where you'll be safe."

"Like you care what happens to me. You locked me in a room and left me there."

"I also risked my life, and my crew's life in turn, for you when I pulled you from the sea. That means you owe me a debt, and I don't know that I'm ready to have you leaving or dying until it's paid." Propping his hands on the arms of the chair I'm sitting in, he brackets me with his arms. "I know you're having trouble believing much of what's happened to you, but even so, you'd do well to keep clear of the boys, lass. They may look like children, but in this world, there isn't room for innocence. In this world, there are few who can even begin to comprehend what the loss of a life means. Most would kill you one day and not remember your existence the next."

I swallow hard. "Are you one of them?"

He doesn't answer right away. "I know well enough what it means to die, if that's what you're asking."

It isn't really, but an urgent thumping shakes the door before I can press him any further. The Captain ignores it at first, but when the thumping sounds again, his brows slam together and he stands, his features dark with irritation. Stalking across the room, he flings open the door and glares at the boy on the other side.

"John, I asked very specifically that I not be disturbed." His words are calm, but they carry a clear threat.

"No time, Captain. Longboats off the starboard side." The boy's eyes are wide, and they dance with fear and, if I'm not mistaken, anticipation. "We're being attacked."

The Captain blinks, assimilating the news in a split

second. "Then what in the bloody hell are you standing here for? Get your arse out there and at the ready!"

A brilliant, almost manic grin splits the boy's face. "Aye, Captain." And with a jaunty salute, he's gone.

"And, you"—he pins me with a glare—"I've no time to get you back to the safety of your quarters, so sit here and don't be making so much as a sound until I get back."

He's gone before I can respond, leaving me unguarded. As the silence settles over the cabin, I try to steady my breathing. He's left me alone, and I have no intention of following his orders.

At first it was such a tiny sound that a leaf might have fallen on it and smothered it. But as it came nearer, the sound became more distinct. And more deadly. The boy fumbled for his mask. . . .

CHAPTER 13

I DON'T KNOW WHO'S ATTACKING THE SHIP, but as long as they keep the Captain and his boys occupied, I don't much care. Keeping one eye on the door to make sure no one else is coming, I go to the desk. I know it's probably futile. Too many strange, unexplainable things have happened for me to really think I'll find a radio or some other clue about why I'm here, but I have to try. There has to be *something*.

I'm reaching for the first drawer of the desk, when the ship quakes so violently, I stumble to the floor. The papers once neatly stacked on the desk flutter around me, settling like scattered leaves. Many of the sheets contain notes scrawled in the same narrow, slanting script, but one sheet is a sketch of a girl with a heart-shaped face and a pert, upturned nose.

There is something familiar about her, I realize, searching my memories for some hint of who she is. For some reason,

I have the uncanny feeling that I *know* her. Her doe-shaped eyes stare up from the floor, like she's been waiting there all along for me to find her.

"Olivia," I say to myself. The word feels strange on my tongue at first, but also comfortable, like I've said it a hundred times before. "Olivia," I say again, louder this time as I try to remember how I know that word and who the girl in the sketches might be.

I repeat the word—the name, I realize—again and again until, eventually, the fog of memory starts to lift. Until I can almost picture her rolling her eyes as she takes me by the arm and pulls me over to her group of friends. The fogginess in my head clears a bit more, and I see her better now, watching me with concern in a darkened London street.

London. That's why the blonde on the deck—Fiona—had felt so familiar. She'd been in London too.

That can't be a coincidence.

"Oh." My breath rushes out of me. I haven't thought about Olivia since I first woke up on this ship and got distracted by the Captain's tales of Neverland.

How is that even possible? How could I have sat in that lonely little cabin for days and *never once* wondered whether she was kidnapped too? Whether she was in danger or whether she was even alive?

Panic inches across my skin as I realize it's not just the memory of Olivia that's hazy—it's everything. I can hardly picture my life before—I feel like it *might* be there, buried somewhere in the far reaches of my mind, but I can't remember it. I can't recall the color of my old room or the hallways where I went to school. The few images that come to me rise up through the thickness of the past, murky and indistinct, like bubbles coming to the surface of a muddy pond. And then the memories sink down again, below the surface where I can't reach them.

Maybe I hit my head when I fell out of the sky, because no matter how hard I try, I can't remember very much of what came before the Dark Ones. But when my fingers brush the cool stones at my wrist, their blue-gray color reminds me of something else. . . .

Eyes. The color of the stones reminds me of the blue-gray of my mother's always-stormy eyes.

I close my own eyes and try to bring her face into focus, but I can't quite manage to recall her features or anything else. All I can really remember is the soft, cloudy color of her eyes and the bright red halo of her hair.

The realization makes me goes cold. If I forget about the world I've come from, I'll never get back. I sink down to the floor and pick up the sheet of paper with Olivia's face on it. I need to feel the paper solid and real in my hand. I won't let myself forget again.

If he takes the girl's life, he will be unbeatable, Fiona had said.

She'd said "he," not "you," when she was talking to the Captain. Perhaps they hadn't been talking about me, after all. Maybe Olivia was the girl they'd been discussing. Which means Olivia could be here, in this world, too. And if *that's* true, if she's the girl Fiona was talking about, she's probably in danger.

"Where are you now?" I say to the picture as the ship rolls beneath me again. Struggling to stay upright, I grasp the desk, but I'm barely on my feet when I hear a sound that makes me go still.

A familiar rustling fills the air, growing steadily as its metallic hum grates against my skin. My throat goes tight as the dark shadows in the corners of the room begin to waver and lurch. They slide from the walls, like they're melting to the ground, and then they begin to slink, almost snakelike toward the center of the room, where they start to collect and swell.

Ignoring the metallic taste of fear on my tongue, I swallow down my rising panic and tuck the picture into my pocket as I run for the door.

Outside the Captain's quarters, I'm assaulted by the sights and sounds of the chaos of battle. Two long rowboats have pulled up alongside the ship, and from them, boys are still climbing up onto the main deck. These boys are easy to distinguish from the Captain's, though—they're dirty and dressed in an assortment of ragged clothes and shaggy furs that remind me of Fiona's.

Boys—the Captain's and these new ones—are *everywhere*, and each is fighting with a vicious skill that takes my breath away. I don't know what to do, exactly. My mind races as I take in the chaos, and I think maybe if I can get to one of those boats, I could try to get away.

But I'm barely down the steps that lead to the main deck before two large boys corner me against the bulwark of the ship. Their faces are painted with what looks like dark flaking mud, so the only features I can make out are the whites of their flat, emotionless eyes. One of the boys is missing the lower half of his arm. There's no blood, though. It just looks like the skin where his arm ends has gone black and the bottom half of it has simply cracked off.

Because I'm still trying to make sense of what I'm seeing, I don't notice another boy dressed in ragged furs moving toward me. In an instant, he has me locked tightly against his rank-smelling body, and his strong forearm is pressing against my neck to hold me in place.

"Captain!" The nearby voice is familiar, but I can't put a name to the sandy-haired boy it belongs to. "They've got the girl!"

Across the ship, I spot the Captain. He is, perhaps, the most vicious of all, his face twisted in rage as his dual blades slash at whatever—and whomever—is in his way. He turns at the boy's call and, when he sees what's happened, he stops dead in his tracks.

"William, Wren, Arthur!" He plunges back into the fight, his blade cutting deep into the boy who had been about to attack him. The small body jerks and then falls, bleeding its life out onto the deck, but the Captain merely steps over it. "Get her!"

As the Captain's boys turn toward the two who have me cornered, I writhe and kick against the ironlike hold of the boy who has me, but I can't free myself.

The three boys the Captain sent—Will and two I don't recognize—circle the two attackers. Their small white teeth are bared, and their sharp blades are poised and ready to strike. In any other situation, three-to-two might not have been a fair fight, but the two larger boys fight dirty.

In the blink of an eye, my captors attack the Captain's boys. Their blades sing with the violence of the battle, and it's not long before they are beating my rescuers back. With a vicious lunge, one of my attackers paints a bright crimson slash across the chest of the smallest of the Captain's crew.

The ribbon of scarlet creeps across his shirt as the boy crumples to the deck, his eyes wide with shock. But the fallen boy's astonishment is more than just from the pain of his wound—it's like he's suddenly come to understand that his swordplay has *always* been more than just a game of pretend.

The Captain's other boy watches the dark stain spread beneath his friend's body as Will continues to beat back my attackers. But when the fallen boy goes still, the living boy's features harden—a subtle shift that narrows his eyes and curls his lips in a murderous sneer. With an earsplitting shriek, he lunges once again into the fray to help Will, his wrath focused less on freeing me than on destroying the boy who's killed his friend.

His attack is so brutally unexpected that his small dagger easily finds its mark. With a vicious thrust, he forces the blade deep into the belly of the one who killed his friend. Then, his eyes burning with fury, he turns to help Will finish off my other captor.

The one who has me seems to understand that his friend probably won't win against two of the Captain's crew, and he begins to back away from the fight. Little by little, he drags me along the deck. Toward the longboats.

I struggle violently to get away from him, pulling with all my strength at his filth-covered sleeve and kicking at his legs. But he's pressing his arm so tightly against my throat, I can barely breathe. Already my vision is starting to go dark around the edges, and my lungs are screaming for oxygen.

Then, just as I think I can't stay conscious for one moment longer, the boy's body goes rigid. All at once, he releases me from his hold.

Gasping for air, I stumble to my knees, and when I turn to look up, I see what's caused him to release me—he's been stabbed. The tip of a dark blade protrudes from his belly. Around it, blood blooms. His shaking hands grab at the blade, like he's trying to push it back through, but it's too late. His body gives a violent jerk as someone else pulls at the blade, and blood gurgles from his mouth as his knees give out and he falls to the deck.

Behind him, the Captain stands, his blade coated with the boy's dark blood. His eyes murderously set on me.

"Get her up from there." The Captain's voice is rough with exhaustion and barely leashed temper.

The battle is already dying down as thin yet strong arms hoist me up from the deck. But I can't take my eyes off the crumpled body of the boy at my feet. It doesn't even matter that he was hurting me, or that he would have tried taking me. . . . I've never seen someone die. And his death was so violent, I can't seem to stop myself from shaking.

"How many did we lose?" The Captain's voice is brutally cold.

"Just four, including Wren," Will says, nodding toward

the small boy who died trying to save me. "Little Davey's injured, but he might pull through."

A tall dark-skinned boy with hair braided like snakes approaches. He's bleeding from a gash above his eye and seems almost shell-shocked as he takes in the carnage on the deck around him. "Where did they all come from?" he asks, his hand shaking as he wipes at the blood dripping into his eye.

"Where d'you think?" The Captain looks out over the deck, his expression grim. His hair has tumbled free and hangs listlessly over his brow. I'd been wrong—his hair like that doesn't soften his appearance at all. If anything, it makes him look even more dangerous. "Burn their boats. Then we'll deal with those who remain."

"But why, Cap'n?" another of the boys ask. "Himself's never attacked like that before, not in broad daylight and not in the middle of the sea."

He glances at Will and then he looks at me, those dark eyes of his as cold and dark as the waiting sea. "That is the question, lads," he says as he scratches at his chin absently with the edge of his knife, but from the way he's focused on me, I'm afraid he already has his answer.

After the attack, when only a pale gray light filtered over the empty land, nothing moved there. Nothing seemed even to breathe. The boy wished that someone had warned him fear tasted of mustard gas—of lilacs and horseradish. . . .

CHAPTER 14

EAVY CLOUDS HAVE ROLLED IN, AND THE air snaps with a new chill now that we are under sail. The island, once no more than a speck on the horizon, has disappeared in the distance. I've been given new clothes to replace the ones that were splattered with the boy's blood, but they aren't as warm as the heavy sweater I'd been wearing before, and I can't quite keep myself from shivering.

Or maybe it's more than cold that has me shaking. When I changed my clothes, I found the crumpled picture of Olivia and was reminded again about how easily I'd forgotten her. How easy it still is to let the idea of her, and the memory of who I was, slip away.

The Captain is standing close to me, watching the progress his crew is making in scrubbing the blood from the deck and setting his ship to rights. He's exchanged his bloodstained clothing for a clean military-style jacket with a double row of large pockets across the front. It must have faded to that grayish, drab green long ago from the looks of it. Its elbows are worn and patched, and the right epaulet—which has long since lost the button that once held it in place—flops listlessly over his shoulder in the gusty wind.

I pull the folded sheet of paper from my pocket. "Is this the girl you were talking about with Fiona?" I ask, watching for his reaction.

He stiffens when he glances down at the drawing, but then he turns to me after a moment. "You were looking through my effects?"

"You left me alone in your quarters. What did you think I was going to do?"

His mouth goes tight, but he doesn't say anything. He just keeps glaring at me with that indecipherable expression of his.

"Her name's Olivia," I tell him, concentrating on the way the word feels on my tongue, the way it sounds before it's carried off by the breeze. "She was in London with me, when I was taken. What are you doing with her picture?"

He scratches absently at the dark scruff on his jawline. "This Olivia," he asks, ignoring my question. "You say she's from your world?"

I nod.

"You're sure about this—you remember it?"

I clench my fists. "I didn't at first. The picture helped."

His brows draw together, and his dark eyes study me for a long moment before he responds. "I'm surprised you remembered at all, lass. Most of the boys don't remember anything

98

at all of your world—no matter how many tales I tell them of it." He narrows his eyes at me, but I'm getting so used to his half-threatening looks that it's fairly easy to ignore this one.

"They're all from my world?"

The Captain's mouth goes tight as he gives a terse nod and confirms my fears. "Not that it's anything more than a story to them now. All they are is who they've become."

I think about Owen and how confused he was when I asked where his parents were, and I wonder if it's possible to forget that completely. Could I really become like the boys on this ship, all thinking that Neverland—or whatever this strange world might be—is the only home I've ever known?

"I won't forget Olivia again—I won't forget any of it," I say, determined. Even as I struggle to hold on to the wisps of memory I've managed to grab hold of.

"As you'll soon learn, Gwendolyn, everything about this world inspires forgetting. If you survive long enough, Neverland will tempt you to abandon the life you knew before, to betray everything you believed you were."

"Is that what happened to you?" I wonder.

But his expression goes stony, and he turns away, dismissing the question and me all at once.

"Wait! What about the girl—Olivia?"

He turns back. "What about her?"

"Can you help me find her?"

He shakes his head slightly. "I'm afraid not, lass. I won't risk any more of my lads. We're heading out to sea, beyond the range of more attacks."

"But Fiona said—"

"The game has changed," he says simply. "Pan has never risked such a brazen attack before. And if he has your friend, as Fiona believes, she's already lost." His words are so blunt, so absolute, I have no doubt they are final.

"Pan?" I ask, and I cannot stop myself from looking at what remains of the battle's carnage. Dark spots still stain the decks. Boys still trickle blood from seeping wounds or peer out of swollen eyes. "But in the story—"

"I did try to warn you that you're not in any bloody story," he snaps. Then he takes me by the arm and steers me back away from the railing of the upper deck, back from the hungry eyes of the boys below.

I pull away from him. "You told me I'm in Neverland. You said there are fairies, and now you're telling me Peter Pan attacked your ship. That sounds an awful lot like the story to me."

His temper is a living thing, but he keeps ahold of its leash. "All of that may be true enough, but whatever you might know of Mr. Barrie's tale, you'd best forget it, lass," he says, his eyes as sharp as his voice. "In this world, the story belongs not to Mr. Barrie, but to Pan. The stories you may know have very little bearing on what happens here. Perhaps Mr. Barrie had some way of knowing of this land. Perhaps this world is where his stories came from. But whatever the case, the stories in your world are nothing compared to the truth of *this* one. Here, Pan uses the tale for his own purposes."

"Like you haven't." I can't help but think of the boys who bled and died for him today. I think of the boy he killed to save me. *To keep me,* I realize with a start.

He blinks at me, as though he didn't expect that reply, but

his expression goes flat, unreadable. "As you said yourself, Gwendolyn, I'm the villain."

Before I can say anything else, the Captain is gone, his long strides taking him across the upper deck and down the steps toward the main mast of the ship. When I go to follow, my two guards pull me back.

"Bring the prisoners forward," the Captain calls.

All around the deck, the boys shuffle, agitated, like something is about to begin. The Captain turns the frayed collar of his coat up against the wind and watches a few of the older boys lead the group of captives forward on the deck below. Each of the prisoners has his hands bound behind his back. Most of them are sporting blackened and swollen eyes or noses crusted with dried blood.

I can't get over how young they look beneath their bruised faces. Or how terrified.

Not that I blame them. The Captain's already severe face seems somehow even more fierce as he looks them over. Many of the swollen eyes follow him as he stalks across the deck, watching his every move, like dogs who have been kicked too many times by their master.

"I'll give you the same choice I give any taken aboard my ship," he says loudly enough for all on the ship to hear him. This, I understand implicitly, is a display meant for his crew as well as for the prisoners. "You can join us and pledge your loyalty, and I'll swear on my life and honor to protect you as my own." He pauses, eyeing them each and letting his words settle. "Or you can walk the plank."

Walk the plank? He can't possibly be serious.

But no one else seems to find what he's saying funny.

"You, there." The Captain points his blade at one of the older boys who's making a point not to pay attention—a stocky guy who's tall enough and broad enough to play linebacker. He's the largest and cockiest of the captives, and he doesn't seem to realize he should be hiding his disdain. The dark-skinned boy with the thick braids pushes the boy forward until he stands in the no-man's-land in front of the line.

"What shall it be, mate?" the Captain asks. "Will you join us?"

The boy doesn't hesitate. "Bugger off," he says, giving the Captain a sharp jerk of his chin. "I ain't joinin' nuffin' of yours. Got it . . . *mate?*"

The Captain cocks his head, examining the boy like he's no better than a roach in the pantry. The Captain turns on him and, in a motion so swift that the boy could not have predicted it, he rams his glove-covered fist into the boy's gut. The boy goes down hard, his moan echoing on the winds as he crumples over, unable to clutch his stomach with his hands bound as they are.

Stepping back, the Captain watches with barely concealed disgust as the boy writhes on the floor, desperately trying to catch his breath. When he has almost stilled and when his breathing is more labored than erratic, the boy tries to come to his knees. But as he struggles, the Captain crouches and lifts the boy's head by his hair. The boy tries to jerk away, but the Captain's grip is too strong.

"I'll ask you once again, lad," he says, his voice carrying over the wind. "Will you join us?"

The boy glares at the Captain, his nostrils flaring in anger or pain or some combination of the two. After a beat, he wrinkles his face and, with some effort, sends a gob of spit directly at the Captain's face.

The boys on deck shift uneasily as a murmur ripples through the crowd, but the Captain doesn't react. He lets the boy fall to the deck as he wipes the spittle from his cheek with a handkerchief from his pocket.

"I see," the Captain says, and I cannot stop the gasp that escapes when he unexpectedly gives the boy a savage kick to the gut. Taking the time to fold the scrap of material into a precise triangle, he places it back into his pocket while the boy writhes in pain at his feet.

With the handkerchief tucked away, he gives a slight nod. Will and the boy with the dreads move forward and flank the prisoner. Together they lift the still-moaning boy back to his knees and jerk his head back, forcing him to look up at the Captain.

"Let's try this once again, shall we?" The Captain pulls his long triangular blade from its sheath and runs the edge of it along the boy's throat. "It's like I've told you, lad. You've got yourself two choices: you can join with us or you can be leaving." His tone is calm, almost conversational, as he gestures to the sea.

A few of the other prisoners in the line whimper, but the Captain doesn't spare them a glance. The defiant boy jerks his head away from the two holding him and glares at the Captain with a cold fury. "And it's like I told you," he sneers, *"sod off."*

The Captain studies him for a moment, his back stiff and straight. "Your choice, lad." He looks to the two boys holding the prisoner. "Gareth, Will, perhaps you could escort our guest off the ship?"

The two holding the boy nod, almost in unison, and start to drag the prisoner to the bulwark of the lower deck. As they pull the stocky boy along, the Captain glances up at me. I can't read the emotion in his features. I can't tell if it's exhaustion from the battle or regret for what he's just done that makes him look so drained. He doesn't bother to watch the progress of the boys or to offer assistance, though. Instead, he climbs the steps back to his perch next to me on the higher deck.

The boy doesn't go easily. At first he collapses onto the deck, making himself into a dead weight, but it doesn't work. Little by little, Will and Gareth drag him to the bulwark of the ship. The closer the boy gets, the more he begins to panic— his legs jerking out desperately to find a foothold, his face turning as white as the sails that flap above us.

I understand his panic. I know too well what's it like to be dragged away against your will. What it's like to feel fear closing up your throat. And I know just how cold and dark and deadly that water can be.

"Captain!" the boy's voice cracks. His eyes are wild with fear now. "Captain, please! I've reconsidered."

I let out a breath when I hear his words, relieved that he has finally decided to save himself. But the Captain doesn't move. Not a muscle in his face shows any signs of softening.

"Please!" The boy is practically squealing now, sobbing, and his screams grow more desperate with each inch he is pulled closer to the railing. Beyond, the sea is quiet. Waiting.

"Go with God, lad," the Captain murmurs, giving the boy a small salute.

The boy's legs go out from under him at the words, and a wet stain spreads on the front of his pants, but still Will and Gareth drag him to the rail of the ship.

"No!" I'm moving before I think better of it, jerking away from the two boys who are supposed to be guarding me before they even know what's happening. "You can't do this." I grab the Captain's arm.

He turns on me, his eyes narrowed, vicious. "Can't I?"

I realize my mistake instantly. Of course he can. This is his ship, his world, and he's the commander of it. "But he's changed his mind," I say, hearing just how weak the words are.

"Has he?" The Captain's dark eyes travel down to where I'm holding his arm. He doesn't shake me free, though. "I wonder. Desperate people do tend to say most anything now, don't they, lass?"

"Please. You can give him another chance. You can show mercy."

"Mercy," he scoffs, his expression strangely calm. "Was mercy what he showed when he came to my ship to kill me and my lads? Was that this *mercy* you speak of?" he asks, shaking his head as though he's already denying the words. "I gave him his chance. I gave him three, in fact, and he'd not take them." He does shake me off then. "Now the others will."

"And if he can't swim?"

"What is it that your stories tell you? Something about death being a great adventure?" Stepping away from me, the

105

Captain gives a sharp nod, and the two holding him dump the boy in.

"No!" I lunge toward the railing, but the Captain's arms are around me before I can leap. The heat of his body surrounds me, and I am trapped against his lean form. He may not be a giant of a man, but he is also no soft boy. Every inch of him is pressed to every inch of me, and every inch of him is unyielding muscle honed by who knows how long at sea.

"What is it you were thinking to do, Gwendolyn?" His voice is soft, rough in my ear. His breath warm against my neck. "Do you think you can save him? He, so much bigger than the wee slip of a girl that you are?"

I should struggle. I should pull away from him and make it clear just how distasteful I find him. But I can't. His voice curls about my brain, and the warmth of him, the solidness of his body against mine, is suddenly too real. Too immediate for me to even process. He laughs then, softly, as though he knows just how weak I am, and the sound of it rumbles up out of his chest and across every one of my nerve endings.

And I hate myself for how weak I am. Because the truth is, the Captain's right—I never would've been able to pull the boy's bulky form to safety.

"He changed his mind," I say again, wishing that were enough to spare his life. Knowing it isn't.

"He made his choice, lass. Long before he set foot on my ship."

With a sputtering noise, the boy comes to the surface, and I almost go limp with relief.

"Ah, so it seems he can swim," the Captain croons in my

ear. "Not that it'll help." His voice is so empty, so devoid of any feeling, that I whip my head around to look at him. The features of his face are hardened—his jaw with its dusting of dark stubble is tight, his mouth a line as flat and uncompromising as the horizon. And his eyes are still steady on the water.

"What do you mea—" But the sound of churning water draws my attention back to the sea and to the boy. All around him, the sea is bubbling. "What is that?"

"The Sisters." I can feel the Captain's eyes on me. "Sea Hags," he says as I meet his steady gaze. "They're a bit like mermaids."

"Mermaids?" I can't tell if he's serious.

"Just a bit," he says, but his attention is already back on the water.

Confused, I look as well. The boy is gone, but the water hasn't stopped churning. As I watch, the surface turns a lurid, rusty pink.

"In your world there are tales of people capturing mermaids for the wishes they're believed to grant. But in this world, the Sisters don't take kindly to those who invade their home." The Captain's usual detachment is gone, his voice strained, and I get the feeling he is not as indifferent as his flinty expression would suggest.

"Wishes," I repeat stupidly.

"Aye. The desires of the heart. Though human desire is such a weak thing, Gwendolyn." His lips are so close to me now, I swear I can feel the heat of them against my neck.

"It is?" I whisper, swallowing hard, forcing myself to hold completely still.

"It is," he rasps, his voice as rough as the waves. "Oh, it may burn and it may chafe, but it rarely devours a person. Not completely. In this world, though, desire is a bit more dangerous. In this world, lass, more often than not"—his lips do touch my neck then, softly, like a prayer— "it consumes," he whispers against my skin.

I close my eyes, trying to block out his words, the heat of his body, the spice of the cloves on his breath, but it doesn't work. He is too close, too *much* for me to ignore.

But then the moment is over. The Captain adjusts me in his arms, allowing some space between us as he gives a small salute to the waves. When I look in the direction of his salute, my legs feel like I've just finished a ten-mile run. The torsos of three figures with skin the color of a bloated corpse are rising out of the pinkish water. The hair clumped to their large heads reminds me of tangled algae. With great yellow eyes and rows of daggerlike teeth that flash from wide-set mouths, they are perhaps the most horrible things I've ever seen.

They're gone as quickly as they appeared, and I can almost convince myself they hadn't been there at all. Except for the bits I won't let myself identify floating in the pinkish water.

Without warning, I'm free. The Captain's arms are gone, and only the cold cut of the sea wind is there to meet me when I stumble in surprise at his absence.

"Now then," the Captain says, making his way once again to the head of the steps. Hands on his hips, his silhouette is stark against the setting sun. He takes his time looking over the prisoners, who are waiting, slack-mouthed, below. "Which of you will be joining your friend?" he shouts, pausing for a long, uncomfortable moment while the implication of his words settles over the decks. Down below, the boys' eyes grow wide with fear. "And which of you will be joining *me*?"

The captives erupt—all of them clamoring to be the first to sign on as crew for the ship. All of them already shouting their allegiance.

"That's what I thought," the Captain murmurs, tossing a glance back at me. He smiles then, a wicked grin that somehow transforms the severity of his face. His smile falters a bit, though, when I don't respond in kind.

He starts to turn away, dismissing me again, and something snaps.

Memories bubble up to the surface of my mind. The details are indistinct, but the emotions behind them are potent. My whole life, I've felt like this—trapped, powerless. I moved because my mom said we had to, I held our lives together when she was falling apart, because the alternative—telling someone, getting help—meant risking everything. But my mom's a world away now. That life is gone. Even now I can barely bring up the details of it, and I don't feel like there's much left to lose.

"What about me?" I demand, drawing his attention back. I don't know if it's the cut of the wind or what I just witnessed, if it was the way my blood hummed at his nearness before, or the cold calculation in his eyes now, but I can't seem to stop shaking.

He raises his brow slightly, mocking me. "What about you, lass?"

"Do you need my allegiance too? Or will you toss me to those monsters?"

The Captain's eyes go dark, his face an emotionless mask. He takes my measure from where he stands, just a few yards away, his mechanical hand balling itself into a gloved fist. "No, Gwendolyn," he says softly, his voice rough and filled a desolation that makes my whole body go still. "It's not your allegiance I want."

*For weeks the boy careened through the days, trying to understand
the strange new world he found himself in. He'd long since realized
that it was not the grand adventure he'd expected. He did not find his
brother. Instead, he found an endless supply of mud and lice and men
with eyes like old knives—just sharp enough to be dangerous. . . .*

CHAPTER 15

THE CAPTAIN'S VOICE ECHOES IN MY EARS AS
I struggle against Devin and another boy who helps
to grab me. I kick and writhe, but it's no use. They
easily outmuscle me, and in a matter of moments, I'm being
carried across the deck and down into the belly of the ship.
The Captain never looks back. The wind lifts his hair, but he
looks as immovable as a statue against the darkening sky and
the perilous sea beyond.

Once the boys have me belowdecks, I can't stop them from
tying my hands together behind my back or from dropping me
unceremoniously onto the cabin floor.

"Captain's orders," Devin says coldly, and then he closes
the door behind him with a violent snap of the latch.

With no real windows in the cell-like cabin, the small
space is dark and closed in. I struggle to get to my feet, which
is no easy task with my hands bound so tightly behind me.

Once I'm up, I try the door. It's locked again, but I throw my shoulder against it and shout for someone to let me out anyway.

No one comes. No one answers. And after a while, my side aches and I'm panting with frustration and fear. Because I don't know what the Captain could possibly want from me.

I settle myself onto the bed, trying to adjust, but it's impossible to find a comfortable way to sit or lie with my arms tied like they are. All I can do is wait, my ears sharp and alert for the sound of footsteps outside the door. For a warning that someone is coming for me.

But the waiting is endless and even with the ache in my arms, my eyes eventually start to grow heavy. And the slow rocking of a boat bound for the open sea coaxes me into a dreamless sleep.

I wake from a sharp pain in my arm. It throbs with every heartbeat, a steady stabbing pulse that aches from shoulder to wrist. My cabin is now completely dark, and my head is fuzzy from sleep. The whole ship is quiet, so I know it must be very, very late.

I try to sit up, but I can't quite find enough leverage at first. It takes a few tries of rocking back and forth, but finally I manage to get myself upright. Which might have been a mistake, because now my head is swimming.

The ship creaks as it lists in the choppy waves of the open sea, and I'm so groggy from my unintended nap that I almost miss the soft *thunk* outside my door. I don't miss the slightly louder moan that follows it, though, or the sound of a body sliding to the floor. Trying to get myself ready for whatever is about to happen, I scoot back, away from where the danger might come.

The door creaks open slowly, and a wavering light just bright enough to obscure my vision precedes its bearer. "Will?" I squint my eyes, trying to make out who just entered, but the strange glow is blinding after the pitch-dark night. "Captain?"

"Neither, I'm afraid." The voice is unfamiliar—a deep, rich tenor that sends a shiver up my spine as it comes to me through the darkness.

When the light comes toward me, I realize it's no lamp. The glow is coming from small orbs that hover in the air, circling around the intruder like tiny planets, their wavering light throwing shadows across his face. With his face half concealed in darkness, I can't tell if I've ever seen him among the Captain's crew.

"Come on then, and be quick about it," he whispers as he cuts my bindings. When he pulls me to my feet, his hold on my wrist is gentle, but I have the distinct impression I wouldn't be able to break away if I tried.

"Wait," I say as I do try to wrangle free from his grip, but I can't. "Who are you?"

He catches one of the bright orbs and lifts it up near his face as he gives me a wickedly charming grin. His eyes are so pale, their irises practically glow in the light of the orb he's holding. They're set above a straight nose and a wide, soft mouth and strong, square chin. I still don't know who he is, but he's definitely not one of the Captain's crew. I would have noticed him.

From the amusement I see shimmering in those eyes, I know he's aware I'm admiring him. And from the smile teasing at his lips, I can tell he likes it.

"I'm the one here to save you, Gwendolyn," he whispers softly, his voice warm and tempting.

"But who *are* you? And how do you know my name?"

His eyes narrow just a bit, giving away his irritation. But the soft, pleasant smile playing on his lips never falters. "I am Pan," he tells me simply, as though that single word explains everything.

Pan, the one who attacked the ship. The reason so many boys are dead.

Instinctively, I struggle harder to break his grip, but it's like he doesn't even feel me.

"I'm here to take you to Olivia," he tells me.

"Olivia?" I stop struggling against his grasp at the sound of her name, and the moment I do, he takes advantage and scoops me into his arms.

"I had no idea the Dark Ones had stolen two from your world," Pan cuts in. "When I discovered it, I sent some of my lads to retrieve you from the Captain, but they failed." His jaw hardens and he glances away, his face shadowed.

"The attack on the ship was a rescue attempt?" I ask, peering through the darkness as I try to read the truth in his response.

"I'm sorry it was not more successful, Gwendolyn." I can't make out his features, but his voice is filled with remorse. "She's waiting for you," he whispers. His pale eyes never leave mine, but he doesn't move. It's as though he's giving me a chance to decide. "If you're ready?"

But I'm not sure.

The Captain told me Pan was the biggest lie of all. But isn't that exactly what Hook *would* say? And it's not like I haven't seen with my own eyes what the Captain himself is capable of—I watched him toss a boy to the monsters in the water. The Sisters, he'd called them. All because the kid hadn't immediately pledged his loyalty. The Captain had refused to show him any mercy at all. Not when the boy begged and pleaded. Not even when he squealed like a scared pig.

"Will your Captain take you to your friend?" Pan asks me.

No. He already told me he wouldn't.

One thing is clear—whoever he is, this boy knows about Olivia. The prospect of finding her, of finally finding someone who is squarely on my side in this upside-down world, is enough to make me stop struggling. It's enough to give this Pan character a chance.

When my chin dips in the barest nod, his eyes light with satisfaction. "Quiet now," he tells me as he eases us into the corridor.

He moves through the tight space as silently as the night, pulling me along easily, but he doesn't immediately go to the steps that lead up to the main deck. Instead, he stops at a short ladder that descends to the very deepest part of the ship. "I've one thing more to do," he tells me, the whites of his eyes glinting in the light thrown by the orbs that follow us.

He motions for me to take the ladder first. My arms still ache, but I manage to keep ahold of the well-worn railings as I inch myself down, Pan following behind me. He's dimmed the small lights that float around him so they're only ghostly whispers of their former brightness. Putting a finger to his lips, he dismounts, and then takes my hands and pulls me toward a glow coming from behind a stack of large wooden crates.

"He won't last much longer, Cap'n," Will says, his voice startling me as it drifts through the darkness.

"You think I don't know that?" the Captain answers.

As we get closer, I see the two of them silhouetted by a lantern hanging from the ceiling—the Captain and Will. They're leaning over a small body laid out on a pallet on the floor. I recognize the boy as the one the Captain was helping earlier—Davey. For a moment I'm not sure if the boy is alive, but then he lets out a small, labored moan.

Will shuffles back uneasily, his jaw tense and his brow deeply furrowed. But it's not the boy's injuries that have Will so tense. In the dim lamplight, I hadn't noticed the large, dark figure waiting in the shadows of the hold. Now that I see it, my breath seizes in my throat.

As the Dark One approaches the Captain, the hold fills with a familiar metallic buzzing. The creature's wings half unfurl and fill the tight space, but the Captain doesn't move to attack. They stand as though locked in an uneasy truce, each taking the other's measure. Then, in a motion so quick that I barely see the blur of darkness as it moves, the creature plunges its fist into the boy's chest.

The small limp body jerks violently in response.

I stagger back at what I'm seeing, and Pan's arms go around me, supporting me gently but also pinning me firmly in place. "Help him," I whisper, my voice ragged with the shock of what I just witnessed.

"Shhh," Pan soothes, brushing his lips against my temples. "It's too late now. Had we arrived a few moments sooner . . ." He trails off, his implication clear—if not for my hesitation earlier, we might have saved the boy.

I watch in horror as the creature's hand passes through the small body, like the boy is no more solid than a ghost. The boy convulses again, his chest lifting up from the floor until his whole body hovers rigidly in the air. When the creature finally withdraws its fist, it brings with it a trailing thread that glows with an eerie luminescence.

The Captain does nothing but watch.

"What is that?" I whisper, unable to keep the horror—the wonder—out of my voice.

Pan's voice is calm, sure, as he whispers in my ear. "It's taking the boy's life, Gwendolyn."

The Captain stands motionless as the Dark One spools the thin luminescent thread around its dark fist before thrusting it forward and offering it to the Captain.

"His life?" I whisper, horrified.

"Well, perhaps not his life, exactly," Pan says.

"Please, Will," the Captain urges, the desperation in his voice uncharacteristic. The Captain and Will are staring at each other across the darkness of the hold, tension simmering between them. "I won't lose you to this place."

"No," Will says quietly, his voice sure. "You won't. Not in that way, at least."

The Captain frowns as though he's understood more in Will's words than I do. "It's already done. And it would give you more time," the Captain urges. "Already, your arm—you know what's there is only the beginning. That mark will grow, and when it does, you'll die."

Will rubs absently at the piece of dark fabric wound around his forearm. "Maybe, but how many times have you told me that there are worse fings than death, Cap'n?"

An uncomfortable silence rears up between the two. "What would you have me do, then?" The Captain's voice is no more than a ragged whisper. "Should I leave all of the lads to die?"

The buzzing thrum in the air grows, signaling the creature's impatience.

Will glances at it warily before he turns back to the Captain and shakes his head as though in defeat. "Do what you must," he says. His shoulders slump as though the fight has gone out of him, and he walks away from the Captain and the dark creature. His steady steps echo through the dark hold as he ascends the ladder to the deck above.

The child's rigid body is still hovering in the air. The boy's mouth is wide, and his sightless eyes are still open in a combination of pain and terror. The Captain doesn't even seem to see the boy though. His eyes are focused on the place where Will disappeared, toward the ladder hidden by the darkness around us, to the deck above. The Captain's face is blank, his eyes steady, and though I can tell he might want to, he doesn't go after Will.

"Watch, Gwendolyn. If you have any doubt of the choices before you, watch what your Captain is capable of."

The Captain has already turned back to the Dark One and is slowly lowering himself to his knees, his head bowed before the dark creature, his eyes level with the boy's motionless body. "Go with God, Davey," the Captain whispers as he crosses himself. "And forgive me what I must do."

The Dark One thrusts its hand forward again, offering the fistful of glowing thread to the Captain. This time the Captain accepts the thread of the boy's life in cupped hands. For a moment he simply holds it, the glow lighting the sharp angles of his face, and I can't tell if it's revulsion or appreciation that makes him pause. Then he lifts his hands and inhales deeply, his lips soft in a rounded O as he breathes in the boy's light. With each breath, the boy's body convulses in the air with an agonized groan.

"You see, Gwendolyn," Pan whispers as I watch the horrible drama play out before me. "Your Captain cares so little for those who follow him, he will drink in the boy's life, and the boy will die." The boy lets out another frail, awful moan. "Imagine, my dear, what he would do to you."

It's not your allegiance I want, the Captain had told me. Is this what he meant? Is this what he had planned for me?

I can't make myself look away from the scene in the dark hold before me. The Captain's face is a combination of pain and relief, regret and horrible delight. With every breath of light the Captain takes, the boy's moans shatter the stillness of the night. With each breath, the small body twitches and convulses, and the boy's skin begins to turn a dusky, mottled gray. Dark jagged lines that remind me of the crew's tattoos snake their way across the boy's skin, until his entire body is covered with a web of them.

Finally, the small body convulses silently with one last, horrible twitch and goes limp, falling back to the pallet. And when his body hits the ground, it shatters into hundreds of jagged pieces that skitter across the floor of the hold.

The curve of an ear settles near my feet, and I let out a strangled gasp.

The Captain goes perfectly still at the sound.

Pan tries to pull us back far enough to avoid being caught, but it's too late. The Captain's wild eyes have already found us in the darkness, and when he sees who it is, and that I am not alone, his face contorts with fury.

"Unhand her," he growls, his blade raised unsteadily toward Pan. His eyes aren't quite as sharp as usual, almost like he's having trouble focusing.

"I don't think she wants to be unhanded." Pan's arms are still around me. "Shall we ask her? Would you like me to unhand you, Gwendolyn?"

I hear his voice, but it sounds so far away. My vision has gone dark around the edges, and it feels like I'm looking down a tunnel. All I can see is the small, fragile curve of the boy's ear lying on the ground near the toe of my boot.

"I'm warning you. Leave the girl," the Captain growls again, his voice even less human this time as it tears from his throat.

"Or what?" I can practically hear the taunting smile in Pan's voice. "Will you kill me? Will you kill her, as well? Perhaps you'll drink in her life, just as you drank in the boy's?"

The Captain growls, lunging forward, but whatever he's done has taken a toll—his legs seem to be too unsteady to hold him, and he stumbles. "Let. Her. Go."

"I don't think I will," Pan says calmly as he begins to back us toward the ladder. "I don't think I could countenance leaving such an innocent here with the likes of you. I've already promised to free her, you see."

"Gwendolyn." The Captain's eyes are wild. Their once-dark irises almost seem to glow in the darkness of the hold, like the fury has lit him from within. "Don't listen to his promises," he rasps. "Nothing but lies." He tries to stagger toward me.

But all I can see is the shattered pieces of what was once a boy scattered across the floor. "And you haven't lied to me?" I whisper. But then my voice grows stronger, more sure. "You told me the Dark Ones could breach the boundaries between our worlds, but you never mentioned that you're working with them."

The Captain only stares at me, his jaw tight, and his dark eyes flashing with some unspoken emotion I cannot place. But he doesn't deny it.

"It's up to you, Gwendolyn," Pan coaxes. The warmth of his arms feels real and strangely secure. "I will not force you. I would never treat you like a prisoner."

The implication is clear—that the Captain *has* treated me like a prisoner. Not that I need to be reminded. My wrists still ache from his crew's treatment.

"Think of Olivia," he whispers in my ear. "I can take you to her."

Olivia. The thought of her shakes me from any wavering. I don't know how much I trust Pan, but I've twice seen with my own eyes what the Captain is capable of. I need to find Olivia. If we have any chance of ever getting home, it will be because we're together, and Pan is offering me that much.

I meet the Captain's eyes and see the fury there hasn't ebbed. "Let's go," I tell Pan.

With a crowing laugh, Pan scoops me up again and runs.

The Captain tries to lunge for us, but he's still too unsteady on his feet. Pan, on the other hand, moves quickly, deftly through the dark ship, guided by his strange orbs. The instant we're above deck, he leaps, and we are in the air.

"You made the right choice, my dear," Pan says, his voice smooth and sweet as honey.

But I can't be sure that I have. I'm even not sure there is a right choice in this strange and dangerous world. I close my eyes, not wanting to see the dark water or the ship receding below me, and, as we mount higher into the sky, the relentless rushing of the air echoes my own clawing sense of dread.

The boy grew to hate all of it, but he hated the darkness most of all, for at night, he couldn't see death coming. That night, like so many others, there would be no sleep. When they called for him to "Stand To!" he wore his fear like a tattered coat. . . .

CHAPTER 16

T HE NIGHT SWEEPS PAST, DARK AND THICK as ink as Pan flies on. I force myself to focus on the glittering stars above us, because I don't want to think about the tender curve of a broken boy's ear. And I don't dare look down.

Pan's body is my only warmth against the chilly air, his arms the only thing between me and falling to my death. But his darkened expression is so sure, so determined, I can *almost* make myself loosen the tight grip I have on his neck.

His face is masked with shadows, but a smile plays about his lips as we fly. I can't tell if it's from the satisfaction of besting the Captain or from the pleasure of the flight itself, but it seems like a secret smile. I don't think it's meant for me. Still, the longer we fly, the more I find myself drawn to him. The more I find myself wanting him to look at me.

Maybe it's because he smells like the night, wild and free

as the wind whipping through my hair, but it takes all my focus not to let myself lean into him. His is a cold scent, distant and empty as a winter day, but that doesn't make it any less enticing. I want to breathe him in, and it's only when he chuckles darkly that I realize I'm doing just that.

Then, before my cheeks can even flush warm with embarrassment, before I can even register how strange it is that I would be so taken by him, we're falling. Or I guess we're diving, but when you're plummeting to earth with no control over the fall, the feeling is about the same. We break through the clouds, the cold dampness of them wetting my cheeks and hair, clinging to my bare arms.

We are still over the endless sea, but the surface of the water is now as smooth as polished glass. It shines pink from the soft morning light instead of the lurid meals of monsters. The clouds and sky glow a rosy amber now, and off in the distance, a sliver of sun is just beginning to peek over the level line of the horizon.

The view from this height is so vast, the feeling of the air rushing across my skin so exhilarating, an overwhelming sensation of freedom rushes through me as Pan glides effortlessly over the water. It's like when I run, when I push myself enough to quiet the worries and the insecurities until I can only feel. Only this feeling is so much bigger, so much more intense. So much more tempting.

The Captain and his ship are nowhere to be seen, but the island is there before us, rising up from the sea like an angry fist.

Pan leans into the wind and makes a course for those

strange shores. We're close enough now that I don't need a spyglass to see the wreath of jagged rocks that protect the island. Their dark surfaces rise sharply from the water, like some long-submerged creature trying to claw the sky with its craggy fingers. No wonder the Captain stays so far out to sea— the waters around the island would be deadly to a ship as large as his.

But navigating these dangers is easy for Pan, who glides easily around the peaks that rise unevenly from the water below. I can't help but think he's showing off a little with how easily he sails through the island's gauntlet. He follows the shoreline to where the sea cuts up through a rocky beach and then follows the water farther, through a narrow pass that leads deep into the island's interior.

I am sure now that I hadn't been imagining what I saw through the spyglass on the Captain's ship. Up close, it's clear the island is moving as though it's alive. Sharp corners of rose-colored rocks flatten to smooth planes as it continues to move and transform itself.

But even as surreal as it all seems, the beauty of the island overwhelms—the staggering heights of the pink cliffs shot through with silvery veins of glittering crystal, the jeweled green of the jungle growth clinging to the rocky land. The flowers dotting the lush green with bright bursts of color are all more vibrant, more breathtaking than anything I've ever seen.

The sheer cliffs of the coastline soon give way to hilltops covered by a thick carpet of impenetrable vegetation. Everywhere below us, the jungle shivers and pulses with life. The broad glossy leaves of the plants ripple in the still morning light, their enormous flowers opening and closing like hungry mouths. But just as unmistakable as the beauty here is a feeling of danger so thick that it stirs in the very air.

Adjusting his course, Pan plunges into the jungle itself. He glides effortlessly along the canopy of trees, and then descends beneath their limbs, continuing along the jungle floor. Branches shift and move, creating a path through the jungle, as though the island is welcoming him home. On and on we fly, until it feels as though there will never be anything more than this green surrounding me, alive and threatening. Eventually, though, the trees ahead begin to thin, and I hear the rushing sound of water.

Pan chuckles at my gasp when we enter a wide clearing anchored by a towering waterfall. He touches down and gently lowers me to my unsteady legs, but he doesn't release me.

Instead he leans in close, like he wants to tell me a secret. "Welcome to Neverland, Gwendolyn."

How long ago was it that the Captain gave me those same words, not as a gift as Pan offers them, but as a threat, a warning? It feels so much longer than a handful of days. And with my memories of the time before so hazy, it's hard to imagine I even had a life before my captivity on the Captain's ship or before I was brought to this world.

I take a deep breath to steady myself and use the opportunity to look around. We are in the center of a wide, level valley. On one end, across a smooth, clear lake, water glints in the morning light as it cascades from a steep rise of rose-colored rock. And anchoring that rock is a towering waterfall that's like nothing I've ever seen. The falls remind me of

126

the tumbled tiers of a wedding cake and each step throws up clouds of mist that shimmer in the soft light. It's like watching a living prism, the rainbows within the mist shifting and dancing over the many pools.

The Captain had tried to explain that we were no longer in the human world. After all I saw on his ship, after all I experienced, I came to believe him, but now, standing here in this place in the very heart of the island, my heart understands the truth. "This really is Neverland," I say with a kind of strangled awe. And if this is Neverland, how much more could be true?

Pan takes me by the hand and leads me forward, closer to the edge of the mirrorlike surface of the lake. "Welcome home, Gwendolyn, my dear."

Home.

A feeling of joy crashes through me, and for a moment I can't help but accept the absolute rightness of his words. A longing wells inside me so startling, so complete, it shocks me.

Because this place *isn't* my home. And I can't let Neverland become my home. But there is something about the land around me that pulls at me. Calls to me in a way I cannot remember ever having felt before.

Covering my reaction the best I can, I gently pull my hand away from his grip and touch the stones at my wrist, forcing myself to remember my life from before. But the memories that surface are hazy and indistinct. And they aren't easy or comforting.

I can't seem to envision any of the places I've lived, but I *can* remember the overwhelming feeling of rootlessness, of being unsettled and out of place time and again. Of knowing that each move we made was only a stop—a pause that let me settle just long enough to almost get comfortable before I'd be uprooted again. But I don't remember any of those stops ever really feeling like a home.

Even through the murkiness of my memory, I know I've never had a place that truly felt like my own. But as I open my eyes again and take in the beauty around me, Pan's words of welcome echoing in my head, there is a traitorous part of me that wonders whether this *could* be the home I've been looking for. With all this beauty around me and the almost comforting pulse of the island beneath my feet, a voice deep inside me whispers, *Would it really be so bad?*

I step back from Pan, unsettled by how easily I almost let myself give in. The Captain had warned me about this—he'd told me Neverland would tempt me to betray everything I once knew. I hadn't understood . . . not really. But maybe now I'm starting to.

I *can't* forget who I am and where I need to get back to. I won't let myself be taken in by this world again.

"Gwendolyn?" Pan asks, his voice filled with concern. When I don't answer, he lifts my chin gently. "Are you well?"

I give a slight nod. "I'm fine," I tell him, finally forcing myself to meet his eyes.

Safe on the ground and with the morning sun finally lighting the world, I take my first real look at him. He certainly doesn't seem like any Peter Pan I've ever seen. He's no child, for one. He's taller than the Captain, but he looks about the same age—Pan, too, is maybe a couple of years older than I am. Though the barest hint of light stubble lines his jaw, his face is missing the worn, exhausted quality I now realize was the Captain's defining feature.

His white-blond hair stands on end in an artful disarray that gives the impression he's constantly in flight, like the wind itself can't keep its greedy fingers out of those unruly locks. Just as I'd suspected back on the ship, he's beautiful. But I see now that he has a hint of darkness to him, a suggestion of danger that doesn't so much warn you away as make you want to lean closer, to learn his secrets.

He's wearing the same tight, jaggedly stitched pants as Fiona and a high-necked vest that exposes the well-defined muscles in his bare arms and chest. The pale skin over his collarbone and around each bicep and wrist is adorned with bloodred tattoos that remind me of something.

It takes a second for the memory to bubble up, murky and indistinct as all the others, and then I realize where I've seen markings like Pan's tattoos before—they're similar to the rune stones my mom has always made and collected.

That recognition helps me remember her a little more clearly—every time we moved, she would take her collection of small, smooth pebbles and line our new windowsills with them. In every new place we went, she found another stone and painstakingly carved a crooked symbol into its surface. She'd wrap each stone carefully and keep them with her until she could set them out on the next window. My mom always said the runes she used were old Celtic symbols for protection—

I reach out without thinking, and touch one of the red markings that adorns the skin below Pan's collarbone. The red lines aren't smooth like a tattoo should be. They're raised, ever so slightly. They're not just tattoos, I realize. They're scars. Someone *carved* these symbols into his skin.

The warmth of his skin beneath my fingertips brings me back to myself and, embarrassed, I pull my hand away like I've been burned. My cheeks are hot with the awareness of how strangely forward it was to touch him like that, but even in my embarrassment, something makes me want to reach out again, something pulls me toward him.

I clench my hands into fists at my sides instead. "What are they?" I ask.

"They were a gift from my mother," he replies with a small smile.

"Your *mother* did that to you?" I say, horrified.

"She did it *for* me, Gwendolyn," he says.

His face is still serene, pleasant even, as he takes my hand and brings it up to his chest again, covering mine with his own. Beneath my fingertips and the raised edges of the carved lines, his heartbeat is slow and steady. His eyes, with their glacial-blue irises ringed by midnight, never leave mine.

"In this world, power requires sacrifice, Gwendolyn. The Queen sacrificed some of her power to bestow these gifts onto me. I accepted the pain, and in return, I received the power they give me. Some allow me to break free from the earth— flight, as you've seen. Others give me the power to speak to the island and compel it to obey," he says, pointing to a different marking.

Then he takes my hand in his, pulling it away from the marks on his chest, and raises it to his lips. Still holding my

130

gaze, he kisses the underside of my wrist softly before releasing it.

I rub absently at the bit of skin that burns where his lips brushed over it. When he smiles again, my skin practically buzzes with heat where his lips touched me. But there's a memory tugging at me, even through the pleasant haze of his attention. There's something I'm supposed to be doing. . . .

Olivia, a small voice whispers, reminding me.

I can't seem to look away. "Where's Olivia?" I murmur, the words thick and unwelcome in my mouth.

I think I see impatience crash through his expression, but it's gone so quickly, I wonder if I imagined it. "She's most likely still sleeping. I thought I would show you my favorite part of the island rather than disturb her so early."

What I want is to see Olivia, but he looks so hopeful—almost shy and boyish—I can't seem to make myself disappoint him. "It's beautiful," I tell him honestly.

"Come." He gestures that I should sit at the water's edge before he lowers himself to the ground, his long, leather-clad legs outstretched comfortably.

The clearing is empty and silent except for the soft rush of water from the falls. No one knows where I am. *I* don't even know where I am. Tentatively, I sit, keeping distance between me and the beautiful boy who's brought me to this place.

On nights such as that one, the boy came to understand that the key to not dying was remembering he was alive. For the world around him was strange, and often it felt like he was dreaming, though wide-awake. So he almost did not trust his eyes when he turned and saw his brother, gray and pale as an apparition, in the dim evening light. . . .

CHAPTER 17

S O THE STORIES ARE TRUE," I SAY, WATCHING the dance of the waters. Maybe the tales weren't accurate, exactly, but . . . "Neverland is real." I glance over at him. "And so are you."

He grins then, a wickedly charming smile that makes my heart kick up in my chest. "It does appear that way, does it not?" he murmurs, his voice soft, coaxing, and again I feel pulled toward him with an urgency I don't understand.

"It does," I agree, but I also remember what the Captain told me about stories and the lies they often hide.

Though it's clear now that the Captain's stories held lies of their own.

"What did the Captain do to that boy on the ship?" I ask Pan.

Pan seems to ignore my question as he lets the tips of his fingers trail through the water of the pool, making small eddies ripple across the glassy surface. Tiny brightly colored fish swim over to investigate. They look like jewels glinting just below the surface. One of the braver fish stills and then, darting forward, latches itself on to Pan's finger with an unexpected violence. He doesn't even flinch. He simply lifts his hand from the water, the fish still dangling from his fingertip.

"We each belong somewhere, Gwendolyn," Pan finally says, examining the fish. "This creature belonged to the water. . . ." The fish's scales are a brilliant sapphire-blue and startling purple, too vibrant and bright to belong in the seas of my own world. But as I watch, the colors fade and tiny black lines begin to snake themselves across the surface of its body. The lines remind me of the cracks that appeared in Davey when the Captain drank in his life.

"But when a creature ventures beyond the safety of its own world, often it can't survive." Pan flicks the body of the fish from his fingertip, and it falls to the ground, where it crumbles on impact into brittle shards that look like bits of broken glass. Dark blood begins to well from Pan's finger, but he ignores it. "Your Captain doesn't belong in this world, Gwendolyn, and so he depends upon the Dark Ones for his life."

I stare at the blood beginning to drip from Pan's finger and think of the way the boy's life drained away from him when the Captain inhaled the glowing thread, and I have a feeling I understand more than I want to.

"You see, my dear, children do well enough here in Neverland. This world is a place for the wild, unruly desires of innocence. But your Captain is no longer a child, and he's certainly no innocent. Without what he takes from those boys, his body would become as fragile as this poor creature's." With a deft flick of his wrist, he brushes the shards of the fish back into the water. The other fish immediately swarm, darting in and out to scavenge the remains of their friend. "As all human bodies become here as they age."

The tattoos. On the ship, the older boys all had dark, scar-like lines that I'd thought might have been some mark of loyalty or rank, but I see now they weren't. What just happened to that fish is happening to all of them.

"*All* humans?" I ask, my voice wavering. I'm not any more of a child than most of the tattooed—no, cracked—boys in the Captain's crew. Neither is the Captain.

"Well . . . perhaps not *all*," Pan concedes. "As you saw in the hold of the ship, your Captain has found a way to avoid such an unfortunate end. When he accepts what the Dark Ones offer, he takes for himself his victim's innocence and youth. The younger the child, the more power it contains, the more time it buys him." His cool eyes bore into mine as his expression goes coldly dangerous. A moment before, the valley had felt like a peaceful, welcoming place, but now there is a dangerous tension radiating from Pan.

"But it will never be enough for him. This world will *never* be a place where he belongs." Pan's features soften, and his mouth curls into a slow, satisfied smile. "Not as I belong," he says, brushing his hand over the soft grassy ground cover between us. Tiny white flowers appear at his touch. "And not as you could belong, Gwendolyn." His cool eyes meet mine, but he doesn't speak for a long, uncomfortable moment.

"Me?" I say with a surprised laugh. But a small part of me

still wonders at the pull I feel to the island, to Pan. "This isn't my home. I don't *want* to stay here," I force myself to say. And it's only partially a lie.

"But it could be," he says simply as he trails his fingertip along my leg, drawing a line of his blood from my knee down almost to my ankle. I can't look away from the dark smudge of his blood on my pants, and can't help but think that he's basically marked me. *But for what?* the small voice inside me asks.

Then, as though sharing the best sort of secret, he bends his head toward mine conspiratorially. "In this world, you could do anything. *Become* anything." The sky has lit completely now, and the pink from the sunrise has all but melted into the bright blue of day. A blue that can't compete with the brightness of his eyes. "I can show you, protect you. Just as my mother taught me."

"So you're not one of the Fey?" I ask, surprised. Until this moment I hadn't known for sure.

"No, but the Queen of this world was the only mother I ever knew, and because of my mother's gifts, I am as close to Fey as any mortal has ever been." He plucks one of the tiny blossoms, and as he holds it, the petals turn from red to pink and then to blue. "For some, Neverland can be paradise. I can give you that, Gwendolyn."

As I reach for the flower to accept it, a part of me also wants to accept the promise of his words. My memories are still so hazy, but the one feeling I cannot shake, the feeling that comes through clear and sure, is how out of my control my life had always felt. Even as I held everything together, each move we made was my mom's choice. Each time I had to start over was because *she* decided.

What would it mean to choose the beauty and wonder of this place for myself?

"You could belong here, Gwendolyn," Pan tempts, offering me the flower. "You could belong with me."

His words stroke at something inside me, something that wants and aches and cannot remember having been satisfied before. I'm not sure what I mean to accept when I reach out to take the flower from him. But I can't bring myself to care. I just want something, *anything*, to feel right and real and true.

But as soon as the stem of the tiny flower is between my fingertips, tiny black lines begin to creep along the petals' surfaces. With a gasp, I let the flower fall to the ground, wilted and gray on the bright emerald of the grass. At the sight of it, the intense wanting that had reared up so suddenly and so strongly crumbles and fades.

I'm not sure if Pan realizes the emotions that have just crashed through me. He doesn't seem to, because a moment later he takes my hand and gently settles it palm down in the soft, grassy growth. Then he covers it with the broad warmth of his own hand, pressing my palm so firmly into the ground, I can feel the uncomfortably sharp point of a pebble, the dampness of the earth. Beneath my fingertips is the constant and gentle throb of an island always changing.

"Listen to Neverland, Gwendolyn. Can you feel it calling to you?" His voice is soft and urgent, coaxing me again to believe that what he's saying might be true.

I want to pull my hand away and rub the heat of his skin

from mine, but I can't. Because it would be a lie. The ground *does* pulse beneath me, like a heartbeat. And there's more—something warm growing beneath my palms. Something comforting and welcoming.

"You don't have to be afraid, my dear. You need only ask for what you most desire, and see if Neverland finds favor in you," he tells me, low and sweet. "You need only call to it, to see if it responds." Pan's eyes are clear and bright now, hopeful as they meet mine. "Go on," he urges. "Try."

I swallow hard, not sure whether the connection I feel to the land is safe—or even real. Not sure whether I can trust his words. But he's looking at me so ardently, and I can't bring myself to disappoint him. I close my eyes, and I do what he asks.

I want to go home, I think because it is what I'm supposed to think.

And once you're back there? the small voice whispers. *What then?*

I want to have a normal life, a normal home. I want to find a place where I fit without pretending to be something I'm not. That's what made Westport feel like home, I remember then—I had someone there who didn't look at me like an outsider, who didn't ask questions that forced me into lies. I had Olivia.

The ground beneath my hands goes hot, burning against my palms as an ache travels up my arms. I open my eyes and jerk my hands away, scraping them against the ground just to be free of Pan and the uncomfortable heat.

He's watching me with an intensity that's almost uncomfortable. An intensity that makes me think he knows what's just happened. All at once, I realize how easily I was taken by his words. How completely I'd fallen under the spell-like pull of his appeal. And I'm shaken by it.

I glance away, because his gaze is too steady and expectant for me to hold any longer. I focus on the broken flower and make myself ask the only question that matters. "Will you take me to Olivia now?"

He considers me a moment longer, and for a second I think he knows everything—how close I came to accepting, how much part of me still wants to. But he smiles, pleasant as ever, and I think maybe I was wrong.

"Of course," he says, standing and offering me his hand.

A minute later we are aloft again, soaring over the tops of the trees, the falls passing beneath us as we make our way farther into the island. Up we fly, toward the craggy center of the mountains, until we come to a place where there is no jungle. He lands in a clearing where there is only the smooth face of a cliff and the barren rock beneath our feet. Behind us, a gaping chasm in the ground separates us from the rest of the island.

"Where are we?" I wrap my arms around myself. The air isn't any colder here, but the bleak landscape sends a chill through me just the same.

"Home," he says simply, a smile teasing at his lips. "This is where I live. Where I keep my boys."

"Here?" I ask, looking around. There isn't anything here but the flinty face of the rock rising up around on one side of us, and the gaping tear in the earth on the other. My stomach sinks. "Where's Olivia?"

"Inside," he says, gesturing grandly to the sheer cliff.

I don't know what he's talking about—there is no door or portal or split in the rock that could be an entrance to a cave. "There's nothing there."

"Isn't there?" he asks wryly.

I look again at the rock, and just as I'm about to tell him, *No, there isn't*, the earth beneath my feet begins to tremble. I grab for Pan's arm as the entire wall of rock begins to move. With a thunderous grinding, the cliff shifts backward slowly, rearranging itself and revealing the silhouette of jagged spires and towers.

When the land finally goes silent, I'm standing in the shadow of an enormous structure. A castle. Or maybe a fortress would be a better description, because it's too massive, too violent-looking to be anything as romantic as a castle. It towers at least six stories above us, hewn from the red-gold rock of the cliff that bore it.

Its walls are solid rock, and its windows are narrow slits high up from the ground. The only opening at all is a deep, dark tunnel that leads straight into the mountain itself. Even without the chasm that cuts it off from the rest of the island, even without the steep bluffs that pen it in safely on all sides, this is not the sort of place anyone could attack easily.

Pan's eyes are dancing, his mouth twitching in amusement as he glances at the grip I have on his bicep. "Ready, my dear?"

I try to pull away, but he stops me by placing his hand over mine and tucking my arm more securely against his body. He smiles then—a truly breathtaking sort of smile—and the look in his eyes is enough to make my cheeks flush with warmth.

I glance away, uncomfortable. There's something about the way he looks at me that makes me think he sees something in me that no one else ever has. Like I am something whole and strong and *important*. Being looked at like that— being *seen*—is something completely new and absolutely intoxicating.

And I don't trust it one bit.

But I've made my choice. Before us, the towering fortress waits. The Captain and his ship feel very far away. London feels even farther. With the warmth of Pan's body next to mine, the scent of him, wild and free as a winter night, surrounding me, and the promise of finding my friend ahead of me, I take one last look at the open sky above and walk on.

The boy had grown ever more sure he might never see his brother again, so he did not hesitate to grasp him in a tight hug once he realized it was no apparition before him. His brother smiled, flashing the crooked tooth in his worn-out grin. "Volunteered to come up to the front," he told the boy. "Couldn't leave you to have all the fun." But the boy knew, from the worry darkening his brother's eyes, that wasn't it at all. . . .

CHAPTER 18

THE ENTRYWAY OF THE FORTRESS IS LIT BY the same floating phosphorescent blobs that Pan had with him on the ship. They hover around us, guiding us through the dark tunnel as we make our way deeper into the mountain. I reach up to touch one that comes close to my face, but Pan snatches my hand away before my fingers can brush against it.

"Fairy lights," he tells me. "Never can tell how they'll react."

From the other side of the tunnel, I can make out the sounds of voices. As the light gets closer, the sounds grow, and the glowing orbs peel off, leaving us. When we reach the end, the tunnel flares open into a great hall with a ceiling that soars stories above. Two sullen-looking boys snap to attention, blades drawn, but when they see Pan, they scuttle to their posts against the wall and avert their eyes.

The Great Hall of the fortress is a mad playground. Everywhere I look there are children, most much younger than the ones on the Captain's ship. A group of small boys nearly runs me over as they chase after an even smaller one. They're all screaming all sorts of inventive curses and brandishing swords that look too sharp to be safe for any game. Other boys, who couldn't be any older than nine or ten, lounge around the edges of the great space, smoking thin, sweet-smelling cigars on thick piles of furs.

"Where did they all come from?" I wonder, struck by the number of them.

"The Dark Ones steal them from your world," Pan tells me. "I bring them here and give them a home," he says, throwing his arms wide.

Rows of torches lining the walls throw their flickering light over the scene before me. They give the whole space an otherworldly quality. But even with the high ceiling, the air in the fortress is dank and stale.

"This all belonged to my mother." He takes a step into the chaos. "When I was a small boy, the Queen and her people filled these halls with light and merriment, and every day was an adventure. Now these walls offer me and my boys protection—from the Dark Ones, from the pirate, often from the other creatures of this land."

"Where's the Queen now?" I ask, moving closer to Pan to avoid being hit by a boy careening after a friend.

"The Dark Ones rose up and overthrew her some time ago," he says, his voice dark and his jaw tight. I wait for him to say more, but he doesn't. "Come. I'll take you to Olivia."

Pan doesn't seem to notice the disorder around us as he leads me through the hall, still holding my hand firmly in the crook of his arm. He deftly sidesteps the piles of broken weapons and an unconscious boy as we make our way to the far wall. Without warning, he scoops me into his arms again, and then we're rising through the air toward a door nearly three stories up that I hadn't noticed before. He gives it a brisk knock before pushing it open and setting me gently inside.

This space is brighter than the Great Hall below, and the air is fresher and smells overpoweringly of the hundreds of flowers that tumble out of vases and across the surfaces of the room—wildly colorful blooms, some as large as my head, others barely the size of my smallest finger, all bunched in bright bouquets and strung up in long garlands.

I'd thought we were inside of a mountain, but there is a window on the back wall, covered with brightly colored silks that rustle in a breeze. With the draping fabrics and the soft furs that cover the floor in a patchwork of color, the whole room reminds me of a sultan's tent. In the center of the space stands an ornately carved canopy bed draped with silky white curtains. And in the center of the bed, half obscured by the diaphanous fabric, is a familiar figure.

"Olivia," I whisper, afraid to move. I have the sudden feeling if I say her name too loudly, the spell will be broken and this will all disappear like a dream.

But it doesn't disappear. She's real.

The second I see Olivia, alive and whole, I can almost believe I might be able to find a way back to our world, because I don't have to find it by myself anymore. I don't have to be alone in this strange place. The one person who has ever come closest to understanding me is here, and we'll find a way back together.

Olivia doesn't see me at first—her attention is focused on stringing daisylike flowers together into a long garland that's already trailing up over the canopy of the bed and halfway across the floor. I've never seen her do anything half so crafty before, and she looks absolutely absurd doing it now.

"Olivia, dear," Pan says smoothly from behind me. "I've brought Gwendolyn to you."

Olivia's hands go still when she hears Pan's voice, and when she sees him standing in the doorway, her whole face softens and her eyes brighten with delight. There is no fear in her expression, no worry.

Then she sees me standing next to him, and her expression darkens. "Gwendolyn?" she asks, her voice as unsure as the look on her face. I can tell she doesn't recognize me.

If I hadn't been looking for her, if I hadn't seen the picture in the Captain's quarters, I don't think I'd have recognized her, either. She's wearing a soft, flowing gown of the palest pink, something Olivia would never be caught dead in. Her long blond hair falls in its usual waves around her face, but her eyes aren't right. Their pale green is too glassy, too distant.

It's what this place does to people, I remind myself as I try to smile, but my face feels stiff with fear.

Pan steps forward into the room, toward the large bed. "Olivia, dear," he says again, his voice soft and soothing. "You remember Gwendolyn, don't you? You told me she was your dearest friend. You asked me to find her for you. And I have."

Olivia's brows draw together, like she's not exactly sure she remembers ever asking for such a thing. But her features soften when Pan offers her his hand. She rises slowly and allows him to pull her toward me.

"Come, Gwendolyn," he says, never taking his eyes off Olivia.

"Liv?" I brush my hair back from my face, tentative as I step toward the two of them.

"Come, Olivia, greet your friend properly."

Olivia gives Pan another questioning look. When he inclines his head in the barest nod, she finally releases his hand and steps toward me, her arms out in greeting. The gesture is formal, stiff, and so unlike the girl who would think nothing of looping her arm through mine. The memory of it rises up in my mind, clear and distinct. But before I can hold it tight, the image begins to fade again.

I step toward her, but her body tenses at my approach, her arms falling to her sides. I'm not sure what I should do or say. I'm not sure how to get *my* Olivia back. "Did the Dark Ones hurt you?" I ask finally, looking her over for some sign of injury.

"The Dark Ones?" Confusion shimmers in her eyes.

"The monsters that took us from London," I tell her gently, trying to remind her. Even with so many of my memories remaining just out of reach, the horror of being taken from my bed has never completely faded.

"London?" She says the word like it feels funny in her mouth, and then she glances at Pan for guidance. He has the same almost pleasant expression on his face he's had all morning, but his eyes are sharp and perceptive.

"You remember what we've talked about, my dear," Pan says gently.

Olivia closes her eyes. "I remember waking up," she says in a stiff voice. "And I remember Pan. He takes care of me." When her eyes open and look up at him, they are soft with wonder and an emotion that looks dangerously close to love. "He protects us all."

"Olivia—" I start to say, but Pan interrupts me.

"I had no idea the Dark Ones had stolen two from your world. Once Olivia confirmed she had a friend, I discovered the Captain had you. I sent some of my lads to retrieve you, but as I said, they failed." His jaw hardens and he glances away, his eyes shadowed. "I'm sorry they were not more successful, Gwendolyn," Pan tells me, the picture of contriteness.

"None of that matters now," Olivia tells him in a breathy whisper before she turns to me. "We are safe here, with Pan. You can forget the rest. All that"—she wrinkles her nose in distaste—"unpleasantness." Then she gives Pan a dazzling smile before settling herself back on the bed to work on her daisy chain again. The determination on her face is so thoroughly Olivia and yet so completely wrong.

"No," I tell her, approaching the bed slowly. "We can't stay here, Liv." I kneel down on the floor next to her and touch her arm to stop her from stringing another flower. "We have to find a way back," I tell her. "I need you to remember so you can help me figure this out."

"Back?" She goes very still under my hand, her expression tense.

"This isn't our home," I say, pushing down the unease I feel under Pan's too-watchful gaze. "This isn't our world."

But she's not listening to me. Her attention is on a point just beyond me—on Pan—and, ignoring me completely, she gives him a slow, private smile.

I ignore the jealousy that twists uncomfortably inside me when Pan smiles in return.

So Pan looked at me. So maybe for a second there I had thought . . .

I don't even know what I'd thought. Of course Olivia would want Pan. With his dark clothes and the scarlet runes decorating his fair skin, he looks like an elfin prince, and of course he would want *her*. She would make him the perfect fairy princess.

None of that matters, though. Like the Captain said, this isn't a fairy tale. We can't stay.

I take her hands and do not let them go, even when I feel her try to pull away.

Olivia glances at Pan, and I get the sense she doesn't know what to do.

"You *have* to remember, Olivia," I say, squeezing her hands and failing miserably to keep the urgency out of my voice. "Think about what our parents must be going through right now," I tell her. By now everyone would know we're gone. Would there be search parties? Would our faces be on the nightly news? "Think about how scared they must be."

"My parents—" She says the second word slowly, drawing it out, but recognition begins to light her eyes. Then her face falls. "My parents are probably too busy to even realize I'm gone." She looks up at me, sadness and anger clear on her face. Then she sees—*really* sees me—and the glassiness in her eyes lifts like a fog.

"Gwen," she says, and now it's *my* Olivia who is speaking. "Are you okay?" she asks. She's touching my face, squeezing my hand. Her expression is urgent, like she's suddenly awoken and just realized where we are.

She slides from the bed and throws herself at me. Her long arms go around me, and for a moment I'm overwhelmed by her hug. For a moment I feel like everything will be okay. "Oh my god. I thought I'd never see you again," she says, pulling away and looking me over.

"I know," I tell her. "Me too. But I'm here. So we'll figure this out."

"See, my dears. A happy ending after all," Pan says.

I turn to him, relief barely settling over me. I'm more determined now than ever that we need to get out of this world and back to our own. "Can you help us get back?" I ask him. There has to be a way.

He frowns. "Only the Fey can truly cross the boundaries between our worlds," he tells me, regret shadowing his expression. "But I shall do what I can. And until then, you are safe under my protection."

"Thank you!" Olivia leaps from the bed with her usual burst of energy to embrace Pan. But she lingers longer than a friendly hug usually demands, and she pulls away slowly, reluctantly. Pan gives her hand a courtly kiss, and by the time he releases it, her eyes have gone glassy again.

My stomach sinks as she smiles dreamily at Pan before turning back to the bed, and her piles of flowers.

"Olivia?" I ask softly. But she doesn't answer.

"I shall leave you to each other, then," Pan says with a small bow, and with an acrobatic leap from the threshold of the door, he leaves us alone in the flowered opulence of the room.

Olivia is already focused intently on her daisy chain. For a moment she was there, but it was only for a moment. I watch her work, and when I understand that my Olivia isn't there anymore, I walk over to the door and look down the sheer drop to the Great Hall below.

"How do we get down from here?" I ask, watching as boys run and shout and do all sorts of violent things to one another.

"Why would we want to get down?" she asks dreamily as she settles back in the plush bed again.

"Why *wouldn't* we?"

"Well, there are the boys, for one. They haven't had a mother in a very long time, and they're not very well behaved." Her voice is hollow and strangely formal, and she never takes her eyes from the flowers in her hand.

As I watch, a boy who can't possibly be older than eight tries to skewer another boy on the end of a long, sharp sword. I remember what the Captain told me about how dangerous *his* boys could be, and I'm suddenly almost okay with not having a ladder.

"Liv?" I ask, closing the door against the noise that rises up from below. Our flowered room falls into silence.

"Yes, Gwendolyn?" she asks, saying my name stiffly. She doesn't bother looking up.

I settle myself on the bed next to her and watch her work

for a moment. The flowers she's threading have velvety petals and stems spiked with thorns. They're like everything I've encountered so far in this strange world—beautiful and lush with an unaccountable thread of danger. The thumb of her left hand is bleeding from being pricked, but Olivia doesn't even seem to notice. She's gone on making her chain, staining the white petals with smears of red.

"You know we have to find a way out of here, don't you?" I'm unsettled by how quickly her eyes went glassy again, and I can't hide the fear in my voice. "We need to find a way back." *Before we can't remember what we need to get back to.*

She bites her lip, and her brows knit in concentration, like she's warring with herself over the answer. But she never looks up. She never stops weaving the stem of one flower into another.

"It's really not so bad here. Pan is wonderful. This world is magical. I've seen *such* amazing things." Her eyes are still soft and unfocused with that disturbing glassy sheen.

I watch her for another minute or two, but when it's clear we're not going to talk anymore, I go over to the lone window and pull back the silky fabric draped over it. The view I find confirms there is no way out of this room except through Pan. Outside, the mountain that the fortress is part of drops off steeply. Below us is water—a cove of sorts with a narrow passage out to the open sea beyond. There is no sign of the Captain's ship. There is no sign of anything on those still waters but the waiting sea.

*When their commander asked for volunteers, there weren't any young
or innocent enough left among them to step forward at first. His
brother looked at him, his eyes tight, commanding the boy to be still.
But the boy was no longer a child. He stepped forward and shot a
look at his brother, defiant. His brother's expression was grim as he
stepped forward too. . . .*

CHAPTER 19

G WENDOLYN." THE VOICE COMES TO ME
through the haze of sleep, distant and familiar. My
cheek brushes against the cool silk of the pillow,
a soft floral scent reminds me of lavender, and for a second,
I think I'm back in London. "Gwendolyn," the voice says
more urgently, and this time I register who it is. And where
I am.

Clutching the blanket around me, I sit up with a start.
"What?" I ask, pushing my hair back out of my face. The light
in the room is bright enough that I know I've slept long past
morning. "What is it?"

"Hurry, Gwendolyn," Pan says, his face inches from mine.
"We must go."

"Go?" I rub at my eyes. I haven't seen Pan since yesterday. It's almost a shock to see him again now—to realize my
memory of how striking he is wasn't a lie. But it's even more

of a shock to find him hovering over me when I'm alone in bed and barely awake.

I'm alone.

"Where's Olivia?" I ask. She was here when I finally fell asleep, long after she did.

"Your Captain has her," he says, his light eyes thunderous.

"The Captain?" I ask as I throw back the covers. I'm still wearing the outfit I managed to assemble yesterday from a selection of clothes that were lying around Olivia's room—a pair of jaggedly stitched leather pants and a tunic I made from tearing off the bottom off a wispy blue gown.

"A hunting party went out earlier—Olivia went with them. I realize now I shouldn't have allowed it, but she was rather distressed after your time together yesterday and . . ." His voice trails off as he gives me a look that is part question, part accusation.

My stomach sinks. I spent most of the day yesterday trying desperately to convince her we needed to find a way back to our own world. At first she just pleasantly dismissed what I'd told her—the little I could remember of our lives before—but by the time evening came, she closed me out completely.

"You were quite exhausted from your ordeal, and still sleeping," Pan continues. "So I thought it might soothe her to get away for a bit, perhaps find some new blooms on her own. A few moments ago, one of my boys returned alone. He said they'd been set upon." His jaw tightens. "I should have been prepared for some sort of retaliation."

We don't waste any time. After I lace up the heavy boots

I got from the ship, Pan scoops me up, and this time, I don'
even hesitate to wrap my arms tightly around his neck. With a
leap, he plunges toward the floor of the Great Hall, pulling up
just in time to sail over the chaos below. As we make our way
toward the entrance, a couple of the bright orbs join us and
follow at his side.

Once we're through the tunnel and out over the deep
trench that separates Pan's fortress from the rest of the island,
he turns and sails over the clear waters of the cove I glimpsed
from my window, out toward the rocky landscape of the other
end of the island.

The ground passing beneath us is rugged and parched.
Because it's completely bare of any vegetation, the never-
ending motion of the island is more starkly visible and erratic.
More violent. The rugged terrain ripples, its rocky surface
cracking and recracking like waves crashing into shore.

Pan's eyes are focused on the horizon and the dense, shadowy fog that rises up in the distance like a wall.

"What *is* that?"

"It's where we're headed, a place called the End," Pan
says darkly. "Once, the Dark Ones were banished there by the
Queen. Though they escaped long ago, that part of Neverland
has never quite recovered. I don't usually allow my boys to go
so far—it's impossible to know what dangers await."

As we approach, I can see a small group of people wav-
ing wildly at the edge of the fog. Their silhouettes are barely
visible against the gray mist. Pan speeds on, descending to
where the group of boy waits, bloodied and beaten.

"They took 'er, milord," one of the larger boys tells Pan as

he settles me to the ground. The boy's speech slurs through a fat lip. "We tried to chase 'em down and stop 'em, we did, but it weren't no use."

"How long ago?" Pan asks, not bothering to concern himself with the boys' injuries.

"Not long," the boy says, flinching as a high-pitched scream echoes from within the fog.

"Olivia," I say, recognizing her voice.

"They must still be close." Pan nods to the boys. "Let's go."

But none of the boys moves. The taller boy shakes his head, his swollen lip trembling. "I ain't going in there," he says, his eyes wide.

Pan takes a menacing step toward him. The boy can't be more than twelve, and Pan is so much broader and more than a head taller. The boy casts his eyes to the ground, but his head still shakes slightly as he nervously refuses the order.

"I think I must have misheard you," Pan says far too pleasantly to match the stiffness in his expression.

"P-please, milord. N-not in there," the boy stutters. "You know the Dark Ones haunt that land."

Pan draws a dark dagger from his belt and lifts it to the boy's neck, tilting his chin up with the tip. The boy won't look Pan in the eyes, though. "Let me put it simply: you may take your chances in there, or you may take them with me. Do you understand?"

A few yards away, the gray mist swirls and swells, inching closer. The day is cool, but a drop of sweat trickles down the boy's temple as he swallows hard and takes a shaking breath. Finally he gives an unsure nod.

"Go on, then," Pan directs, the dagger still in his hand.

The boys raise their weapons, holding them at the ready as they step hesitantly through the curtain of mist. For a moment we can still see them, but then they disappear completely.

He holds out his hand to me. "Stay close to me, Gwendolyn."

"Me?" I shift back again, away from the fog and from Pan.

"Of course. I can't take the chance that this is a trap. Even now the Captain could be waiting to have off with you the moment I'm gone. I won't leave you here in the open, unprotected."

"But . . ." The fog looks like a living thing. It's already swallowed up Pan's boys. I'm not in any hurry for it to swallow me.

Another wailing scream that sounds too much like Olivia comes from deep within the fog before I can find the words to refuse him.

"Come," he says, grabbing my wrist before I can stop him. Pan's hand is like a shackle as he pulls me through the curtain of mist, and a moment later we're inside.

Behind me, I can just make out the slightly brighter light of the day, but this fog is not like the one that hangs over London. There's nothing natural about the dry, dusky air around us. There's no warmth here. No thick dampness to explain the murkiness around us. It's like stepping into a vacuum, a cloud of nothingness. Like we've left Neverland behind.

Even with the orbs to guide us, I can't see more than a foot in front of my own face once we're within the cloud. Even Pan, holding my wrist as he is, looks blurry and indistinct. But the fog isn't silent. Sounds echo in the gray mist, bouncing off one another and multiplying. All of us call for Olivia, and soon we're surrounded by a hundred iterations of our own voices, all shouting the same name.

Pan pulls me along as one of the glowing orbs leads him into the murk. The ground is uneven, littered with stones and debris, and beneath the thick soles of my boots, I feel the crunch of brittle things I don't want to identify. At one point I trip over something that looks to be shaped like a shoe. But I think of what the boys said about people not returning from the End, and I don't look too closely.

Pan catches me when I stumble over something larger. "We need to move faster," he tells me. "Olivia will be in a great deal of danger if we don't find her before she finds the end of the island."

"The end of the—" I think of the sharp drop-offs that form the coastline, and I shout more frantically. But only the sound of my own voice comes back to me, taunting me with her name over and over.

Finally, after what feels like minutes or hours—I can't tell anymore—Pan turns to me. "I'm so sorry, Gwendolyn, but—"

"Pan!" Olivia's voice echoes back from four directions at once.

Pan goes still, listening to his name repeat in the mist surrounding us.

"It's Olivia," I breathe, relief shuttling through me. "We found her!"

I can barely make out Pan's expression as he continues to listen to his name echo around us.

"Well, what are we waiting for?" I ask.

He doesn't answer right away, and I think he might not

have heard me. But then his eyes flicker, glancing at me, and after another moment, he gives me a terse nod. "Are you alone?" he shouts.

"Yes!" The echo of Olivia's voice surrounds us. "Hurry!"

"Stay where you are and shout for me again," Pan calls.

After a moment Pan's name comes again from within the fog. And again.

Time loses all meaning as we inch along, trying to follow the sound of Olivia's voice in a deadly game of Marco Polo. Sometimes we turn toward her call, only to realize we're following an echo. Finally, though, I see the golden glow of Olivia's hair ahead of us in the thick fog.

"Olivia!" My voice bounces off the fog and comes back to me, all excitement and relief.

With it comes another sound, though—a too-familiar metallic hum, a buzzing pulse that makes me reach for Pan. "The Dark Ones," I whisper, but he's heard. His dagger is already raised in warning.

Around us, the edges of the fog seem to be growing darker, and the echoing voices that have been chasing us for who knows how long begin to die away. Until the only sound is the rustling hum of the Dark Ones themselves.

Pan's eyes track through the gloom for the source of the sound. "Quickly," he commands, directing me toward Olivia's silhouette. She turns when she hears our footfalls, her eyes wide with fear, but when she sees who it is, she leaps for Pan, who folds her into his arms.

"There, there," he whispers as he strokes her hair. "All is well. I have you."

She lets out a sob, which is muffled by the fabric of his vest. "The boys came out of nowhere," she tells him, not loosening her hold. The volume of her voice grows with every word. "We weren't even that far from the tunnels, and then . . . they just left me here. I didn't know what to do or where to—"

"You're safe now," Pan tells her, running his hand over her hair. But his eyes meet mine through the hazy mist as the rustling buzz grows louder. The Dark Ones are getting closer.

"We need to go," I whisper, looking down to see shadows creeping along the floor around us, circling us. "Now."

But it's too late to run. The shadows swirling around our feet are already surging and growing as they form themselves into a trio of the dark creatures. When they're fully formed, they unfurl their wings, stirring the gray fog into whirling eddies.

Pan moves to shield us with his body as the glowing orbs that guided us through the mist attack the Dark Ones, darting at the creatures like angry bees. Where they hit, the Dark Ones' flesh hisses, and the smell of burning leaves filters through the air. It's not enough to stop the creatures, though. The fairy lights are no more than a nuisance, nothing like the Captain's fireballs that brought them down from the sky.

Furious, the largest of the dark creatures strikes out at the fairy lights, swatting the glowing orbs away with an inhuman growl as it continues to stalk toward us. Pan doesn't so much as flinch. The hand holding the dark blade of his dagger is steady as he thrusts in the direction of the Dark Ones, and when the creatures see what Pan is threatening, they go surprisingly still.

I can practically feel their anger lashing through the air around us. The buzzing hum pulses and grows to a deafening pitch, but they don't come any closer.

"Go," Pan says. "Touch the lights."

"What?" I don't understand until one of the orbs buzzes around my head.

"It will take you to safety. Touch it," Pan orders. "Now!"

Olivia doesn't hesitate. Without any argument, she grabs at the orb hovering around her face, and in a flash of light she's gone.

"Go, Gwendolyn."

"But . . ."

There are three creatures and only one of him. The other boys disappeared long ago. It's not that I really think there's anything I can do to help him, but leaving him alone with those creatures seems wrong.

He tosses me a devastating smile, as though the Dark Ones aren't pawing at the ground just feet away, as though their wings aren't already beating in rage. "I can take care of myself, love. They can't touch me as long as I have this," he says, giving his dagger a wave.

"It's just a knife," I tell him. Certainly enough to slit the throat of a boy, but it's barely big enough to prick the creature's side.

"It's iron, Gwendolyn. Even a scratch would be lethal to them. Go on. I'll catch up after I've given you a head start."

I look at the dagger he's holding. It's so small compared to the size of the Dark Ones, which tower over Pan. I can't imagine it could do much to protect him from them.

"Go!" he roars, and this time the impatience in his voice makes me jump.

Without any more hesitation, I reach out and grab the orb flickering near my face. My fingers slide through its icy density, and the world flashes white.

The boy stood next to his brother and waited for their orders. Each of them hummed with a nervous anticipation as they waited, believing they were ready for what was to come. "Stay behind me," his brother said. "You cover my back, and I'll be at yours. . . ."

CHAPTER 20

I COME TO WITH THE SUN BEATING DOWN ON my face and the rocky ground rippling beneath me. My head aches, and my vision is a little blurry, but I can make out Olivia a few feet away on the ground. Above us the gray mist swirls malevolently, like a storm is brewing within it.

No one else is around. None of the boys seem to have made it out of the fog. There's no sign of the Captain or any of his crew, and there's no sign of Pan.

I sit up, my head swirling with the dizziness of what just happened. The fairy lights are gone too. We're alone at the end of the world, and this part of Neverland is barren all around us. My limbs feel shaky and unsure, but I crawl the few feet over to where Olivia is lying on the ground and gently try to wake her.

Olivia coughs and moans, and then with shaking arms, she

pulls herself up and looks at me. "Gwen?" she says, her eyes unfocused but strikingly clear. They've lost the glassy quality that I fought all day yesterday.

"You remember me?" I pull myself up straighter and try to focus on her. The pink gown she's wearing is torn and soiled. The left sleeve hangs loose, half ripped from her shoulder by someone or something.

"Of course." But then she looks around, noticing her surroundings with a start. "What happened? Where are we?"

"The Captain tried to take you, and we found you in the fog. We're somewhere called the End," I tell her. "Pan's still in there."

"Pan?" she says uncertainly, her eyes narrowed. "What are you talking—"

Before she can finish her question, the mist swirls again as something dark shifts within its depths.

"Look out," I say, reaching for Olivia to pull her back. But I stop—it isn't a dark creature that's emerging from the cloud. "He made it," I whisper, relief catching in my chest at the sight of him.

As Pan steps out of the gray mist, his eyes are alight with triumph. There isn't a scratch on him. He gives me a wry smile that has me smiling in return. But then his expression grows serious. "We should go. I don't trust the Captain or the Dark Ones not to return."

"But the boys," I say, thinking of the one who was so scared, of the others, who marched into the cloud as though death were an impossibility.

"There's nothing I can do for them now," he says, and the

blunt matter-of-fact tone of his declaration makes me take a step back from him. He's not even going to try.

"But—"

"What's important is that we get you both back to safety," he interrupts, and though I want to argue, there's something in his expression that warns me it would be a mistake. "We're safe enough in the light of day, but we need to get back before nightfall," he explains, eyeing the fog warily. "Unless, of course, you wish to meet more of the darkest Fey when they're at their strongest?"

After he says that, the rest of my objections seem pointless.

By the time Pan pulls Olivia to her feet, her eyes are already starting to lose the clearness they had just moments before. He tucks her under his arm, and she moves closer, taking full advantage of the protection of his body as he offers me his other hand. His grip is sure as he pulls me effortlessly to my feet.

My head is still swirling, but I resist the urge to lean into him as Olivia's doing. Too much has happened. I need space to figure out what I think of it all.

"I'm glad you made it out," I tell him, a peace offering.

"I assured you I would. After all, I have this." He pulls his dagger from its sheath and offers it to me. Reluctantly, I take it.

It's heavier than it looks, and though its blade is dark, it has a silvery shine that looks like it's coming from within the metal.

"This is really all it takes to scare one of those things?" I ask, glancing up at him doubtfully. The metal feels warm in my hand.

"That's not just any knife, Gwendolyn. It belonged to my mother, the Queen," he explains. "Long ago the Queen traveled across the boundaries into the human world to find something to defeat the Dark Fey, who so often attacked her court in their attempt to take over this world. She brought back this—a dagger forged in iron and human blood and silver. Together they are deadly to the Dark Ones. To all Fey," he said, nodding into the mist and taking the dagger back from me.

"She used that blade to kill the King of the Dark Ones and to banish what remained of his court to the far ends of this land so her people could live here in safety. They know well enough what this is capable of," he tells me as he tucks the dagger securely back into the sheath at his side. "And they're smart enough to avoid it."

"Why don't you just kill them all with it, then?" I ask.

"It's impossible to kill a shadow, Gwendolyn. The Dark Ones can only be killed when they're fully corporeal, and they have the inconvenient habit of melting into the darkness they're born from. Besides, without the Queen to hold them in check, there are far too many of them for any single blade to do the job."

I frown at his explanation. And I can't help but glance at the dagger. He's probably right—there's no way that such a small weapon could defeat *all* the Dark Ones . . . But I only need one or two to get us home.

Pan's expression flickers then, as though he's sensed the

164

direction of my thoughts and doesn't approve. "As I was saying," he tells me, his voice unwavering, "it's time we go."

Since he can't carry both of us at the same time, and the fairy lights seem to have been lost in the fog, we spend the afternoon walking back to his fortress. Once we cross the flat, rocky stretch of land I saw from the air, the terrain begins to climb steeply into the mountainous middle of the island. I worry a little about making it all the way to the top—it's been so long since I've done anything physical, and I'm already breathless only a quarter of the way up. Still, the burning ache as my tired muscles struggle up the incline is almost pleasant. It reminds me of something I'd felt before, something comforting and real from life in my own world. But before I can figure out what it is, Pan stops at a rocky outcropping and leads us through a hidden passageway that cuts directly into the rocky hillside.

As soon as we enter, more of the glowing orbs snap to attention and circle us, but as though realizing we're not a threat, they simply light our way through the winding curves of the silent tunnel. On and on we go, through a narrow passage that seems endless. The air is close and has a coppery smell that reminds me of old pennies, and the walls often pitch at odd angles, so we have to duck or maneuver around them.

By now, Olivia's eyes have gone completely glassy. As we walk, she occasionally steals glances at me, but I can tell that when she looks at me, she doesn't recognize me. From the stiff set of her shoulders and the way she takes advantage of every opportunity to pull Pan's attention toward her, I don't think she sees me as anything but a threat.

Eventually, we come to a place where the tunnel we're following opens into a cavernous room. The dark stone of the barrel-shaped ceiling is shot through with veins of scarlet crystal that glimmer like garnets. With the rocky walls steadily moving around us, it feels as if we're standing in the middle of a beating heart.

All around the sloping walls, a series of identical openings lead off in different directions. None of them are marked in any way, but Pan doesn't even slow his steps.

"Where do all of these go?" I ask, glancing back over my shoulder as I try to remember which tunnel we've just come through.

"Various places in Neverland. Though I would caution against exploring on your own, my dear. Never can tell where you might end up. This way," Pan says, gesturing toward an opening on the far right.

Though this new path is drier than the last, the walls are sloped steeply on either side. In certain places, Pan has to crouch to keep moving without hitting his head. And all around us, the walls of the cave are in constant movement. Pebbles rattle, falling to the floor as the rock undulates in its constant dance.

I look warily at the ceiling of the tunnel. "Is it really safe to be down here?"

"We haven't much choice. There's no other way to get back to the safety of my home except these tunnels. The entrance we used yesterday would be far too difficult and treacherous of a climb from this side of the island. There's good reason why the Queen picked this location for her stronghold."

As we walk on, I think of the thick walls of the fortress, the impenetrable-looking facade. I think of the fairy lights that guard every entrance and the dagger, which is supposedly so deadly to the Fey, and I can't help but wonder how anyone managed to penetrate the defenses the Queen had built up around herself. If she was all-powerful, I can't imagine how the Dark Ones rose up and overthrew her after she'd already killed their King.

When the stone walls of the cavern around us tremble with a sudden and unusual amount of force, Pan goes still, his body tense as though readying himself for a collapse.

"It never stops, does it?" I ask. Yesterday, watching the land shift in its never-ending dance as we sailed over it was enchanting—magical, even—but this far beneath the surface, the constant movement seems more dangerous than anything else.

"It wasn't always like this," Pan says, his eyes scanning the ceiling of the tunnel before he leads us on. "When the Queen was in power, the island bent to her will, and all who lived on it were protected, but when she fell, so too did the protection her power provided. Since then, this land has grown evermore unstable. Recently it's been getting much worse," he tells me. "I've done what I can with the gifts she gave me, but I'm not strong enough to hold this world alone. Without her power, Neverland will eventually tear itself apart."

I can hear the din of the Great Hall clearly now, but I stop and stare at him. "But you asked me to stay."

"I did," he tells me. "I think you belong here, Gwendolyn. I think there's a reason you found your way to this world."

Olivia's eyes flash as she shifts in Pan's arms, pulling herself closer to him as though staking her claim.

Just then the land trembles again, sending showers of rock and debris down onto our heads. Olivia tucks herself closer to Pan, and I reach for the wall to steady myself as it quakes. For a second I think it's never going to stop. The pulse of the island is so erratic beneath my palms, so violent, that for a moment I think the ceiling above us will cave in.

But the moment I touch it, my hands go warm. My whole body goes hot, like I've touched a live wire, and the quaking earth pulses once, twice . . . and then goes completely still.

I stay close the wall, waiting for the violent quaking to begin again, and after a few long moments, the mountain slowly starts moving. When I'm sure it's not going to start shaking again, I pull myself away from the wall, eyeing the tunnel around me, ready just in case.

"You should be finding a way out of this," I tell him as the rock around us settles into its usual, more gentle undulating rhythm. "Instead of convincing other people to stay here to die with you."

He turns to me then, giving me his full attention. "I have no intention of dying, Gwendolyn. And I'm not looking for a way to escape this world." The determination in his tone leaves no room for argument. "I would do anything to save it."

His steady blue gaze meets mine, a challenge if I've ever seen one. But a challenge to what?

"There's a way to stop it?" I ask. "To save Neverland from destroying itself?" And from destroying everything and every-one within it, I realize.

"I believe there is," he says, his expression steady and calm. "And by saving Neverland, I shall save us all. Would you not pay any price to do the same?"

When he says it like that . . . Maybe he's right. Maybe we're not so different. I'd pay almost any price to get home, wouldn't I? To make sure Olivia gets home too?

But Pan misreads my silence for disagreement, and his expression changes. His earnestness is replaced by a look so intense, so unflinching, I can't seem to find the words to explain.

Not that I have time to anyway. From the length of tunnel ahead of us, a rapid patter of footfalls draws Pan's attention away from me.

In an instant, his dagger is out and ready. But this time the danger is only a small boy, one not even as tall as I am. Pan doesn't lower his knife. "What is it?" he snaps.

The boy stops short and eyes the knife before he looks up and meets Pan's eyes. "We're under attack, milord," he says breathlessly. "Hurry."

"What?" Pan grabs the boy by the arm before he can take off again. "What are you talking about?"

"Pirates," the boy says, his uneven teeth glinting in the flickering light of the orbs. "Attacking the fortress."

"Impossible." Pan's expression is a mixture of denial and fury. "They wouldn't dare, and even if they did, they'd never get past the trench."

"They already have," the boy says. "They're at the gate, and I don't know how much longer we can hold them."

The boy wanted to tell his brother that he did not need to be protected, for he knew that was why his brother was there, in that place with him. But when he went to speak, he was struck by how his brother's face reminded him of home, and he could not find the words. All at once, he saw clearly how far he'd ventured from the safety of that other world, and he wondered why he had ever left. . . .

CHAPTER 21

PAN SENDS THE BOY OFF IMMEDIATELY TO rally the others before he turns to Olivia and me. "I'll return you to your room," he tells us. "Their breaching my defenses means there's a traitor among us, and I need to be sure you're safe."

Around the corner ahead, the tunnel widens and then, after another turn, opens into the Great Hall. The usual chaos has been replaced with something more frantic. No boys lounge on furs now. Everywhere they gather their weapons and dart off in all directions. Despite the frantic energy around us, Pan is strangely calm as he pulls us through the muddle of bodies, pushing aside any child who dares to get in his way.

When we reach the far side of the hall, Pan presses his hand to the rock wall. A moment later a great rumbling sounds through the fortress, shaking the ground with such a violent aftershock, I have to reach out to steady myself. The entire wall is moving ragged shards of stone begin to protrude to form a steep, uneven staircase up to our room.

Pan takes Olivia's hand and helps her mount the first of the large boulders so she can begin the precarious climb. When she's well on her way, he pulls me forward. But I hesitate.

"You're just going to leave us there without anything to defend ourselves?"

"You'll be safer there than anywhere," he says. "Once you're up, I'll retract the stones, and no one will be able to reach you." Lifting me easily by the waist, he sets me onto the first step. Then he takes my hand in his and presses his lips to the underside of my wrist. Heat flares at the place his lips touch me. "I'll not let him have you, Gwendolyn," he says with a determination that has my cheeks flushing hot. "I never let him take what's mine."

For a moment, I don't pull away. I feel as though all I can see is the clear blue of his eyes. For a moment, I feel that same tug toward him, that overwhelming urge to just agree with whatever he demands of me, to give him anything he wants.

But then he glances up, breaking our gaze. Without the steady intensity of his attention, I feel almost lost.

The intensity of that feeling is enough to bring me back to myself—to make me realize how quickly, how easily I fell under his thrall again. And enough to scare me.

When I turn to see what's caught his attention, I realize Olivia has already reached the top. She's watching us with narrowed eyes from the doorway above. From the dark look she's giving me, she saw Pan kiss my wrist. And she's not happy.

I pull my hand away from Pan and give him a weak smile before I turn to the steps. *I'll explain,* I think as I start to climb toward Olivia. I'll calm her down and try to get *my* Olivia back. She was there this afternoon, if only for a moment. I have to believe she's in there still, somewhere behind the forgetting Neverland inspires. I have to believe I can remind her, because the longer I'm in this world, the more I see and experience, the less clearly I remember the world I came from. The more easily I feel pulled by Pan's temptations. And the more I understand we have to find a way back soon, or we'll never get back at all.

Once I've stepped into the room, the stairs retract with another thunderous grinding noise, leaving us stranded high above the growing commotion in the Great Hall. The boy had been right—the gates didn't hold. The last step has barely retracted back into the wall before the Captain's crew begins flooding into the Great Hall.

All of them have their blades drawn to attack. Sam is there, leading the charge. Devin wields his sword with devastating accuracy, cutting down any of Pan's boys who dare to get in his way. Even soft-eyed Owen looks more fierce than I would've ever imagined he could be as he lumbers into the fray.

"You'll never win, you know." Olivia's voice comes from behind me.

At first I think she's talking about the battle below. At first I think that she knows a part of me is rooting for the Captain.

"I don't know why he brought you here, but he doesn't

need you. And you can't have him." Her brows draw together, and her pale green eyes meet mine, challenging. "He's mine," she says sharply, as she grabs for my arm to force me to face her.

She misses my arm and snags my bracelet instead. I feel the fragile string give way, and time goes slow and still, like my limbs are frozen, and all I can do is watch helplessly as the blue-gray stones fall, ricocheting off the uneven floor.

It's not until I hear the first of them strike the stone beneath my feet that I can make myself move. I lunge for the beads, frantic to keep them from careening out the door and down to the Great Hall, but they roll away from me, bouncing in too many different directions all at once.

"Help me," I plead.

But this Olivia doesn't care. This Olivia doesn't remember my mom or our world or even our friendship. This Olivia sees me only as a threat, not as someone trying to save her. She stalks over to me, the shadow of her squared shoulders casting a pall over the ground before me. When she speaks, her voice sounds like someone else.

"I should have known what you were up to from the beginning," she says with a hollow viciousness that makes tears burn in my eyes. She takes another step forward and kicks some of the stones out of my reach. A couple of them clatter across the floor and out the open door. "Pan is *mine*. He came for me. He saved *me*."

"Olivia—" I say, but my voice dies when I see her standing above me. Her eyes are wild and angry, the eyes of a stranger. Not the eyes of my friend.

"I won't let you take him from me," she says, and her voice is so cold, so unlike her that I don't doubt *this* Olivia will keep her word.

I try to collect a few more loose stones. "I don't want him," I whisper, as much to myself as to her. And this time, it is not a lie. I pluck up the last of the beads that haven't tumbled down to the Great Hall and close my hand around them, not understanding how everything could have gone so off course so quickly.

Below, Pan's boys battle the Captain's. Pan himself is among them, fighting with a graceful economy that none of the other boys possess. Where the other boys slash with bloodthirsty violence, Pan's movements are frugal, elegant, even. It also helps that he's not bound to the ground. Flying gives him the advantage of surprise and the ability to sail over a boy and cut him from behind before his victim has a chance to turn.

Suddenly I see Owen, his plump hand holding a short sword and slashing wildly at Pan. I can see the smirking arrogance across Pan's face as he thrusts his dagger forward, pushing Owen back toward the fray. The boy's chest heaves great panting breaths, and for a moment he holds his own. Then I see the gleam in Pan's bright eyes, and I realize that he's only toying with the boy.

Pan's knees bend ever so slightly, and I know that in a moment he will be aloft, and Owen will be doomed.

"Owen!" I scream, trying to warn him.

The boy's eyes look up to find who called his name, but it's a mistake to take his attention off the fight even for a second. Pan's already in the air, already over and behind him, and the same moment Owen's eyes meet mine, Pan drives his dagger deep into the boy's back.

"No!" I scream as Pan's blade finds its new sheath. Owen's eyes go wide, his face contorted in a kind of shocked agony. "No," I whimper. But my protests are worthless. Owen—the boy who was so easily flustered by a kind word—has already crumpled to the ground, his blood a terrible flower blooming across his back.

Pan glances up at me, his eyes bright with the rage and the delight of battle, and he smiles before he gives me a jaunty salute and plunges into the battle once again.

"No," I moan, unable to take my eyes from Owen's still body. Because I know his death was partially my fault. Maybe even entirely my fault.

But his death is only one of many. And I'm helpless to do anything but watch.

Angry tears are burning at my eyes when I hear a scratching from behind me. I turn in time to see a gloved hand grasp the edge of the window, and a moment later a head of night-black hair appears. Then dark eyes meet mine.

"Rowan?" The name comes before I can stop myself, but the moment the roundness of it curves my lips, I realize I've never called him that before.

He's as startled by my use of his name as I am, and that momentary surprise softens his sharp features. Then his grip on the sill of the window slips, and his expression is once more serious. "A little help, lass?"

There is such a look of panic on his face that I scramble over without thinking twice and, grabbing ahold of his arm, I help to pull him into the room. Olivia makes a keening sort of sound and backs away to the safety of the bed.

"What are you doing here?" I say as he pulls himself to his feet.

He rights his jacket by giving it a few sharp tugs to smooth it into place.

"I thought it was fairly clear," he says, gesturing to the window. "I'm rescuing you."

"Rescuing me?" I say, incredulous. He looks so earnest, so serious that I almost laugh, but then I stop myself. "You can't seriously think I'm just going to fly off with you after what you did to Olivia?"

"I don't bloody well fly," he grinds out, taking me by the hand and starting to pull me toward the window. "And I haven't done anything to her." He glances over at her. "She seems well enough."

"You attacked her earlier," I tell him. "You left her for dead at the End."

"The End?" he says, his expression twisting in confusion. "I've done nothing but try to reach you since you flew off with *him*, lass. I've never had the pleasure of even meeting your lovely friend," he says, extending his hand toward Olivia as though they've just been introduced. The Captain gives a roguish grin, but Olivia flinches away, her eyes wary.

"Then your crew did it," I said. "Which amounts to the same thing. She could have died out there."

The Captain goes very still and turns to me. "My crew has done nothing save work night and day making sail to rescue you. I've no idea what you're on about."

"But Olivia—"

"I'm not here for Olivia," he snaps. "I'm here for *you*."

I blink at the resolve in his tone, speechless for a moment. And then my thoughts turn darker as I remember everything Pan told me about how the Captain survives in this world. "Why me?"

But the Captain doesn't react the way I expect.

"I—" He runs his gloved hand through his hair, mussing it so a dark lock falls over his forehead. Then he looks up at me, and his expression is bunched with confusion "You left," he says simply, as though he's still trying to understand how or why it happened.

"Of course I left!" I back away from him again. "It's not bad enough you feed kids to sea monsters, but you let the Dark One kill that boy," I say, my voice rising. "And then you took his life."

I see the moment when he understands what I'm referring to. His brows draw together, and his whole expression goes serious as he stalks toward me. "It was the Dark One that took his life," he says, grabbing my wrist and pulling me toward him with a sure tug.

I try to jerk away, but I can't escape. "I saw everything that night, Captain. I know exactly what you did. I know why you did it, and I know there was part of you that *enjoyed* it," I say, thinking of the look of horror and rapture on his face as he had taken that glowing thread.

"You know *nothing*," he says, jerking me closer yet, until I'm forced to tilt my head back to look up at him.

"I know enough," I say, refusing to back down.

"Do you?" he growls. "You knew, then, that the boy was dying, aye? That he'd been sliced clean through the gut. That when the infection hit—as it would have—his would not have been an easy death?" His mouth goes tight, and the expression on his face is like flint, his features so sharp and hard, ready for the strike that will make a spark. "And I suppose you knew as well that, had I not accepted what the Dark One offered, the boy's death would have been for nothing?"

"You expect me to believe that excuse?" I ask, searching his face for something to give away the lie in his words.

"I don't rightly care what you believe, lass." He releases me then and backs away, putting enough space between us that I can almost breathe again. "I know the truth," he says darkly.

"And what is the truth?" I challenge, but he doesn't answer. "Why would the Dark Ones offer you anything? Unless . . ."

My mouth falls open. How stupid I've been not to see what was staring me right in the face this whole time. "No . . ."

His eyes narrow at me. "Unless what, lass?"

"Unless you're with them," I whisper. "Or unless the Dark Ones are with you."

Though his brows rise slightly, as if he's surprised by my words, his expression doesn't otherwise change.

"Unless you're the one who sent them to London in the first place." I think of the blonde on his ship, the one who was also in London, and the air in the room feels thin, dangerous. "Is that why you've come back for me now?"

"You think *I'm* the reason you landed in this world?" the Captain asks, all humor gone from his voice.

"I ended up on your ship. I saw you working with those monsters," I say, putting the pieces together. "And I saw Fiona in London, before I saw her on your ship."

"You think *I* brought you here?" The Captain doesn't give me time to respond. He's already answering, his voice growing louder with each point he makes. "You're not exactly what I look for in my crew," he says, narrowing his eyes at me. "You're pretty enough, to be sure, but not exactly handy in battle, aye? Every time I turn around, you're needing rescuing, and here I am again, risking myself and mine to save your ungrateful behind only to have you throw *this* accusation at my feet."

Olivia, who has been watching the entire exchange, whimpers behind me, and I understand why. With his white-hot scar and wicked dagger, the Captain can cut a terrifying figure when he wants to. And right now, he definitely wants to.

But I won't be intimidated. "No one ever asked you to save me," I say as I take a step toward him. I glare up at him, my temper spiking.

His mouth is so near that if I just lifted a bit onto my toes—

"No. No one bloody well did," he says, stepping away suddenly. He runs his hand through his hair again, disheveling it even more.

I've never seen the Captain so rumpled, so undone. It makes him seem that much more human—and that much more dangerous.

He turns back to me, his expression grim, mocking. "I suppose you believe your new protector will be taking over the task of saving you now."

"I don't need him to save me," I snap.

"Well, that's a relief, since I doubt he'll be doing anything of the sort." The Captain pins me with his eyes. "You see, lass, if you want to know who it is that commanded the Dark Ones to bring you to this world, you'd do better to look to Pan than to me."

"Pan?" I ask, thinking of what he's told me about his mother, the Queen. "He has more reason than anyone to hate the Dark Ones."

"Does he?" The Captain smiles, but it's not a pleasant expression. More a baring of his teeth than anything else. "All lies, Gwendolyn, tied up in a package of pretty words. I did warn you of that."

"And I'm just supposed to believe *you*?" I charge, feeling suddenly unsettled and less sure of anything than I was just moments ago.

"I've never lied to you about who or what I am, lass."

I huff out a hollow laugh. "You left out enough."

"I've never promised to ply you with pretty words." His grim mouth tightens. "But it's not a lie when I tell you Pan brought you here because he intends to use you. And it's not a lie when I tell you he'll not allow either you or your friend to return to the world you came from. Especially not you, Gwendolyn."

"Why not?" I ask, suddenly unsettled by how quiet his words have become. How his eyes are clouded with something that seems like regret.

His expression goes tight. "There's more to all of this than I've time to be explaining to you right now. Come with me, and I'll tell you all." He doesn't demand this time. He simply holds out his hand again, an offering. "It's past time for us to be going."

The battle is still raging below, and the sounds that carry up to me remind me of the look on Owen's face when Pan's dagger found its mark, and the amusement on Pan's face when the boy's body dropped to the floor.

But I've seen what the Captain can do as well. I've seen him kill just as ruthlessly. And I've seen him take an innocent life. Neither of the two is safe. Neither is innocent.

"I'm not going with him," Olivia says from where she's been watching our conversation unspool.

"Then stay," the Captain tells her without ever looking away from me. "Come, lass. Before it's too late." He has offered me his hand but nothing else.

"But it's already too late, Captain," Pan says from the open doorway.

The boy warmed his hands so no one would see how they trembled on his gun. His brother never shook before battle—just closed his eyes briefly and then faced whatever was to come. As though his brother had found a way to accept the pointlessness and the waste of the lie they found themselves trapped in. And the boy hated his brother for it, just a little, the way that only brothers can hate. . . .

CHAPTER 22

EVEN THOUGH HE SPEAKS TO THE CAPTAIN, Pan's pale blue eyes are fixed on me. "Gwendolyn, my dear, perhaps you'd be so kind as to step aside?"

The Captain's sword is drawn, and in a blink he's in front of me, blocking me from going to Pan.

"I'll not let you have her again," the Captain growls.

Pan gives him a bored look. "Then again I shall have to remind you, the choice is not yours to make."

The Captain steps forward, his blade at the ready. "I've heard you've been spinning your tales, Peter," he says, snapping out the syllables of the name with a mocking cadence.

"Don't, boy," Pan warns, his voice dangerous.

"Still playing at your fairy tales, I see," the Captain taunts as he lunges with a swift step forward. Pan parries easily, though, avoiding his dagger without much effort at all.

"I don't play at anything. You know that well enough."

"Aye," the Captain says, pushing me back toward the bed, away from the fighting, as he circles left. "I know a great many things about you. I wonder, though, if you've bothered to tell Gwendolyn your secrets. Or if you've just tempted her with your many lies."

Pan follows the Captain's movements easily. "I've no need of lies." Pan swipes savagely, and again the Captain meets him, their blades crossed, face-to-face. "Gwendolyn chose *me*, Rowan. She'll choose me again." He pushes the Captain back viciously. "And again."

"And if she doesn't?" The Captain's face has gone murderous, but his voice remains calm as he rights himself, ready for Pan's next move. "Will you leave her to die like you leave the rest that cease to be of use to you?"

"Why wouldn't she choose me?" Pan drawls, circling farther to the right. "I saved her from the likes of you, didn't I? And I can give her anything she wants."

"Not anything, apparently," the Captain says, baring his teeth. "You haven't taken her back to her world, have you?" he asks, following Pan's movement and preparing for the next attack. "Does she know that you could?"

I'm moving before I can think better of it, before the Captain can stop me. "What's he talking about?" I ask Pan as I step in front of the Captain, between the two of them.

Pan shrugs. "They're the desperate words of a desperate man, Gwendolyn. You saw with your own eyes who the Dark Ones work for, did you not?"

When I turn back to the Captain for some explanation, I see his expression has gone stony. Before he can say anything,

Pan grabs my arm and pulls me safely behind him. In a blink Pan has the Captain's back against the open doorway. Pan lunges and the Captain parries, but the heel of the Captain's polished boot catches on the edge of the floor and he bobbles, his arms flailing to catch himself.

Pan lunges again, his dagger lashing out viciously, knocking the Captain back again.

But there's nowhere to go. The Captain's foot finds air, and he stumbles backward, only barely catching himself on the edge of the floor before he can fall to the hall far below.

He's still clutching his blade in his hand and struggling to pull himself up from his precarious hold on the ledge when Pan approaches him. The Captain goes still when Pan crouches down, looming over him, but only for a moment. "Is this how you imagined you'd meet your fate, boy?" I can't see Pan's face, but I can hear the anticipation in his voice.

The Captain's jaw goes tight as he struggles again to pull himself up.

Pan simply shakes his head. "I must admit, this isn't nearly as amusing as I thought your demise would be," Pan says, feigning disappointment. "And not nearly as satisfying as I hoped." He raises a booted foot and brings it down, crushing the Captain's hand—his real hand.

The Captain howls, his face contorting as his hand lets go of his blade, and his whole body slips farther. Pan picks up the Captain's sword, examines it for a moment, and then brings the point to the Captain's throat. "Ah, that's better," he drawls, amusement tinting his voice. "Done in by your own blade. Quite poetic, isn't it, Rowan?"

The Captain's dark eyes meet mine, and I see real panic there. And fear. The expression is so foreign, so strange-looking on the sharp lines of his face, I'm moving before I can think better of it. Before I can think through the implications of what I'm about to do, I grab Pan's arm and pull him back. "No!"

Pan turns to me, his eyes narrowed and his mouth curled up into a snarl. Gone is the beautiful boy, and in his place is something cold and dangerous. His blue eyes are empty of any feeling but rage. Still I don't let go of his arm.

"Why ever not, Gwendolyn? He brought his rabble into my home, to kill my boys—why should I spare him?"

"If you do this, you'd be no better than he is," I say, careful not to look at the Captain. I keep my eyes on Pan, begging him without words to relent.

Pan's eyes narrow as he considers me. For a moment that feels like an eternity, the Captain hangs from the doorway, sweat beading on his forehead with the effort of trying to pull himself back up.

Whatever he's done, whatever he might be, I can't stand by and do nothing. I saw the Sea Hags, and I know the risk he took to pull me from the water. I owe him this much. "Please," I plead. "You don't need to kill him to win. You can be better than he is."

At first Pan doesn't show any sign of having heard me. His jaw remains tense, his whole body ready to attack as he glares at the Captain. But then his shoulders relax, just a little, and he glances at me, his expression hiding more that it reveals.

"Quite right, my dear," Pan says after another long moment.

Then a dark smile flickers across his face. "But then again, I've always been better than he is."

With a flick of Pan's hand, the vining garlands that Olivia made begin to snake their way along the floor and wrap themselves around the Captain's wrists. Blood wells where their thorns dig into his right arm, but he barely flinches. He doesn't scream or plead his case. His dark eyes are steady on me as the ropes of green begin to drag him off the ledge, lowering him down to the Great Hall.

I run to the doorway to see Pan's boys gathering below. When the Captain, still struggling against the vines, finally makes it to the floor, the boys set upon him.

"You said you wouldn't kill him," I say to Pan, who is watching the events unfold with a gleam in his eyes.

Pan glances at me. "Worry not, my dear. My boys know well enough that I'd be very displeased if the Captain's death came at any hands but my own."

I'm not as sure of the boys as Pan is though. With his hands and arms wrapped tightly in the vines, the Captain doesn't have a chance to defend himself against the blows he's being dealt by the feral pack of children below. After a moment, one raises the Captain's metal arm aloft like a trophy.

But some of the glowing orbs have started to gather around the group of boys. With a flash, one of them explodes in a burst of light that has me blinking away, and when I look back, I see a person is standing where the orb once floated.

Or not a person, exactly, but a creature that looks so much like Fiona, I don't have any doubt he's Fey. His naked torso is covered in the same strangely iridescent scales that covered

Fiona's body, and his head is topped with the same white-blond hair.

The boys in the hall below go completely silent, and the one who was about to deliver a kick to the Captain's face lowers his foot as, one by one, the glowing orbs flash with blinding brightness and transform into more of the blond Fey. The sixth and final orb explodes in light and reveals Fiona, standing stone-faced over the Captain's body.

I let out a shaking breath in relief as she bends down to examine him. With a quick jerk of her head, two of the other Fey come forward and hoist the Captain up by his arms. I wait for the boys to attack, but they never do. They just watch with uneasy expressions on their young faces.

"Show our guest to the hold," Pan calls down.

I whip my head around, confused. On the ship, Fiona talked to the Captain as though they knew each other—more than knew each other. She talked to him as though they were allies. For a moment I thought she came to rescue him, but it's clear from the expressionless look on her face, she hasn't.

Pan smiles at my confusion. "Fiona's been loyal to me from the first, Gwendolyn."

"But she was on the ship," I protest.

"Yes, she was—at my behest. She brings me information and keeps me apprised of the Captain's plans. Rowan has no idea." Pan smiles, a slippery curve of his mouth that lights his eyes with amusement. "Though I suppose he does now."

When the order was given, they crept slowly, cautiously, out into the barren stretch of land between safety and death. His brother's eyes were alert, watching for danger to reveal itself. The boy should have been looking as well, but he could not take his eyes off the misshapen lump that had once been a soldier a few meters away. . . .

CHAPTER 23

THE BODIES OF THE FALLEN BOYS ARE already waiting for us when Pan leads me and Olivia out of the fortress and to the edge of the trench. The dead boys are uncovered and unprepared for their final rest, and their skin is ashen and unwashed. The blood of battle still marks their clothing and is already congealing at the edges of their wounds. Many of their eyes remain open, as though accusing the heavens for the cruel fate they've found themselves victim to.

Some are Pan's boys, but most belong to the Captain's crew. In death they seem even younger than in life. That patina of danger they'd carried on the ship like a badge of honor has rubbed away, leaving only the faces of children behind.

They are never going to know another day. They're never going to grow up to become the men they might have been. And in this world, no one will even remember them. No one will mourn their loss. In days, or maybe even hours, no one will even remember them.

I wonder about the people they left behind. I wonder if anyone from our own world still waits for them to come home. I wonder if anyone waits for me.

Two older boys lift the first body—Owen. Grabbing him by the shoulders and feet, they unceremoniously heave his familiar freckles and ruddy hair into the pit. Then they reach for the next boy. I feared Sam on the ship, but now as I look at his broken body, I can hardly remember why.

When they lift him roughly, Sam's arm flops like the dead weight that it is. Part of it is missing, but there is no bloodied gash like so many of the other bodies wear. Instead, like the boy who attacked me on the Captain's ship, the lower half of his arm is simply gone, as though it cracked off along the line of his jagged tattoo. No blood. No bone. Just empty blackness where his arm was once attached.

Is this what happened to the Captain's arm? Is this what drove him to accept the life the Dark One offered that night?

Pan is standing to my left, with Olivia tucked close to his other side. He's watching the proceedings without any visible emotion as one body after another is lifted and tossed unceremoniously into the gaping pit. When Olivia turns and buries her tears in Pan's shoulder, he comforts her without sparing me a glance. Ever since I plead for mercy on the Captain's behalf, Pan has looked at me with barely concealed disappointment.

I can't really be sorry for what I did, though. I couldn't have watched the Captain die like that. On his ship, he told

189

me that he'd saved me and that I owed him a debt. I consider that debt forgiven now, because Pan gave me what I asked for—he's spared the Captain's life. For now, at least.

But I can't stop wondering why the Captain tried to make me believe Pan was the one who controlled the Dark Ones? After what I'd seen him do on that ship, I would have thought he'd have come up with a more believable story.

"Come, ladies." Pan pulls Olivia closer and extends a hand to me. "Let us put this whole messy ordeal behind us, shall we?"

"I'm going to stay for a while longer," I say, not taking his hand. My gaze is still steady on the last of the bodies.

I need time away from the chaos of the fortress. Time to mourn for the boys who died today—to witness the loss, even if no one else seems to understand the finality of it. Even though I understand that, in this world, time is probably the last thing I have.

And I need time away from Pan. One thing became painfully clear the moment Pan admitted Fiona was working for him—he *does* have a way to get us back. Fiona was in London, and if she's on Pan's side and not the Captain's, she could take us back there. If he wanted her to.

So why doesn't he want her to?

"Come in before dark," he says after a beat of uneasy silence, not a request but a command. I give him a vague nod, and he takes Olivia in, leaving two of the fairy lights behind to guard me.

I stand in that pointless vigil long after the last body disappears into the gaping mouth of the trench. When my legs grow tired, I'm still not ready to face what waits for me in the fortress. I know Pan's boys will already be pummeling one another, sating their appetites, and sleeping lazily in half-drunken stupors. I know the fortress will still be filled with the Fey, their watchful faces blank with careless indifference as they stand guard.

Sinking to the ground, I press my palms against the pulsing surface of rock to steady myself, wanting so badly to be able to go back and make different choices. To believe my mother, to leave the light burning and the window shut, to stop Olivia from coming to London. To stop any one part of this from happening. Beneath my palms, the ground grows suddenly warm, and heat licks across my skin.

And then as quickly as it flared, the heat is gone.

I pull away and stare at my hands. There's no sign of a burn, no sign that anything at all just happened. Still, I *know* I didn't imagine it, just as I'm more sure now that I didn't imagine it at the falls with Pan—or in the tunnel, when I thought the island would bury us alive.

I stare at my palms for a long moment before I slowly lower my hands to the ground again, wondering all the while. I close my eyes and concentrate on the heartbeat of the island and—

"You play a dangerous game, Young One."

I startle at the voice behind me and pull my hands away from the ground, tucking them into the soft folds of the tunic I'm wearing as I turn. No bright flash warned me of Fiona's approach, but she's there behind me, her bright hair a beacon in the dimming night.

"I'm not playing any game," I say as I glance over my

shoulder, where the chasm stands waiting. It's not lost on me that we're alone. The other fairy lights Pan left with me are gone.

She stalks forward, her steps as graceful as they are predatory. "Are you not?" Her voice is as menacing as a swarm of wasps. "What were you attempting, then, with your hands pressed as they were to this world?"

"Nothing," I say, feeling immeasurably stupid for having even tried. Fiona cocks her head, expectant, clearly unwilling to let it go. "Pan told me Neverland answers those who belong here. I was just trying . . ." But it feels too ridiculous to say the words aloud.

"And *did* this world answer your call, Young One?" she asks, her eyes narrowed dangerously.

"No. I mean . . . I don't know," I admit, uneasy under the intensity of her stare.

"Perhaps it would be better for all of us if it did not." She takes another threatening step forward.

I don't ask the question I want to ask. Instead, I make myself stay perfectly still as she continues to stalk toward me, almost herding me to the chasm's edge.

"The one who calls himself Pan has long searched for one to whom this world will answer." She cocks her head to one side. "One of the Queen's own blood."

"The Queen?" I ask, my skin going cold as I take a step back.

"One who is more than human. And less than Fey," Fiona continues. "One, perhaps, such as you."

Sharp needles of warning are prickling across my skin, urging me to run, but I have nowhere to go. A few steps more, and I will tumble back into the dark abyss that has already claimed many bodies today. And in front of me, Fiona blocks any escape.

I shake my head in denial. "I'm not *any* Fey," I say, curling my fingers into my palms.

"Pan believes so," she says. "He believes you could be the heir to the Queen's True Child, the Fey prince she left in your world many ages ago in exchange for the human child who became Pan. He has long heard whispers of this Fey prince and the children he left unprotected, a halfling with the Queen's blood—the Queen's *power*—in its veins. It is why he sent his Dark Ones to find you and bring you to this world."

"No," I say, shaking my head. Because she's wrong. "The Dark Ones overthrew his mother."

"The Queen was *never* his mother," she snarls. "The one who calls himself Pan was nothing more than a plaything for her. When she grew bored with his weakness, she cast him out of her palace, banishing him to the farthest reaches of the island. She never expected him to survive. But she'd given him too much of her own power, revealed too many of her secrets." Fiona's sharp teeth glint in the night as she sneers at me. "Instead of dying, he found the Dark Ones, and they were more than willing to lower themselves to a mere human in exchange for the opportunity to exact their revenge for their fallen King."

I take a shaking breath, willing her to be wrong. "But he hates them," I counter.

"Of course he does," she hisses. "He hates *any* reminder that he is not truly Fey, that he is *weak* and *dependent* upon our power." Her mouth curves into a mocking smile.

"But I've seen—"

"Only what Pan wishes you to see," Fiona interrupts, taking a menacing step toward me. "He showed you the Captain's greatest secret in order to turn your affections, did he not? But Rowan is not alone in requiring the assistance of the darkest Fey to survive in this world. Pan also needs the lives they bring to him.

"*This* is why he has searched for one of your kind. He thinks he can claim the Queen's power from your blood, the same as he has claimed countless human lives over the ages. And he believes that with that power, he could rule this world once and for all. Without need of the Dark Ones' assistance. And with complete power over this world and my kind."

I shake my head in denial, even as Pan's words echo in my memory: *I'm not trying to find a way out of this world. I would do anything to save it.*

"I'm not—" But I can't even say the words. "I *can't* be."

The way Fiona's looking at me makes the prickling across my skin a hundred times more painful. "It is true that you do not seem as we do, but the one who calls himself Pan believes in your promise. For he is sure now that the other girl holds no such power. But you, he has a great interest in."

"No," I say. "I'm human. My mother's human, and . . ."

"And?" Fiona drawls. "Who is your sire, Young One?"

I take a step back in shock. *My sire , . . my father?* "I don't know," I tell her honestly. "But he can't be . . ." But when I start to step back again, my heel reaches the edge of the chasm, sending a few small bits of rock tumbling into the depths.

Fiona only smiles. "Perhaps not . . . but I wonder, then, how you came to have these?" Fiona reaches out a single, claw-tipped finger and lifts the necklace I'm wearing made from the few blue-gray stones I managed to salvage from my bracelet. "Humans call these *deora sí*. Fairy tears," she says with a sneer. "A stupid enough name, but such a powerful and dangerous gift can only be bestowed by one of the Fey."

Before I can stop her, Fiona gives an abrupt jerk, and the thread breaks. The second the stones fall away, her finger transforms, the sharp, clawlike nail shrinking into a softly rounded manicure. I'm too surprised by her transformation to bother to worry about the stones at first. Instead of the Fiona I'm used to, a lovely and very human-looking girl stands before me. Her skin isn't iridescent, and her teeth are completely normal.

She smiles—a perfectly normal smile now—but there is something in her eyes that gives away her otherness. "Yes, Young One. They allow you to see through our glamour, but they are not what has hidden you from *him* for so long," she says, licking at the air, lizardlike, as if to taste it. "There is some other power doing that work. You would have been discovered long before now had you not been protected by those who were loyal to the Queen's True Child. Someone knows of what you are. Someone has protected you quite carefully."

With a shaking breath, I crouch to scoop up the few stones that remain. The second my fingers touch them, the Fiona I know is back. And touching them, I remember something else—a room in London, the foggy voice of my mother as she slipped the bracelet onto my wrist.

Is this why my father had given my mother the bracelet? Why she gave it to me? All those years, could it have been the reason she could see the monsters, and the reason I could see the truth of what Fiona was in London?

I stand back up and face her again. "Why are you telling me any of this? I thought you worked for him."

With a hiss, Fiona glares at me. "I work only for my own kind. Pan believes in my loyalty, and that gives me power to work against him. To free my people and my world. But if you reveal your true self to Pan, if you give yourself to him, all my work will have been in vain."

"I don't plan on giving myself to anyone," I tell her. "Your plans are safe as far as I'm concerned."

"It is not enough." Fiona runs her long tongue over those awful teeth. "You've chosen to betray the one ally my kind have in this world. Without the Captain, who will stand with my kind against the one who calls himself Pan? The Captain must be freed." She gives me a smile that makes the prickling sensation across my skin intensify until it's almost painful.

Understanding what she intends me to do, I take another step back. But there is nowhere else to go. As I stumble toward the chasm, Fiona's hand snakes out to grab my wrist and hold me by one arm as I dangle over the gaping pit. She doesn't immediately pull me to safety.

"You expect *me* to free him?" I ask, trying not to let myself look down at the blackness beneath me.

"The Captain is your only chance to escape from Pan, to *ever* see your miserable world again."

I can hear the soft, distant echo of the shower of rocks I

knocked loose from the edge of the chasm. My mouth dry, I plead with Fiona: "How can I save him? I don't even know where Pan's keeping him."

"I can get you to the place where he is being held. Once he's free, the Captain can help you find your way from the fortress." Her grip feels like a vice as she jerks me back to solid ground.

I let out a ragged exhale, fear still squeezing my throat.

"Then we understand each other?" the Fey says, satisfaction dripping in her tone.

I glance up, still trying to catch my breath. Her expression is so arrogant, so sure, the panic running through me falls away. "Not even close, Tinker Bell."

Her expression transforms into something cold and truly terrifying, but I force myself to stay calm. I've jumped from one mistake to another out of fear. This time, I need to understand more. I still don't completely trust the Captain, and I need to know what I'm choosing.

"I need time," I tell her. "To consider."

Her eyes narrow at me, but to my relief she takes a step back. "I will give you one thing more . . . to *consider*. A gift, you might say, between distant kin." She licks her lips, like she can taste my fear and uncertainty. "Fey power cannot be taken. It can only be bestowed. Guard your secrets well, Young One, and be careful with what you offer him." She gives me a smile that I can feel prickling at my skin. "Be careful of what you surrender."

The pinpricks turn into a thousand razor-sharp slices, and I feel like I'm being flayed alive. And in a sudden flash, the world explodes in light, and Fiona is gone.

197

At first the field was quiet, and for a moment the boy felt an unspeakable excitement. Finally, the adventure he had so wanted was his. Then, quick as a thought, a shell burst overhead, lighting the field. Exposing them all. It hung, still as a star, flickering above as though it were alive. . . .

CHAPTER 24

ONCE MY EYES ADJUST AGAIN TO THE EVENING light, I head back into the fortress. I need to find Pan. I need to figure out if anything Fiona has just told me is true. But I'm no sooner through the entrance when a boy I've never seen before runs up to me. He's barely as tall as I am, and he can't be more than ten or eleven. Still, with the thick club he's holding and the wild look in his eyes, I take a step back.

"You were there, weren't you?" he demands, taking another step toward me. "Today, out at the End. You went with Himself, didn't you?"

"Yes," I tell him, inching back as I eye the club.

"Did Liam return with you?" he asks, taking a step even closer yet. "I haven't seen him. And then with the fighting . . ." His voice trails off, as though he's unsure of what else to say. He chews on his lip nervously, his eyes darting wildly from side to side, like he's afraid to look at me.

From the state of it, I'd say he's been chewing on his lip for a while now.

"I don't know," I say, trying to inch around him. I don't want to be the one to have to tell him that no one came back from the End except Pan, Olivia, and me, but the boy is insistent. He won't let me go.

"Himself said it would be fine. Just a bit of fun. But Liam ain't come back yet, and I'm starting to worry."

"A bit of fun?" I ask, confused. There was nothing fun about the morning's excursion. The boys we found out at the End were beaten and bloody, and the gray mist. . . . I get a chill every time I think of what could have happened out there.

"It was just another game," he tells me. "I should have insisted for us to be on the same side. Liam's my best mate, see. We're always on the same side, but . . ." He looks up at me. "You sure you didn't see him?"

"What do you mean, a game?" I ask, ignoring his question.

The boy's wide eyes regard me as though I'm something of an idiot. "Same as always. A bit of fun is all."

The way this boy is acting, the things he's saying have my instincts on high alert. "What about the Captain?" I ask.

"I dunno, but I 'spect whatever's left of him is locked safe in the dungeon down below. I didn't get a swing at him, though," he says, his brows drawing together in disappointment.

"This morning, I mean," I say, trying to get the boy to focus. "You were with Olivia this morning. Didn't you see the Captain out at the End when you all were attacked?"

His face scrunches in confusion. "Weren't no Captain," he tells me. "Just a bit of fun with us lads."

My stomach goes tight, and ice slides down my spine. "If there wasn't any Captain," I ask slowly, carefully, "who attacked you?"

He straightens his spine, tightening his grip on his club. "No one attacked me. Not this time," he says defensively. "I should've maybe gone with Liam, but I had a chance to be on the hunting squad for once. Couldn't pass up a chance like that, now could I?"

"I don't know," I say weakly, not wanting to accept what I think he's implying. "You're saying the Captain didn't attack you? That it was just a game to take Olivia out there?"

The boy starts to answer, but then his gaze jerks up and focuses on something behind me.

"Gwendolyn," Pan says, sidling up next to me and wrapping an arm around my shoulders, easy and calm. "Are you well?" he murmurs, his clear eyes conveying the depth of his worry.

"I . . . Um . . ." I look at the boy, who's now talking to himself, his eyes studying the floor as he shuffles nervously in place.

"This one wasn't bothering you, was he?" Pan asks. When he turns his attention to the boy, Pan's face transforms itself. All traces of warmth are gone.

"No," I say quickly. "I'm fine. Everything's fine. I was just wondering where you and Olivia had gone off to and I was talking to . . . uh . . ."

"Amir," the boys supplies meekly, staring at his feet.

"Yes. Amir. I was talking to Amir," I tell Pan with what I hope is a believable smile. It takes everything I have not to pull away from him.

Pan is still examining the boy. "Why are you not with the others?"

"I was, milord," he says, his eyes still downcast.

"And yet here you are before me. I wonder why that is?" He motions for one of the other boys to come over. "I think this one has need of some help to find his way. If you'd be so kind?"

The other boy, a tough-looking kid with his head shaved smooth and blood crusted at the edge of his nose, takes Amir roughly around the shoulders and leads him off as Pan turns his attention to me. I give him my best attempt at a smile, but when his eyes go tight, I end up glancing away.

If what the boy said is true, maybe there hadn't been any attack this morning after all. Maybe the Captain hadn't lied when he said he didn't go after Olivia. My breath catches at the thought—at what that would mean—but I force myself to relax, to appear calm, so Pan won't guess where my thoughts have gone.

"Terribly sorry about that," he says with an easy smile. "I gave strict orders for my boys to leave you and Olivia be, but they are rather keyed up from our victory."

"Where *is* Olivia?" I ask, trying to keep my voice as level and normal as possible as I ignore his apology.

"She was rather upset by the events today, so I've settled her into my own chambers. She seems to be more comfortable there."

"I'd like to see her," I say, trying to keep the panic out of my voice.

He gives me a doleful look. "I don't know if that's wise right now," he says slowly. "She's resting quietly, and I think it's best if we allow her to recover. I've come to escort you back to your room," he says, tucking my arm around his. "I'm sure you're quite worn out from all the excitement today."

"I'll see her tomorrow, though?"

Pan leads me around a pile of boys wresting over a fur. "Of course," he says easily as he presses his hand to the far wall. With a grating rumble, the stones begin to move, forming the steep staircase from before.

When the walls of the fortress finally go silent, Pan gives me a pleasant smile and holds out his hand to help me onto the first step. But I ignore him and climb up on my own.

Pan's eyes are sharp, a stark contrast to the easy expression on his face, but he takes my hand in his and presses his lips to my wrist. "Sleep well, Gwendolyn."

I pull my hand away and force myself not to wipe off the part of my skin that tingles with warmth. "Will you leave me the steps?" I ask. "I don't want to be trapped up there alone," I say as meekly as I can.

Impatience flickers in his gaze, but the serene smile stays on his face. "Of course. You're not a prisoner here, Gwendolyn. I do still hope you'll come to think of Neverland as your home."

"I really think we need to get back to our own world," I say. "Perhaps Fiona could take us?"

His expression flickers. "I don't *quite* think that would be possible." He doesn't add anything more, and I know there's no point in pushing him further. Unless, of course, I want to hear more lies.

"You said you would help us," I remind him. "You promised."

"And I will, my dear," he says, his mouth turning up into a smile. But it doesn't quite reach his eyes.

They were trapped. Between safety and death. Between what they were and what they might have been. The earth quaked under their feet as fire and brimstone rained down upon them. The boy, clutching his rifle like a talisman, realized then his mistake in believing himself brave. "We're going to have to move," his brother told him. "This is just the beginning. . . ."

CHAPTER 25

B Y THE TIME MORNING BREAKS, I'M EXHAUSTED. The cloying scent of the flowers, the things Fiona told me, the decisions I have in front of me—they all kept me up for most of the night.

It's not that I trust Fiona. The only thing I believe completely is that she's out for her own good. And it feels too unbelievable to think I could be part Fey, but my mom had been worried about something. All night I've been thinking, trying to pull up memories of the world I came from, and the thing I remember most is my mom's fear and conviction that we were being chased by monsters.

Monsters that turned out to be real.

There was always somewhere to go, though. Always another stop that would calm her for a while, and I can't help but wonder if Fiona was right to believe that someone had been helping to protect us. I can't help but wonder if my mother had always been right about my father leaving to protect me.

What is certain is that Pan lied to me about being able to return us to our world. He could, if he wanted to, but it's becoming clearer he doesn't. And I can't quite make myself dismiss what the boy told me the night before. The more I think about it—the confusion on the Captain's face when I accused him of attacking Olivia, the sureness in Fiona's voice, even the speed at which Pan knew what had happened and where Olivia was—the more certain I am that the Captain wasn't involved with what happened to Olivia yesterday.

But why the elaborate ploy? Was it just to get me to distrust the Captain? Or perhaps there was something more going on—some scheme to make me trust Pan. Or maybe it was some sort of test of what I am. I think about the challenge in his eyes in the caverns after the world stopped shaking, and I can't help but wonder if I passed or failed.

I need answers, and I know there are none to be found in this empty room. I have to find Olivia. She might not remember me or the world we came from, but *I* remember—parts of it, at least—and I won't give up on getting us back.

Using the wall as a brace, I make my way down the uneven steps as quickly as I can. Once I'm safely on the ground, I'm halfway across the Great Hall before I find a boy who isn't still asleep.

"Have you seen Olivia?" I ask.

He blinks at me. At first I think he doesn't understand, but then he heaves an irritated sigh and waves for me to follow him. He leads me through the tunnel we used the day before, back to the cavernous room where the other tunnels branch out in all directions. "The gardens," he says, pointing to the tunnel on the far right.

"You don't want to show me the rest of the way?" I ask hopefully. He just glares at me and turns back toward the Great Hall.

I stare at the dark opening for a moment, wondering if I shouldn't just go back and wait for Pan to bring me to Olivia. Maybe I'm jumping to conclusions. After all, he left the stairs, as he promised, and he said I could see her today. . . .

No. I don't *want* to wait for Pan. The whole point of my finding Olivia is to get her away from him. I need to get her alone so I can try to talk some sense into her without his easy, tempting smiles pulling her away from me.

I move along at a steady pace, and when the white walls of the tunnel flare open, I find a cavernous space that houses a maze of gorgeously blooming gardens. It's not dark here like in the rest of the fortress. The walls remind me of an opal, and the patches of multifaceted stones above me bathe the whole garden in soft light.

Everywhere I look, plants bloom in lush disarray. As in the jungle, every few seconds they begin to shift—ruffled roses the size of my hand transform into smiling snapdragons, and brilliantly colored daisies morph into the elegant fluted petals of lilies. Flowers I cannot name transform into colors I've never imagined.

One that draws my attention is a vining plant with fluted flowers that looks so much like something I've seen before. For a moment I remember seeing a flower like that, one that glowed with a strange amber-orange light. I can almost picture it. . . . But then the trumpet-shaped blossoms pull inward, and when they reemerge from the stems, they've transformed themselves into ruffled blossoms.

The moment is gone, and the ghost of the memory right along with it.

Still a little unsettled by my inability to really remember, I turn my attention back to the problem of the gardens. The thought of getting lost in their maze of thorny hedges and flowering trees has me hesitating. But their abundance of blossoms tells me for sure there was no reason for Olivia to venture out of the fortress yesterday. She could have found anything she wanted from the relative safety of these gardens. Which makes me even more certain than ever that Pan lied about the attack. If anything, he was the one who put her in danger by having his boys take her out to the End.

Another thought occurs to me—maybe he did that on purpose. I think of his expression when Olivia's voice came to us through that fog, and I'm not sure anymore if it was really relief I saw there. Maybe he never intended for Olivia to come back. . . .

Then, deep from within the lush green landscape, I hear the distant sound of familiar female laughter, and I don't hesitate any longer. I step toward the thick wall of vegetation, looking for a way in.

Almost as if they sense my presence, the plants shift, an invitation to enter. I hesitate for another moment, wondering whether this is just another trap. Maybe this is just another way that Neverland is trying to draw me in and keep me from ever getting home. But then I hear Olivia's laugh again, and I put aside my fear and enter the green alley of branches.

The space made by the parting of their branches is narrow and, at first, seems to dead-end a few yards ahead. But as I walk, the plants move to guide me through the heavy green. When I reach the dead end, I only have to wait for a moment and the hedges rearrange themselves to create a new path. I walk and walk, following the trail that appears before me and growing more and more convinced I'm lost, but every time I think about turning back, I hear the laugh again, and it is so clearly Olivia's, I keep moving. After a while, the sound grows louder, and I start to grow more confident. With each step I grow more sure that I will turn the next corner and find my friend.

But when one of the dead ends refuses to shift, I'm forced to stop. And when I turn back, the path I've just come from is gone. I'm suddenly trapped in a room of leaves and thorns.

"No," I say, trying desperately to find an opening in the hedges. The path can't just have disappeared like that. But the branches and leaves shift and grow, knitting themselves even tighter and making themselves even more impermeable.

My breath goes tight—It *was* a trick, and I fell right for it.

I shout for help, hoping Olivia—someone—will hear me, but the dense branches around me swallow the sound. Worse, the room of green begins to feel smaller. The branches of the hedges haven't stopped steadily swelling, and the more I try to free myself, the more they shift, pinning me with the pricking of their thorns. No matter how I struggle, I can't move.

Forget about this world—I may never get out of this maze. Someday some lost boy is going to find what's left of me pinned into the greenery, like a leftover ornament on a discarded evergreen.

Then—just as I think I will never see the light of day again—the branches part slightly, creating a small window-like opening. Behind me, the hedge grows thicker, pushing me toward that space. It's like the maze itself wants me to see what's on the other side, which should be enough to warn me away. But I don't have much choice. The more the branches behind me swell, the more impossible it becomes to avoid looking at what's on the other side.

And what's on the other side is Pan and Olivia lounging on the soft ground, half undressed, and wrapped around each other in an embrace so intense, my cheeks flame at the sight.

I try to tell myself this is not *my* Olivia, but nothing gets past the hollow ache I feel as Pan's arms pull her closer. *If Pan has her, she's already lost,* the Captain had told me. I didn't want to believe it—I *won't* believe it.

I can't ignore the possibility that the Captain could have been right. *Maybe I'm already too late,* I think as Pan's hands roam up Olivia's long slender legs, over the flat lines of her bare stomach. And the way Olivia responds to him—pulling him to her, entwining her leg with his with such urgency and unbridled fierceness, I don't doubt that she's chosen this.

Except I can't help but remember how *I* had felt pulled toward Pan. I can't help but think how easy it was to let myself fall under his spell—and I'm more sure than ever it was some kind of a spell. There's no way the intensity of what I felt toward him could have been real. And I'm not sure it's real for Olivia, either.

But there's nothing I can do, trapped like I am.

And I can't seem to look away.

As they kiss, the soft light of the cavern throws long shadows on the ground behind the two of them, and at first those shadows perfectly mirror their intimate dance. But as they deepen their embrace, Pan's shadow moves. It doesn't move like a shadow should, though. Instead of mirroring Pan's own movements, it slowly untangles itself from Olivia's shadow. The shadow never breaks its connection to Pan, but it stands, prying itself up from the ground until a perfect dark silhouette lurks over the couple.

A sinister hum begins to grow as other shadows in the clearing make their way toward Pan's, and then bit by bit add themselves to it, until they begin to take on the form and shape of one of the Dark Ones.

Pan glances up from the progress he's making down Olivia's neck. His eyes light with anticipation when he sees the Dark One is fully formed and ready.

The dark figure moves closer and then slowly rests its clawlike hands on Olivia's shoulders. She doesn't recoil as the tips of its claws sink into her skin. Instead, she lets out a soft, satisfied moan at its touch.

When the Dark One withdraws its fingertips from Olivia's shoulder, it brings with it that same faint trail of luminescence I saw harvested from the boy. Pan barely pauses in his thorough savoring of the skin on Olivia's neck to lap at the offered thread. But when he does pause, his eyes light in a sort of ecstasy before he begins to consume it.

To consume *her*.

This isn't the violent taking I saw in the hold of the Captain's ship, though. Olivia doesn't writhe in pain. Her body doesn't contort stiffly, like the boy's on the ship did, and she doesn't fight him. From the soft noises she's making, from the way she pulls Pan even closer, angling her neck even farther so he can nuzzle into it even more, it seems like she's enjoying what he's doing to her.

Paralyzed by the horror of what I'm seeing and the regret that I can't stop it, I can't seem to do anything but watch as a dark line begins to travel down Olivia's arm from her elbow to her wrist. Across the hand tangled in Pan's wild hair.

I know with a sickening certainty that if he continues drinking in her life, that line will grow. She will turn as brittle as the boy in the Captain's ship. And then she'll fall to the ground, pieces of a shattered porcelain doll that can never be put right.

I can't let that happen.

Struggling against the hedge, I start to scream to warn her, but the branches retaliate by pulling me back into their thick, thorny arms, pressing their broad, glossy leaves against my mouth. Silencing me. The hedge closes itself quickly, but not before Pan hears my voice and his eyes find me. Just as the leaves block my view, I see those eyes flash with an anger more dangerously feral than any of his boys.

"Gwendolyn," he calls, confirming what I feared—he saw me. He knows that I understand what he's capable of. He knows I saw the truth of what he *is*.

But I have nowhere to go—the branches are immovable.

"Gwendolyn?" Pan's voice is closer now. His voice has softened, and I can tell he's trying to sound as pleasant and charming as always, but there's a hollowness in his tone that doesn't lie, and I know if he catches me, it won't be good. Because Fiona was right—it *isn't* only the Captain who uses the Dark Ones. And if she was right about that, how much more of what she said might be true?

I slam my fists against the thorny branches, ignoring the way they scrape at my skin. "Let. Me. Out!" I shout, pushing at the dense growth with all my might.

Shadows begin to swirl at my feet, and I shove harder. "Please!" I cry at the immovable branches. "Fiona!"

Without warning, the branches behind me part enough that I fall to the ground.

I'm still panting from the effort of my escape. Around me, the hedge has gone still, and one of the fairy lights now hovers near me, pulsing and growing brighter with each beat as it shivers, as though from the increase in energy.

I glance back at the trembling foliage—I can't leave Olivia here with Pan. I know now for sure just how dangerous he is. And I know this world has made Olivia powerless against Pan's seduction. But there isn't time. The darkness is already gathering around me, the branches already rustling as they part to let him through.

I don't want to leave Olivia behind, but I won't be able to help her if Pan has me. I'm no good to Olivia if I'm dead. With panic fluttering in my chest, my skin cold with fear, I don't hesitate any longer.

The moment I feel the orb's searing cold light on my fingertips, the world tilts. In a flash of blinding pressure, the cavern around me quivers, and then it disappears completely.

His brother asked if he was ready, and the boy nodded, but it was a lie. "I'm sorry," he started to say to his brother, knowing that he needed to put everything he meant in those three syllables. But his brother's expression went hard as he shook his head to stop the boy from speaking. "There'll be time enough for that after. . . ."

CHAPTER 26

WHEN I COME TO, THE LIGHT IS GONE. It takes me a second to remember what's just happened, but I have no idea where I am.

It's dark—a dense, unnatural darkness that I recognize too well. The scent of moldering leaves is all around me. I hear a whispering rustle somewhere in the distance, and the echo of the metallic sound grates against my nerves. It all marks the unmistakable presence of the Dark Ones.

The darkness is so thick around me, so deep and dense, it's easy to imagine that I don't exist at all. It brushes against my cheek and inches like ice down my spine. It spins me into itself until I am completely lost, until I can't tell my past from my present, and suddenly, I'm there again, in that mysterious forest. . . .

The forest surrounding me, the night breathing slow and steady, and my heart racing in my chest with a terrible joy.

A rustling, a scuttling scrape that sounds like the wind coming alive. And the forest dressed in night, and something is out there, waiting. A voice in my head, dark and sweet, whispering to me. But I can't make out what it says.

A wailing moan comes out of the darkness—not the night of that image, but the deep dark night of where I now am. I blink, shaking a little as I come back to myself, but the ghost of the memory is still there, just on the edges of my consciousness. I have the sense that I could almost grasp it and discover what's hidden there, but . . . I back away instead and let the memory fade into the darkness that inspired it.

Another moan greets my ears. Shaking, I listen to it reverberate through the spaces around me, and as it echoes, I realize that I've heard that moaning wail before—it's the sound I heard each night I was a prisoner on the Captain's ship. That can't be a coincidence.

I make up my mind to follow the noise, and begin to inch my way forward. I don't know how long I've been moving through the dark when I come up against a wall—a dead end. The screams haven't come for a few minutes, and I have the sickening feeling I'm lost.

"Who's there?" A voice comes out of the darkness and stops me cold. A soft scuttling sounds at my right, and then the voice speaks again with an urgency that conveys fear as much as the demand itself. "I can hear you breathin'. I know you're there."

I recognize that voice. "Will?" I feel for a space in the wall, something that would explain where the voice is coming from.

There's no answer at first, and then, cautiously, "Who's that?"

I move toward the sound again, following the wall until I come to a small opening, just big enough for my arm to fit into. "It's me. Gwen."

"Gwen?" I hear him shuffle toward me, and then I feel the surprising warmth of a human hand touching mine. "What are you doing here?" He does not sound overly happy, but considering it's Will, I'm not really surprised.

"I don't know," I tell him honestly.

"Your friend Pan didn't send you?" His sarcasm is palpable.

"No." I grasp his hand firmly. "He didn't. He doesn't know I'm here." *Wherever here is.* "At least I hope he doesn't." Because after what I saw him do to Olivia, I'm in no hurry to see him again.

The moan comes out of the darkness again, this time closer than ever before, and the complete desolation in it makes my blood go cold.

"What is that? Is one of the boys hurt?"

Before he can answer, the darkness goes blindingly white.

"Good. You have found them." Fiona's voice comes from the source of the light. "You do not have much time."

I see then what I'd felt in the darkness. Will's face looks out at me from a narrow space between jagged rocks that both shoot up from the floor and hang down from the ceiling of the cave to create a cage. It looks like they're trapped in the jaws of some huge stone beast.

The familiar moan comes again, a soul-chilling sound of

pain that has me peering through one of the narrow openings. In the darkness of their cell, I can just make out the Captain on the floor. He's curled into himself and writhing as though he's in extraordinary pain.

"Is he hurt?" He doesn't seem to be bleeding, but I can't be sure.

"No more than he ever is," William says.

But Will *is* hurt. His arm has been tied to his body with a sling made from his own shirt. There's still blood seeping through the soiled material. Peeking out from the edges of the bandage on his other arm, the one he had back on the ship, a deadly black line creeps up toward his elbow.

When I look up at him, his jaw goes tight, and he covers the bandaged arm with the one in the sling, as though he knows I understand.

I look away as the Captain moans again. "Maybe you should try to wake him?" I say, chancing a glance up at Will.

"Be my guest," Will says darkly. "Last time I tried to bring him out of it, he nearly took off me head. Bloody wicked left hook he has. Best to let it pass on its own."

But whatever it is doesn't seem to be passing. Even with our talking, even with Fiona's light, the Captain hasn't stirred. His skin is sallow and slick with sweat, and the sleeve of his left arm flops listlessly over him in an empty embrace. He no longer looks like the cold, buttoned-up Captain I'm used to. He looks younger and much more human than I've ever seen him.

"What's wrong with him?"

Will narrows his eyes at me. "And I should tell you, when it's your fault we're in this bloody awful mess?"

"It's not exactly like he was honest with me," I say, but I can't quite dismiss my guilt.

Will staggers a bit as he steps forward, his bruised face again illuminated by a beam of light. "He was as honest as the likes of you deserved."

"The likes of me?" I blink, outrage stiffening my spine.

"Yes. You," he says, poking a grime-covered finger sharply into my chest. "Double-crossing little—"

"I saved his life," I cut in.

"Enough!" Fiona's voice echoes through the darkness around the halo of her light. "We do not have time for this." Impatience flares in her eyes.

I turn to her. "Why did you bring me here?"

Fiona cocks her head at an unnatural angle and glares at me. It's a strangely inhuman movement that has me taking a step back. "Did you not call me? Have you not made your choice?"

"This isn't what I meant," I insist. "I needed to get Olivia away from Pan."

"It is too late for her," Fiona says simply.

"No. Take me back. Now."

Fiona's lip curls to expose the sharp tips of her teeth. "If you have any hope of saving your human friend, or your own miserable existence, there is only one path for you now. It does not run through Pan."

"I need to go back," I demand.

But before I can finish, the light around Fiona flickers, and we are once more plunged into darkness. I hear Will's panicked gasp, his frantic shuffling as the air goes heavy with the smell of dampness and decay. The skittering hum of the

Dark Ones is still a ways off, but the sound is growing, coming closer with each second that passes. If she leaves us here, in the darkness, they'll find us.

"Fine!" I shout, not wanting them to reach me.

"Fine?" Fiona's voice buzzes in the darkness.

The humming pulse of the Dark Ones is closer now. Louder still.

I clench my hands at my sides. "What do you want me to do?" I grind out as the rustling buzz of the Dark Ones begins to surround us. But Fiona doesn't answer. "Whatever you want, I'll do it. Please—"

In a flash, the light around Fiona returns to its original brightness, and the swelling buzz in the air falls silent as the Dark Ones retreat back into the darkened corners of the caverns. The Captain is still writhing in his sleep, unaware of what just happened. But Will is huddled back against the wall, his hands up as though ready for a fight.

Fiona's mouth is already curved into a viciously satisfied smile, her sharp teeth glinting. "I thought you would see it my way."

I glare at her, wishing I could argue. Wishing I had Pan's dagger.

"You will get the Captain to safety," she tells me, as though this is already an established fact. "Rowan knows the way through these tunnels, and with you as his hostage, the one who calls himself Pan will be more cautious."

"And then what? There's nowhere to go," I say, remembering the monster-filled sea, the dangers that lurk on the ever-changing island.

Fiona's eyes go dark, the pupils glossy and fathomless. "And then, Young One, you will free my Queen."

I gape at her. "Your Queen is gone. She was defeated by the Dark Ones."

"Defeated, yes, but not yet destroyed," Fiona says, her voice buzzing with a dangerous satisfaction. "My Queen created this world, and is the source of all within it. Without her, this world—the island, the seas, and everything in them— would have already ceased to be. The one who calls himself Pan knew this.

"When he and his Dark Ones rose up against her, they did not destroy her. Until now the one who calls himself Pan has been able to do no more than hold my Queen as his prisoner, keeping my people hostage to his demands and the dagger he stole from her. But she grows weak, and as her power fades, so does this world. Find where Pan has hidden her and free her, or you shall die along with Neverland."

"Find her?" I ask Fiona. "You're not going to tell me where she is, at least?"

"She don't know," Will says with a smirk.

Fiona glares at him, but doesn't dispute what he said. "You will have all you need once the Captain is free. He knows more about the one who calls himself Pan than any other." Fiona smiles her sharp-toothed sneer. "They are great friends, you see."

"*Were*," Will corrects quickly, glaring at the Fey. "They *were* friends. Before."

"And they're not now?" I ask, glancing between Fiona and Will, trying to determine who is telling me the truth.

"No," the two answer almost in unison. At least they agree on that much. . . . Not that it makes me feel any better. But at least now I understand why Fiona was so anxious for me to free the Captain.

Fiona lets out an angry hiss. "I may need your Captain, but do not forget *you* are expendable, boy."

"You only need him because he knows where your fairy godmother is," Will says with a sneer. "The Cap'n knows well enough that the minute he tells you, there won't be a single reason for you to keep any of us alive. It's the only thing that's kept you honest with him." He scowls. "Well, as honest as any of your kind *can* be."

Fiona gives Will a disgusted look before she turns to me again. "The time has come for action, Young One. As long as *you* are in this world, there is the risk that Pan could take what power you possess and destroy the Queen. If that happens, *nothing* would be able to stop him from doing or taking what he wants—not even the boundaries between the worlds." Fiona stalks toward me, letting the implications of an unstoppable Pan sink in. "You will go from this place, and you will free my Queen."

"And then what?" I ask, my skin crawling as she advances.

Fiona's mouth curves back into a dangerous smile. "And then I will kill the one who calls himself Pan and free my people."

"But what about *us*?"

Her lip curls. "I'm sure my Queen will show favor on the ones who have freed her." She tosses the bag at my feet. "You will have need of these."

I bend down to look in the package, and find it contains a couple of blades and the Captain's mechanical arm. I narrow my eyes as I look up at her. "That's it? I'm just supposed to take your word for it?"

Will snorts and, for once, we're in agreement.

"You no longer have a choice, Young One. Pan knows what you've seen, and if he discovers you here, the time for pretty stories will be over."

"You told me yourself that he can't take my power, whatever power that may be."

Fiona continues to smile dangerously. "True. But you are not completely immune to the dangers of this world, Young One. Your human blood makes you susceptible to Neverland's charms. How long do you think it would take before your feeble memories of that other world disappear completely? Until you are no different than your empty-headed friend? How long did it take for her to abandon herself to this world?"

Days. It only took days for Olivia to lose herself. And my own memories are not much better. Fiona's right. I have to find another way home. Because if Pan gets me, I doubt he'll try plying me with his charm this time.

"I'll help you free your Queen because I want to get home, but I'm not leaving here without Olivia," I tell Fiona. "Not after I've seen what Pan's capable of."

"She is not necessary," Fiona hisses in a voice as sharp as her teeth.

"Necessary or not, I won't go anywhere without her."

Her eyes narrow. "If I assure her safety?"

I'm about to argue it's not enough, but Will stops me.

"Have her swear on the life of her Queen. Iffen she does that, the girl will be safe until we can get back to her. Maybe even safer than if Olivia comes with us. Fiona's type—they can't break their oaths. It's the only reason there's any Dark Ones still doing Pan's bidding."

"But they help the Captain," I point out.

"Because the one who calls himself Pan made an oath with only a small assembly of the Dark Fey," Fiona explains. "The rest were content to assist in defeating my Queen, but they are not *bound* to him. Even those who made the oath promised obedience, not loyalty." She gives me another sharp-toothed smile, as though she finds it amusing the Dark Ones have managed to exploit this loophole. "But the boy is not wrong. My kind cannot break oaths without being unmade by them. If you do as I require, I will make sure the human girl comes to no harm."

"That's not enough," Will says, glancing at me. "Make her swear it on her Queen's life, and then let's be on with it. Because I don't want to be here when Pan realizes that you're against him now."

"And that's it?" I ask, doubtful.

Will starts to answer, but Fiona interrupts him.

"Pan may already be coming for you," she taunts. "If he finds you here, I will not protect you."

I glare at her. I don't like the idea of leaving Olivia behind again, but I'm not sure I have a choice. "Fine. Swear on the life of your Queen that Olivia will come to *no* harm while I am freeing your Queen—not from Pan, not from you, not from *anything* in this world."

Fiona narrows her eyes with each clause and additional

word, but she makes the oath. The words are no sooner out of her mouth when, in a flash, she's gone, leaving us only a swiftly dimming orb behind for light.

"Do they always do that?" I ask Will, rubbing at my eyes.

"If you're lucky, that's all they do," Will mutters.

We stare at each other uneasily. "I still don't know how I'm supposed to get you out of there." The bars of their prison are made from solid rock. I run my hands across them, trying to find some weakness or hidden opening, but I don't see one. "Maybe you should wake your Captain first? He might have some idea of what to do."

As predicted, waking the Captain's not easy. The second Will touches his shoulder, the once-aimless writhing turns violent. As the Captain thrashes, his fist connects with Will's face with a sickening crunch.

Will barely acknowledges the blow. "It's time to go, Cap'n." Blood dripping from his nose, he gives the Captain a hard slap across the face.

The Captain blinks awake, muttering a string of curses. "William?" He pushes Will off his chest and props himself up, squinting into the light. "Did Fiona come for us?"

"She left," I say dryly.

It takes him a moment before he notices me. "Gwendolyn?" I can hear the confusion in his voice. "Why is she here?" He doesn't exactly sound pleased.

"Apparently, she has seen the error of her ways," Will tells him with no small amount of irony. "Come on, then." Will is already pulling the Captain up onto unsteady legs.

"Has she?" The Captain frowns, not looking at all convinced as he staggers to his feet. I can't exactly blame him, considering it's partially my fault he's stuck in there. Still, it could be worse. He could have fallen to his death. Or Pan could have run him through with his own blade.

"Can we blame me for everything later? We need to figure out how to get you out of there before Pan figures out where I am and comes for me." I'm still feeling the rocky bars, looking for some weakness. "I don't even see a place for a key."

"There's no key that'll open this cage, lass. You'll have to use what you are," the Captain says.

I go still when the meaning of his words registers. "Not you too," I say, shaking my head in denial. It is one thing for Fiona to believe I'm part Fey, but for the Captain to?

And then something occurs to me. "When did you know?"

He hesitates and his mouth goes tight, but then he seems to realize there's no way out of telling me. "When you were on my ship. Fiona told me of the girl Pan had captured, but when Pan's boys attacked my ship, I knew she'd been mistaken," he says, never looking away from me.

"Why didn't you tell me?" I charge. "You could have warned me. I never would have gone with Pan."

His dark eyes are steady, composed. "You wouldn't have believed me, lass. You could barely believe you'd found yourself in Neverland."

I open my mouth to argue. . . . But he's right. I wouldn't have believed him. Not then. I'm *still* not sure I believe it.

On the other side of the opening, his eyes are hooded in shadow. "If Fiona imagines you can open this, you must at least try, Gwendolyn."

"I don't know how," I whisper.

He frowns softly, as though considering the problem. "This island is of the Queen, and if you are of the Queen as Fiona believes, you'll be able to speak to it," he tells me softly. "You've only to desire it, lass."

Like it's that easy. But I shake off my frustration and press my hands against the cool rock that separates me from Will and the Captain. Closing my eyes, I concentrate on the pulse of the island, hoping I will again feel that flare of warmth. But no matter how hard I try, nothing happens.

"It's not working," I tell them.

When I open my eyes, the Captain is rubbing at his bruised chin and considering me. "I'd say you're not wanting it badly enough, lass."

"Of course I want it," I snap.

"No. You don't," he says, ignoring my spike of temper. "You may say that you want us free, but you don't really mean it. Not completely."

"Figures," Will mutters behind him, shifting uneasily.

But I *do* want him free, and I peer through the opening to tell him, when he speaks again.

"You know you *need* to free us. Part of you may even want to. But here"—he reaches through the narrow opening and brushes my hair back from my eyes before he taps gently at my temple—"here, you worry you're making another wrong choice. You worry I'll be angry. Or perhaps you worry I'll go back on my word and take your life. Perhaps you worry you're not enough."

I start to deny it, but the warmth of his fingers sizzles along my skin as he traces down my cheeks, my neck, heating me in places far beyond the reach of his touch. I step closer to the rock that separates us, leaning into the comforting warmth of his hand. "I don't know how," I whisper, the overwhelming ache of that defeat shattering the last of my resolve. Because he's right. I *do* worry that I'm not enough to do this.

"You don't have to know. You just have to want."

"I *do*," I plead.

"You must want it with the whole of your being, Gwendolyn. This island is of the Fey, and the Fey live and breathe desire. It creates them, sustains them. But in its purest form, desire has no thought of fear or misgiving. Neither can you."

He's so close to the bars that I have to angle my head up to look into his eyes. Even with the jagged rock between us, I can feel the warmth of his body, the gentle brush of his breath as he speaks. My heart beats unevenly in my chest.

"You can only *want*," he whispers, his voice soft and tempting. He is so close that I can smell the familiar spice of clove, the crispness of the sea air that not even the sweat and grime of battle can overpower, and I *do* want. Unaccountably, what I want is *him*.

"You can do this, lass. You stood toe-to-toe with me time and again, and never once flinched. You stepped in front of a madman, your back straight and your shoulders squared against the devil himself as you plead for my life." Then he lowers his voice, and what he says next is only for me. "You're more than enough, Gwendolyn."

And in that instant, I believe him. My fears fade away, and all my doubts are suspended, because I *want*. And what I want is nothing more than to feel his body against mine. So I can know what it would be like to put to rest, once and for all, the simmering tension that always seems to boil over between us.

And the moment I let myself admit that desire, the moment I lose my hold on propriety and logic and self-preservation and fear, the stone goes hot beneath my hands. A pain, alive and sharp, shoots up my arm. Before I can pull back, the stone between us disappears, and I tumble into his arms.

*His brother was not looking at him, but into the field before them.
"Run," his brother commanded, "and keep running until we're out
of this, understand?" The boy nodded, unable to find words. "Don't
stop, no matter what happens."*

*The boy understood then what his brother intended. Suddenly.
Fiercely. "I won't leave you," the boy said—an unbreakable oath. . . .*

CHAPTER 27

I LAND AGAINST THE CAPTAIN'S CHEST WITH
a thump, and the unexpectedness of his body against
mine—the heat and strength of him—has me scrambling
away. The corner of his mouth tilts, just a bit, but then he turns
from me, all business once again.

I wrap my arms around myself and rub at an ache that
throbs near my shoulder. I feel suddenly cold and uneasy. The
rocky bars that were between us are completely gone. I don't
understand what happened, but I can't deny the result—*I
did this.* I made them disappear, and that knowledge settles
uneasily into the hollow space in my chest.

The Captain isn't paying any attention to my own per-
sonal identity crisis, though. Relief washes over his face
when he sees the steel hand and, turning his back to me, he
has his shirt off and the arm reattached in a matter of seconds. Miraculously, the cold dead metal springs to life, the

fist clenching and opening as a smile of satisfaction lights his face.

"Come," he says as he pulls his shirt back over his bruised chest. "We've not time to be wasting."

Led by the dimming orb Fiona left us, we make our way carefully through the dark tunnel. The Captain seems to know the way, but the tunnel is endless. Beyond the halo of its swiftly waning light, I can hear the rustling of the Dark Ones in the distance.

The Captain has me by the wrist, and I struggle to keep up with his long steps as he leads us through the tunnels. "Do you really trust Fiona?"

"No," Will says as the Captain says, "Yes."

"That doesn't exactly inspire confidence." I try to wrench away from the Captain, but with a sure tug of my arm, he pulls me on.

"She wants to be rid of Pan," the Captain tells me as we walk. "As long as we're of use to her in doing that, she'll not lead us wrong."

"And when we stop being of use to her?"

The silent tunnel echoes with our footsteps in answer.

I try to jerk away again, which only causes me to stumble, but before I hit the ground, the Captain catches me against him. "Careful, lass," he says softly.

"What happens when we stop being of use to Fiona?" I ask again, trying to ignore the way my skin feels against his.

"I've not told her of the Queen's resting place for a reason," he says darkly.

Once I stop struggling against his lead, we make better progress. Soon the tunnel grows wider, and cool air streams in from an opening ahead. On the other side of the opening, we find ourselves in a larger cavern, long and narrow with a strip of sky above us. I look up as we walk, marveling at the unexpectedness of that ribbon of blue, and this time I trip over something that has me stumbling to my knees.

Not something, I realize too late. Some*one*.

Or what used to be someone. The corpse is bloated and ripe with decay. The skin on the boy's mottled face is stretched so tight, it's started to split apart, leaving white slashes of naked bone poking through the dark, gaping wound. All at once, the smell of it hits me.

Before I can scream, the Captain pulls me away from the body and covers my mouth with his hand. "Hush," he whispers into my hair. "We don't know if we're alone."

I swallow down my scream and the bile that rose with it, and give him a weak nod.

"This way," the Captain says. "Quietly."

There's no reason to worry about being overheard, though. No one waits there except the already forgotten dead, who lay scattered in broken heaps in various states of decay. We are at the bottom of the trench. The place where Pan tosses the bodies of fallen boys.

Eventually we reach a place where the trench ends in a sheer wall of rock, which is split by a narrow passage barely big enough for a person to fit through. By now the fairy light Fiona gave us has long since disappeared, and the crevasse before us looks deep and dark.

I pull back. "I'm not going in there," I say, thinking of the way the Dark Ones hunted in the other tunnels.

The Captain lets out an exasperated huff of air. "We're almost there, lass. A little bit more and we'll be at the cove, where the tender awaits. From there, the ship's only a short distance, and we'll be safely to sea."

I give him a doubtful look.

"Aye, you're right. Though we *will* be safer than we are here," he says. "Will, would you lead us?"

Will gives a tense nod. He takes another few seconds to search the reaches of the trench and the sky above us, and when he's certain—or certain enough—we aren't in danger, he ducks down and wedges himself into the narrow opening.

"After you," the Captain tells me with a half bow.

"You're sure about this?"

"I just sent the boy I love as a brother ahead of you. If there was danger to be found, he'd certainly find it first." When I still hesitate, he urges me on. "Go on, then."

The split in the rock is narrow and every bit as dark as I feared it would be. William's steady footsteps echo ahead, leading us deeper into the rock, and a moment later the Captain enters behind me. Together we follow the tunnel's increasingly steep incline through the darkness. As the light recedes behind us, my certainty wavers and my steps slow.

"A little farther, lass," the Captain encourages each time I pause to catch my breath. "We're nearly there."

But the crevasse is dark and deep, and for a while, I'm not sure I believe him. Feeling our way with hands pressed against the damp rock walls that surround us, we walk so long in the silent, dark crevasse that I start to wonder if we'll ever get out. But the Dark Ones are not here. No unsettling images stir me, and no rustling rattles my nerves.

Then, in the distance, I see a faint sliver of light.

With each step, it grows steadily larger and brighter, so I pick up my pace. Soon I can make out Will's entire silhouette twenty or more feet ahead of me as he comes to the end of the tunnel and steps into the light. Behind me, the Captain is still close on my heels, and in a few feet more, I also reach the other side.

I step out of the tunnel and onto a narrow ledge that clings to the edge of the cliff. Below me, the cove I could see from my room with Olivia sparkles in the sun. I raise my hand to shade my eyes, trying to figure out where Will has gone to. It's not until the Captain exits the tunnel a second after me that I understand that something has gone terribly wrong.

Suddenly I am in the Captain's arms, but it's not like before. His steel hand is around my throat, and his other arm pins me securely to him.

"What?" I start. Then I see what's caused him to attack me.

Hanging in the air before us is Pan, and he has Will dangling wretchedly from his injured and still-bleeding arm. Will's face is white with pain as his legs flail in the air.

I force myself to stay as still as possible. The way the Captain is holding me has to be a mistake. It has to be part of the act, just as Fiona proposed. But the way his hand is pressing into my throat doesn't feel fake. Nor is the way my breath has been cut off from the pressure of it. I wanted so badly to believe that I'd made the right choice this time, but his grip is tight, and I don't doubt he's capable of what he threatens. With the strength of his steel fist, it would be an easy thing to snap my neck like a bird's.

"Let him go," the Captain growls, "or the girl dies."

"I don't think you really want me to do that, do you, Rowan?" Pan says, and to punctuate his point, he lets his grip slip a little before he catches Will again. Will lets out a high-pitched wail of pain and fear all mixed into one.

"Hold on, William," the Captain says, adjusting his grip on me without easing it at all. I wriggle violently, but I can't get away. "If you kill him, I'll make sure you never get the girl," he growls. "All those years, all your plans will have been for nothing, because I will snap her neck and take away your last chance at defeating the Fey of this world."

"Please," I try to say, but nothing comes out but a choking sound.

Pan is silent for a long moment before he speaks. "Well played, Rowan," Pan says with no little admiration. "It seems I've taught you well."

"You've taught me nothing," the Captain sneers.

"Now, that's not *quite* true, is it?" Pan retorts, a dark smile playing at his mouth as his eyes meet mine. But then he turns back to the Captain. "Just leave the girl to me, and the lad is all yours."

"No!" Will's face goes stony as he shakes his head. "Don't listen to him. You know what you have to do—take the girl. Save the rest."

Pan laughs, a low, humorless chuckle that makes my skin go cold, even under the warmth of the sun. "Oh, it's much too late for that. There's no one left for you to save."

A menacing growl rumbles in the Captain's chest, and I notice then what I hadn't before—in the cove the Captain's ship is waiting, its sails still in the windless day. Its decks are empty.

"What have you done with my crew?" the Captain growls, tightening his grip around my neck.

"That *is* the question, is it not?" Pan's eyes dance with cold delight. Suddenly an explosion tears through the silent calm of the day.

"No!" The Captain's voice is filled with rage and pain, but his grip never loosens. Below us, his once gleaming ship is nothing but a ball of riotous flames. Black smoke billows as fingers of orange-red fire climb up the tall masts. "They were but *children*," he rasps, his chest heaving against me in ragged bursts.

"Ah, yes. The ever-protective Captain. So kind and caring to the boys under his protection." Pan's smile is terrible now. "Until, of course, he kills them. Jealous I beat you to it?"

"You are a *monster*," the Captain rages. His grip is so tight and fierce, I can't help but whimper. My neck is at such a severe angle that my shoulders are starting to ache.

"Perhaps," Pan says pleasantly. "Or perhaps *someone* took the lads to safety before this terrible tragedy occurred. Perhaps *someone* has them under his protection . . ."

The Captain goes very still.

" . . . for now," Pan finishes.

"They've done nothing to you," the Captain says. His muscles are rigid against my body, and I couldn't escape if I wanted to. "They mean nothing to you."

"But they mean everything to you, Captain, don't they? And I think you'll do most anything to protect them." Pan's face turns serious then. His crystalline eyes go stormy. "Give me the girl, and I'll let them live, including this one," he says, nodding to Will. "You won't be so lucky, of course, but then, you've nowhere to run. Nowhere to go. Save your boys or watch them die, but either way, the girl will be mine."

"If I give you the girl, you'll assure their safety?" the Captain asks.

I struggle against his grip, trying to wriggle free. There's no way I want to go back with Pan, not with the way he's looking at me, all anger and anticipation lighting his eyes.

"Of course," Pan says. "I've no reason to harm them, so long as they renounce their loyalty to you, of course."

"And Will, you'll ensure his life as well?"

"No!" Will says, writhing against Pan's grip. "It's not worth it, Cap'n. *I'm* not worth it."

"Never doubt that, Will," the Captain says, and the desperation in his voice chills me.

I try again to writhe away from him. He will do this, I realize. He will hand me over to Pan to save his boys, to save Will. In truth, I'd probably do the same, but that thought doesn't comfort me any.

"Make your choice," Pan says, dangling Will more precariously now, teasing the Captain with his friend's death.

Will's eyes are sharp with pain, but they are no longer filled with fear. "You know what needs to be done," he tells the Captain. "You've delayed long enough." Then, with a violent wrenching, Will twists and rips at the bandage on his arm.

It falls away, revealing the black, menacing crack. And before Pan realizes Will's intention, Will thrashes, pounding at the crack with his fist.

Pan's eyes widen as he realizes what Will's about to do, but it's too late. With a vicious shout, Will smashes his fist through the cracked skin, and the weight of his body does the rest. One moment he is staring at us with challenging eyes, and the next, he's gone. Fallen to the depths below.

"No," the Captain rasps, his breath hot against my skin. His muscles quiver, and I can tell it's taking everything he has not to let a sob break free, not to toss me aside and go after his friend.

Pan only laughs, examining the lifeless hand he's still holding before he tosses it aside. "You can still save the rest, Captain. Give me the girl."

The Captain is shaking against my back. His muscles tremble in their unyielding hold, but he doesn't release me. "I'm sorry," I hear him say, but I don't know who he's speaking to, and I don't have time to figure it out. Without any warning at all, he hurls us both off the cliff, to the sea below.

His brother shook him. "If it comes to that, you will leave me behind. If it comes to that, you keep going. Swear to me!" But the boy wouldn't. And then a shell screamed so close that the time for promises was at an end. . . .

CHAPTER 28

THE CAPTAIN'S ARMS ARE A CAGE AROUND me as we plummet to the sea. The force of our fall sucks us both far beneath the surface. The shock of what just happened has me gasping for air, but the moment I feel the salty water rush into my mouth, I force myself to focus. Then I'm kicking up toward the light, the water above burning a lurid red-orange from the fire of the ship.

When my head breaks the surface, I gasp again. At first I can't see anything but the churning sea and the dark smoke from the burning ship hanging above us. But then strong arms secure themselves around me, and a hand goes over my mouth before I can scream.

"Swim, lass," Rowan orders. "And swim hard."

Relief shudders through me. *He didn't give me up,* I realize. *He chose me.*

And for what? He must be completely insane, because

there is no way we will be able to get away from Pan, not when he can attack so easily from above.

I don't argue, though. Black smoke hangs heavy in the air, blanketing the sky and giving us some measure of cover. Even though the water burns my eyes and chokes me with every misplaced breath, I do my best to keep up with Rowan's steady strokes. I push and push until my legs ache with the effort of my kicks.

By the time we clear the wreckage of the ship and make our way across the open water, my muscles are screaming. I've been cooped up too long in ugly little cabins or pretty flower box rooms, and my legs feel weak and ineffective as I kick against the heavy drag of the current.

But when something cold brushes against my leg, I grab for Rowan.

"What is it?" he shouts, turning back to see what's caused my distress.

"I don't know," I sputter, my arms and legs churning frantically to keep myself above the waterline. "I felt something." I can't make out anything in the depths below except murky shadows along the ocean floor.

He pulls me closer, his eyes serious and determined. "We have to go *now*, as fast as you can. And don't be looking back."

"But—"

"The Sisters," he says simply, his eyes tense with fear. I give him a nod, to let him know that I understand, and he takes my hand and begins to pull me along.

The Sisters. Those horrible monsters that turned the sea

pink with the meal they made of that boy. The Sisters, with their corpselike skin and tangled masses of seaweed hair.

A dark shape moves along the ocean floor.

"Swim!" he demands, and this time I'm able to make my body obey. But there's laughter hanging in the air above us. I don't need to look up to know that it's Pan, floating safely above the deadly waves, waiting for us to leave the cover of the smoke. Mocking the pointlessness of our situation with his dark glee.

Rowan sees I'm lagging and he reaches for me, tugging me through the water as something cold and large moves beneath the waves.

"It's not much farther," Rowan calls, helping to tug me through the currents. The mouth of the cove is still about fifty yards off—a distance that seems endless to my aching arms and exhausted legs.

We'll never make it without Pan or the Sisters catching us first. And even if we do, then what? All that waits beyond is the open sea.

But Rowan hasn't given in, and neither will I. The water churns, and the cold bubbles rising from below turn the sea around us icy. Still we swim on, him pulling me every so often, refusing to stop.

"Rowan!" I scream. Through the choppy waves, I see the massive creature.

I flail with a sudden spasm of terror, and my uneven strokes can't keep my head above the waves. I come up again, sputtering for breath, trying to make my arms and legs work together to keep me afloat.

I thought the Sisters were terrifying before, but I didn't understand. Not really.

The creature rising from the depths below is covered in a mossy layer of algae and speckled with bright patches of white. Barnacles, I think at first. But I'm wrong. They're bones. Strings of skulls drape across the huge body of the beast, a horrible necklace of its trophies.

Both Rowan and I struggle against the pull of the water, which sucks us toward the creature as it rises from the deep. The opening of the cove is closer now—maybe thirty yards away. But the Sisters are closer too.

I can't make sense of what I'm seeing, though—this can't be the Sisters. As the creature rises, its great body coming to the surface, I realize that what I thought had been three mermaids is actually one enormous creature with three torsos and three heads. Its tangled masses of hair hang limp from its three large misshapen faces as it breaks through the surface of the water. Its body is the size of a whale, and it has tentacles that flail about, slapping at the water as it continues to rise up, up above the waves.

One of the giant tentacles rises, high above us.

This is the end, I think. *After everything I've been through, this is how I will die.*

The creature brings its massive tentacle down again, using it as leverage to turn in the water. Away from us.

Toward Pan.

"For the love of all that's holy, I need you to swim, Gwendolyn." Rowan's voice comes to me like a dream as I gulp water and air and try to make sense of what I'm seeing.

They are not attacking us. Perhaps they didn't see us, or maybe they just don't care, but the Sisters have risen out of the water, a dark mountain of tangling limbs and horrible faces, and they are attacking *Pan*.

Rowan pulls me along through the water, and this time I don't hesitate. I force my legs to kick a few times more. I force my arms to crawl after him through the water, and we make it out of the cove—out to sea—before Pan can stop us.

On the count of three, they ran, each crouching low to the ground. As they went, the earth shook, like demons from below were rising to join the battle. The sky was alive, and bullets buzzed like hornets past the boy's head. It was madness. And in the madness, the boy lost track of his brother. . . .

CHAPTER 29

B Y THE TIME WE REACH A ROCKY BEACH, WE are both so completely exhausted that we collapse without any thought of Pan following us. Or anything else, really.

Some time later I wake with Rowan sitting close-by. His legs are pulled up to his chest, his arms wrapped around them, like he's trying to hold himself together. His eyes are taking in the sun as it sets over the endless sea, and his face is drawn and pale against the white slash of his scar. I have a feeling he's thinking of Will. Of all the boys he lost today.

He chose me, I think.

Back in the cove, I was so sure he would hand me over to Pan to save his crew. But he didn't. He chose *me.* The guilt and the terrible hope that knowledge inspires make my eyes burn and my throat go tight. I don't understand it. He loves those boys so fiercely. Why would he choose me instead of saving what was left of his crew?

He sees me stirring, but he doesn't speak or make any move to help me up. We're on a broad, flat rock that's still radiating the heat from the day. Around us, the world is quiet and still. With the calm ocean lapping at the shore below, it would be easy to believe that nothing is wrong. That he hasn't just lost a brother. That I haven't just abandoned a friend.

"What now?" I ask once the sun has lowered itself into the sea.

"We haven't much choice. We'll do as Fiona instructed. We'll find the Queen and we'll free her." He runs a hand through his damp hair, pushing it out of his eyes. "Then we'll hope for the best and try to get you and your friend back to your world."

"You'll help me save Olivia from Pan?" I ask, surprised that he would offer without my asking. Especially after what he'd said before, on his ship.

"Aye, though we'll have to be waiting until morning, as it's not safe to venture into the island so late in the day. It should be safe enough to stay here for the night—if Pan hasn't come after us already, I doubt he'll venture out in the darkness."

"He has before," I say, thinking of the night he came to me on the ship.

"That he has, but he knows now my lads and I had help getting into his fortress. He'll be more on guard, less willing to trust his safety to Fiona and the lights of her kind for protection."

I want to tell him that I'm sorry about going with Pan.

About the choice Will made. I know words can be powerful things, but I'm not sure there's a single combination of sounds or syllables worthy of the loss he's just suffered.

"I'll build us a fire," he says after a while. "It should keep us safe enough for the night."

He sets about his task quietly, leaving me on the warmth of the rock to watch him meticulously gather debris, which he piles in a small mound. Then, using the steel of his fingertip to strike sparks against the dark stone, he carefully feeds the embers bits of dried seaweed until they flicker into flame.

When the fire is burning, he lays his coat and his shirt out on the rock so they can dry in the warmth of the fire, leaving his lean torso bare in the deepening twilight. Muscles bunch and move under his damaged skin, but this time, the sight of his scars isn't so shocking. Nor is the steel arm, as it glints in the firelight.

Ignoring the heat that has built in my cheeks, I strip off my own damp boots and socks and warm my toes in the heat of the flames. We sit that way until long after the rosy sky has turned dark. Neither of us willing to break the uneasy stillness with words.

In time the fire grows large enough to cast a steady glow, shielding us from the darkness beyond. My toes are warmer now, but I'm still shivering from my wet clothes.

He frowns at my chattering teeth and takes his coat from the rock, feeling it for dampness. Satisfied, he offers it to me. "Strip out of those and wear this instead."

I give him a doubtful look as I consider the outstretched coat.

"I'll turn my back. Go on," he says, thrusting the coat forward.

I take it from him and wait until he's turned away from me. "Fiona said you and Pan were friends once," I say as I strip out of my wet shirt and pants as quickly as I can. The question's easier to ask when I don't have to face that dark look of his.

He doesn't answer right away, so I pull on the warm heaviness of his coat. It hangs to mid-thigh, long enough that I'm covered but still short enough that I feel uncomfortably bare. When I wrap it around myself, I'm surrounded by his scent—spicy and heady—the scent of the sea and the wind. And of Rowan.

Rowan. I've been thinking of him as that name since . . . when? I'm not even sure. But sometime between when I saw his dark head appear in the window of Pan's fortress and now, the Captain began to disappear for me. Now all I see is the boy beneath the title. The boy with eyes dark as the night sky.

"I'm ready," I say, settling myself across from him, covering my bare legs as best I can with his coat. When he turns back, his gaze brushes over me, and even though I'm completely covered, I feel unaccountably bare.

"I know you're not friends *now*," I tell him, trying to distract him and myself. "But something had to have changed. . . ." I let my voice trail off, not wanting to voice the question directly. But he understands my meaning.

"Don't paint me the hero, lass," he says stiffly. "The only thing that truly changed is that I learned a new way to kill."

I frown, but I don't allow myself to react, and I don't press

244

him. The stiff set of his shoulders and the self-loathing I hear in his voice are enough to tell me that he judges himself more harshly than maybe even I could.

I wait, giving him the time he needs, and eventually, he speaks again.

"Though it's no excuse, Pan tricked me into taking that first life. He thought it would bind me to his cause. Instead, it had quite the opposite effect." The firelight flickers across the sharp features of his face, shadowing his eyes, so I can't quite make out the emotion there. "You see, the Dark Ones are quite curious beings, Gwendolyn. As you've well seen, they've the ability to harvest life, but what is a human life save the memories it carries? Without memory, there is no empathy, no humanity. Without memory, we are not ourselves."

I think about my hazy memories of that other world and how unsettled I feel because I can't recall them. I think about Olivia, how different she is without any recollection of who she once was. And I find I can't disagree.

"When I took that first boy's life, it gave me more time in this world. But it also gave me the child's long-buried memories. They helped me to remember the world I came from, the person I'd been. Otherwise, I might never have left Pan's keeping."

"But you *did* leave," I say, focusing on what seems most important.

"Aye, I did." His eyes meet mine. "I began to see Pan's games for what they were. He believed himself to be a bloody hero, and I came to believe he needed a suitable villain. Someone who could stand against him in this world."

"I can't imagine he let you go willingly, though," I say, the question in my voice clear.

"No, that was Fiona's doing. Because she knew I'd been close to Pan, Fiona believed me to be useful. It was she who helped me escape from the fortress. And she who arranged for my ship and my arm"—the clockwork hand clenches, as if to accentuate his point—"which she enchanted, so I could stand against him as a true equal."

"But you never did help her free the Queen," I charge. "You didn't even tell Fiona where Pan was hiding her."

"I couldn't." He glances across the fire to where I'm sitting. "Do you think Pan just has the Queen tucked into a cage somewhere? Perhaps in a chest or behind a locked door in the Great Hall of his fortress?" He shakes his head. "He's buried her in the heart of the island, and none of the Fey who remain are strong enough to unearth her—Pan made sure of that. It took the Queen's power to put her there, and it would take the Queen's own power to call her forth again."

"Because of the runes on his chest," I realize.

"Aye. Pan's used his power well. Fiona and her kind aren't of the Queen's own blood, so there's nothing they can do to release her." Rowan leans forward to stoke the fire. "Not that I let Fiona know right away, mind. But that secret would have been no use to my lads if Neverland had continued to tear itself apart. So I told her of what Pan had done to keep her Queen hidden for so long. Because until he's defeated and the Queen is released, none of my lads have a chance to return to their world."

"That's why Fiona was in London," I say, understanding. "She was looking for me too."

Rowan's expression is clouded with regret. "And for that, I'm sorry. Had I known then what I know now—had I known you—I would have allowed this whole bloody world crumble to dust before I uttered a word."

"That wouldn't have stopped Pan," I told him. "It wasn't Fiona who finally got to me. One way or the other, I think I was always going to end up here. But I'm not sure if I can do what Fiona thinks I can," I tell him honestly. "That thing that happened in the dungeon—it was the first time I've ever managed to do anything remotely Fey-like."

"You'll do what you can, and we'll take our chances, because we've no other choice. I don't have a ship. I don't have a crew. . . ." he says, his voice faltering, his eyes closing against the pain of his loss.

"You loved them," I say, seeing it so clearly in the pain written across his features.

"Aye, but I've killed them too. Just as he does." He meets my eyes. With his jaw shadowed by more than a day's growth of beard and his hair mussed and hanging idly over his forehead and his chest bare in the flickering firelight, he looks very much the pirate he claims to be.

But he also looks tired and worn from trials I can't begin to imagine.

"If I were braver, I'd have chosen death long ago," he tells me, a confession and explanation all at once. "In that way, Will was far stronger than I've ever been." His eyes bore into me, daring me to condemn him. Or maybe asking me to forgive.

I'm not sure that I can do either.

"Weak as I may have been, I've tried to use my life as best

I can. As long as my life can serve to protect even one lad, I can't regret the path I've chosen," he says, his words tumbling before me, like he's trying to get everything out before he loses his nerve.

He holds himself stiff and his face purposely free of emotion as he waits for my judgment. I can sense it in the air between us—his expectation that I will turn away from him now.

But I find I can't. I've only been in this world a short time, and how many of my own choices have I come to regret?

I stand slowly, careful to keep his coat pulled around me, and make my way to his side of the fire. He doesn't so much as move or blink. He simply stands and waits. The pain and regret and dread in his eyes are so clear, it brings tears to my own.

Gently, I twine my fingers through his, feeling both the warmth of his true hand and the soft leather of the glove covering the metal one brush against my skin. Surprise lights his eyes, but he still doesn't move. He doesn't tighten his fingers around mine or even breathe.

I tilt my head up to him and quickly, before I can think better of it or lose my nerve, I rise up on my toes and press my lips against his. His mouth is warm and firm beneath mine but it is also immoveable.

That doesn't matter.

This isn't a seduction. This isn't me throwing myself at him or trying to stoke some passion deep inside his stoic reserve. This kiss is simply a choice.

For days I have been tossed from one danger to the next.

Misled, tempted, tricked. Used. For days I have not known which way to turn, what the truth was, or who to trust. But the ragged emotion in Rowan's voice, the calm resolve and unadorned words he used to tell me his story, felt more honest and more real than anything has felt yet in this world. So I give him a single kiss, lips pressed simply against lips, with no expectation and no purpose other than to show him my choice.

I let go of his hands and look up at him. His arms are still at his sides, but I see his fists are clenched, as though in an effort not to touch me, and I can't help but smile.

The boy was stuck in that vast landscape of wire and bone. He could not go on without his brother. But he also could not go back. Then his brother was there—just off to the left, running with his arms out. And for a moment, relief washed over the boy, because he could see the field ahead, dark and clear, and the safety of the land just beyond. . . .

CHAPTER 30

ATER, I SLEEP CURLED INTO ROWAN FOR warmth, my head propped against him as he keeps watch. At some point, though, the exhaustion of the day must have overtaken him. At some point he must have fallen asleep and let the fire die, because the sound of rustling and the smell of damp leaves wake me.

When I open my eyes, Rowan's arms are still around me, and the bulk of his body is slumped over mine as he sleeps. But the fire has gone out, and the inky darkness already surrounds us.

The damp, aged odor of the Dark Ones intensifies as they gather. I feel the wet brush of their still-ghostly bodies closing in, and I start to shake Rowan, to try to wake him, but before I can, I'm swallowed by the darkness, and I can't hold off the images that assault me, tipping my world dangerously on its axis until I tumble again into memory.

I am back in the same forest, the cool air of the night whipping through my hair, stinging at my cheeks, and a voice whispers words I cannot understand. *The forest reaching for me, urging me on.* That grating rasp is everywhere, echoing around me, reminding me. *The path was so clear before. The craggy fingers of the dark trees reaching for me. Pulling at me. Encouraging me. Beckoning me.*

But now that I have been to the untamed wildness of Neverland, I realize the trees in those memories have always been simply trees. They are not what I truly fear, nor what I was running from—or perhaps to—that night.

Cold and dark and the forest reaching for me as I run, but I am brushing aside its spindly branches as the voices whisper.

And then the image shifts, and my mom is there, her blue-gray eyes wild as the sky before a storm. Her face this close to mine, her breath sour and hot. "You have to forget this. You cannot speak of it ever again. Not to anyone, Gwendolyn. Do you understand?"

And suddenly the dark woods surround me and I'm there again, remembering other things I'd so long ago shoved down deep, pushed back into the unexamined corners of my mind. Things that make my heart race, my breath come fast and excited with wanting something I can't explain. Things that make me want to run into the night, my arms open wide.

Outside the safety of Rowan's arms, the Dark Ones are still gathering, their bodies like the wind rustling through dry leaves, but I can't seem to stop myself from plunging down into the dangerous waters of my own memories. I can't seem to stop myself from drowning in the images of the forest that night.

The warm fall night going cold, and I am lost.

The image shifts again, and I'm no longer in the woods. *The spinning brightness of police lights throwing jagged shards of color across the dark trees. Heavily jowled men with serious faces looming over me. Their mouths moving, but I can't make out their words, because instead of human voices, a rustling buzz echoes from their lips.*

And then my mom is there, taking me away. Her thin arms are strong around me. How could you? *her voice whispers, her blue-gray eyes stormy and lined with worry.* Don't say anything more. Forget, *she commands.*

But how could I have forgotten?

I'm remembering now, and the memories feel like the sharp point of a knife stabbing through the tender skin of all that I thought I was. It's impossible. It can't be anything more than a bad dream. But there's more waiting for me in those memories, some devastating truth that the darkness teases me with.

It isn't your fault, *my mother tells me, and even then I could hear the lie in her voice.* I will keep you safe, *she says.* This will never happen again.

And again I feel the point of a knife, sharp and wicked. The burn of memory.

And I'm screaming, crying. The tears are hot on my face as my mom says hush, my girl. Hush. And as she shakes me, her grip is as painful as the freshly knifed wound in my arm.

But those are not my mother's hands holding me. My cheeks are still cold with the wet slick of tears that coat them. My arm aches from the phantom cut, but it's Rowan's voice that comes to me urgently through the darkness.

"Come now, lass, wake up," he whispers, his hands tight on my arms.

My eyes flutter open, but it takes them a moment to adjust to the glow of a small fire. "What?" My voice is hoarse as it scratches free from my throat, and his hands become more gentle on my arms.

"The Dark Ones," he whispers. "They'd have taken us for sure if your screaming hadn't woken me. You must have been dreaming."

But that didn't feel like a dream. It had felt like a truth— like I was there again, living it again. I'd gone into the forest, chasing a voice, and when I came out, everything had changed. That was the first night my mom had packed our bags without warning so we could disappear before dawn.

"I'm going to let go of you now," he says, and I clutch his arm in response. "To add more to the fire," he tells me gently, his hand in my hair. "Easy now. It'll take but a moment."

He releases me then, and for a moment I feel adrift. Lost once again. The dark Fey move, rustling their great wings near, but they are unable to get any closer because of the light of the fire. Still, I almost feel myself beginning to fall into the memories once more.

Memories I now crave.

Rowan's face is tense in concentration as he feeds the flames, never taking his eyes from his work as the fire grows. And as it grows, crackling to life, it pushes back the darkness, until the bright halo of light is even larger.

Then Rowan takes me into his arms again, tucking me between his legs, my back against his chest. "All's well, lass," he whispers. But his body is tense, and I know his words are more comfort than truth.

Beyond the glow of the fire, I can still hear the Dark Ones circling. I can sense their frustration, their disappointment that they cannot reach us. Beyond the glow of the flames, Neverland is nothing but darkness. Even the stars seem to have turned away.

My muscles still quiver, my nerves jangle from the overload of fear and adrenaline, and my mind is thick with confusion about what just happened.

Rowan adjusts his body, bringing me closer to him. In the circle of his arms, I feel safe from the dangers of the night. But even the strength in his arms and the protection of his body aren't enough to brush away the memories.

The Dark Ones forced me to face my own truth. They plunged me deep into a past I had let myself—forced myself—to forget, and they revealed a truth I didn't want to remember about what my mother had done to protect me.

All those years of my mom worrying, all those moves from one small nowhere town to the next that I never understood. I do now. I *remember*. That night in the woods. The monsters chasing me through the darkness—until I made it out, just in time, to where there was light. I *knew* the monsters were there, but no one believed me. Except for my mom.

You must've imagined it, the policeman said, his heavy jowls wobbling as he shook his head.

She's just a kid, they whispered, looking at me with grown-up eyes that made my stomach ache. *A scared and confused kid.*

But my mom believed me. *You have to forget,* she told me, her words as sharp as a knife. *You can't talk about this ever again.*

I can't help but rub the scar on my arm.

It's not a vaccination. Or maybe it is, but not in the way I always believed. Not in the way I let myself remember. I was so young, I barely understood what was happening when my mom iced my arm and took out her silver knife.

I was so scared of what had happened in the forest—the way the darkness had tempted me away from the path and into the unknown. So I did what my mom commanded. I locked the memory of that night down deep, and I never let myself think about what happened after that.

But I can't say any of that aloud. Not yet. And he doesn't ask me for it. Instead, he sits in the silence with me, and after a long while, he speaks softly, close to my ear. "There's no shame in being afraid, lass. I know a bit about dreams, myself."

I don't know how to tell him that what I'd experienced wasn't simply a dream, so I don't say anything at first. I just watch the fire flicker, listening to the scuttling stir of monsters in the darkness beyond the safety of its glow. I think of the way Rowan was when I found him in the tunnels. I remember the wailing screams I heard almost every night I spent on his ship, and I understand then, I am not alone in fearing the secrets the darkness can reveal.

"Will you tell me?" I whisper, hoping his words can push away the memory of my own horrors.

He's silent for a long moment, as though gathering his

strength, and when he speaks, his voice comes out not as the steady cadence of a tale well told, but as the uneasy whisper of a man confessing. "It's not always the same," he says. "Sometimes I dream of before, sometimes of after, but most often, I dream of the night it happened." He stops then, silent and still, and I think for a moment that he will not—maybe he cannot—go on.

But the memories I've unearthed have made me selfish. I need to feel less alone. I need to know I am not the only one carrying the impossible weight of memory this night. "The night *what* happened?" I ask, pushing him more than I have any right to.

"The night I killed my brother."

But then the sky went red with hellfire.

And his brother was there, screaming something the boy could not hear.

And then he was not.

CHAPTER 31

·

THE WAY HIS VOICE BREAKS AT THE WORD *brother* makes my heart ache for him. I wait, watching the fire flicker before me, taking some comfort in the warmth of his body against me, trying to offer him some comfort in return. I'm not sure, though, if I want him to speak anymore or to stay silent.

"My whole life, all I wanted in the world was to be like my older brother, Michael. When the war started, we were both too young to go, but we followed the battles and the news like it was the grandest of adventures."

His words are not what I expected, and I'm confused. "Which war?" I ask, trying to catch the thread of his tale before it spins away from me in the night.

"The Great War, of course. What other would there be?" he said, his brow creased in confusion.

When I do the math in my head, my vision swims. World

War I was a hundred years ago, but Rowan doesn't look older than twenty. I hadn't even considered that time in Neverland could be different than time in my own world. How long had we been gone already? Weeks? Years? The idea sends a shiver of ice through me not even the fire roaring before me can melt.

"There have been plenty," I say weakly.

"They promised our sacrifice would be the last." Rowan pauses, as though gathering his courage with his words. "I should have expected that would be a lie as well," he says darkly. Then he releases me and sets to work adding more debris to the fire. He is careful not to look at me as he speaks.

"The day Michael turned eighteen, he enlisted, of course. I was so bloody jealous of him the day he left. My mam was crying her eyes out, but Michael's smile lit his whole face. I didn't see him again for almost a year, when he was on leave. He looked so completely different—my Michael and yet not. There he was in his starched uniform, all gleaming with the bits and bobs he'd won for doing what soldiers do. When my time with him was over, he put me on the train for home, but I didn't go. I found myself in a recruitment office, telling the man behind the desk I was nineteen years old. I could tell he didn't believe me, but it didn't matter. He took my name, and I signed the paper, and it was done."

"How old were you really?"

He glances back at me. "That was the spring of '17. I'd just turned sixteen the month before."

Sixteen—he looked older than that now, but not nearly as old as he should have looked. "And they took you? Without any proof?"

"And why wouldn't they? They needed men, and I was close enough." His eyes turn back to the fire, and I know he is there, reliving his brother's death again. "I never imagined it could be like that. They'd told us tales of blood and glory, of adventure and honor. And we went willingly, rushing toward our fates." As he studies the fire, his mouth turns up, a wry smile that doesn't reach his eyes. "You'd think I would have seen Pan's tale for the lie it was sooner."

I don't know what to say to him, so I don't speak. I simply sit as witness to the story he tells.

"Michael thought he had to take care of me." He huffs out a rough laugh. "He probably did at that. But it was my fault he went on that patrol the night it happened. I was angry at him for trying to mother me, so I volunteered. I was so convinced I was ready to be a man. So bloody convinced of my own bravery. Of course he volunteered as well."

He glances up at me again then, his eyes filled with the pain of all that happened. "I was the only one who made it off the field alive that night. And I barely made it at all," he said, gesturing toward his arm.

"That's what happened to your arm?" I ask, thinking of the scarred skin on his shoulders and back.

He gives me a terse nod, but doesn't say anything more.

He raises the steel hand then and clenches it, watching it move with the kind of terrible wonder he must have had in his eyes the first time he learned that his own arm was missing. Finally his voice comes again, small and broken in the darkness. "I don't know what happened after. I woke in a French hospital without my arm and in more pain than I ever dreamed

259

imaginable. I was in such desperate shape, I'm not sure why they even bothered to try saving me. Just as I'll never be sure of why Fiona brought me here.

"At first I thought I'd died and gone to heaven, save my brother wasn't here, but it wasn't long until I forgot about Michael, about everything before this world. . . . Until I took that first boy's life—that's when the dreams began.

"Now, every time I close my eyes, Michael is there. Laughing. Dying. Over and over, and no matter what I do, I can't change it. I can't stop it." His breath is ragged. His voice no more than a whisper. "The dreams torture me with what I've done, but they've saved me as well, for without them, I'd have been lost long ago. Without them, I wouldn't be able to stand against Pan or protect the boys from dangers they can't understand."

I want to tell him that it wasn't his fault, but I know the words are meaningless. Instead, I take his hands and thread my fingers through his, offering what silent comfort I can, but he doesn't speak. We sit in the silence for a moment before I turn his gloved hand over in mine. "May I?" When he doesn't pull away, I carefully peel away its soft leather covering.

The hand beneath is truly a miracle of engineering. Every one of the pieces is decorated with filigreed scroll-work, and it moves with an effortless grace that belies its mechanics.

"It might not be so bad if I didn't have to remember what it was to be whole," he says softly.

I want to tell him he's still whole, but I don't feel like

muddying whatever it is growing between us with lies. "It's part of you now, though." I turn a bit so I can face him properly, then I open my hand and lay it palm to palm overtop his.

"It's not quite the same as the original, but it serves me well enough for most things." He pulls away and raises the metal fingers to touch my cheek. "For other things, though, I find it sorely lacking."

He raises his other hand, then, and frames my face with his hands—metal and flesh, one hard and unfeeling, the other callused from unknown trials. Both equally Rowan.

I force myself to stay completely still, my heart beating wildly in my chest as he sifts his true fingers slowly through my hair, rubbing at the short strands. I wonder what he sees when he looks at me. Pan saw power. The boys in my own world looked at me next to Olivia and maybe saw a pretty girl, just not pretty enough.

I know he wants to kiss me again, just as I know this hesitation is his way of asking.

Yes, I think. Because if I have to die here—and I'm beginning to think it's inevitable I will—I want to know him again on my lips. I want him to want me that way, this surly pirate of a boy who would sacrifice anything for those under his protection. Anything, it seems, but me.

But he misreads the hitch in my breath and pulls away abruptly, moving back from me. His blank expression tells me that maybe I've made him dig far deeper into the pain of his past than anyone has a right to, but I can't say I'm exactly sorry for it. I've finally met the person behind the mask of the

261

Captain. The boy who chose to play the villain in order to battle a monster who calls himself a hero.

Rowan unfolds himself from the ground, leaving me cold and alone in the light of the fire. "Get some sleep, if you can, lass. We've a long and trying day ahead of us, if we're to do what must be done," he tells me. And then he steps away from the glow of the fire and into the darkness beyond.

When he woke, finally, terribly, on something rough against his cheek and reeking of death, he thought he had been delivered to hell. It had been a mistake. All of it. A horrible mistake. But the angel was there, gentle. Or if not gentle, at least sure . . .

CHAPTER 32

I N THE MORNING, THE AIR BETWEEN US IS charged with an unsettled energy, and I'm not sure what to say to Rowan. We stare at each other for a few moments in the soft light—moments when I think maybe he'll close the distance between us and kiss me—but he turns his back so I can pull on my own clothes instead. When I'm once again dressed, I offer the coat back, and he takes it with a stiff formality that makes everything that happened the night before feel like a long-ago dream.

"The straightest path to where the Queen lies is to follow the water, though to do so, we'd have to venture out into the sea once more, and I'm not all that willing to test the Sisters' mercy a second time." Rowan points toward the dense green jungle that teems with life beyond the rocky shores. "We'll have to cut through the jungle. Straight north to the heart of the island." He pulls out the dagger Fiona left us and hands it to me, handle first.

I don't reach for it. "What am I supposed to do with that?"

"Pray you never need to use it," he says, offering it again.

I take it finally, weighing its solid body in my hands. It's lighter than Pan's dagger, and in the morning sun, its blade glints silvery instead of the strange dark glow of Pan's. I tuck it into the waistband of my pants and hope I don't skewer myself before I need to use it.

"Ready?" he asks, his expression as sharp and guarded as I've ever seen it.

"Not even a little bit."

When we step into the lush green of the jungle, the sound of the sea fades away, but the trees aren't silent. As soon as we enter the teeming canopy, I can feel the trees pulse around me in warning.

This is nothing like the dark forest of my childhood. It's like nothing I've ever seen—even flying through the canopy of trees with Pan didn't prepare me for the experience of being *inside* of it. The vegetation around us is wild and unearthly, colored every shade of green imaginable. Some of the plants have leaves as large as my arms stretched wide. Others are spindly, with needlelike outgrowths that look as sharp as razors.

Strangely enough, even though the air is close here— almost claustrophobic—I don't feel afraid. Or I suppose I should say that I feel uneasy but not unwelcome. Like the garden within Pan's fortress, the plants of Neverland's jungle twist away as we walk to reveal a winding path through the dense undergrowth. The island itself seems to be directing us, and I can't tell if Neverland is guiding us to the Queen because it wants to be freed or if this is just another one of its traps. I should be terrified of how very *alive* it all feels, but after all I've been through—and after everything I've done—fear seems like a luxury I can't afford.

With each step I take following Rowan up the steep incline toward the very center of the island, my confidence falters, though. We climb and climb through the jungle, but we never seem to get anywhere. All I can do is follow him, step after step, mile after mile, making one twisting turn after another.

Once or twice, fairy lights appear, dodging in and around us as we make our way. Rowan ignores them, but they make me nervous. I don't trust Fiona's loyalty as much as he seems to, and I can't help but think the lights are probably watching us, maybe even reporting to Pan. I almost expect him to be waiting for us around every turn, but he never is.

Eventually we come to a clearing where the path we're on divides into three different trails. The one to our right leads into the undergrowth. To our left, another snakes away through a grove of enormous trees. Ahead, a third, identical path leads in an equally unclear direction.

As Rowan considers which to take, I ease back against the smooth trunk of a tree and let myself slide to the ground. My feet ache from the rocky and uneven climb, and I need a break, even though we can't afford to take one.

Behind my back, the tree I'm propped against moves, rippling into some new shape. All around me the other trees shift and settle, re-forming themselves into new trees and other configurations. The paths disappear as enormous plants sprout up and cover them, and other paths emerge.

Rowan curses at the sight of it. "Bloody stupid—" But he never finishes.

The jungle has gone suddenly and deathly still. His eyes meet mine, the question in them echoing my own.

"What is it?" I ask. All around us, it feels as though Neverland itself is holding its breath, waiting. But it's not an easy silence.

"Come on, lass." Rowan holds out his hand to pull me up, but before I'm even on my feet, a faint rustling fills the air around us.

The dark undersides of the leaves begin to shift as the shade beneath them starts to move, creeping along the thick green stems like a swarm of ants, collecting and gathering on the loamy jungle floor. The earthy humidity that has been our companion all morning seems to drain from the air as the coolness of night filters into the clearing. And as the chill brushes against my skin, the green-gold scent of the jungle is overwhelmed with a familiar odor that speaks of the sweetness of rot and the dustiness of memory.

The shadows creep along the ground, encircling us like a giant serpent eating its own tail. Then they begin to billow and grow, until we are penned in by them. Until the darkness begins to block our view of the jungle beyond.

When the shadows begin to lick at our feet and ankles, I'm assaulted again by the images from my past. *The forest reaching for me. Calling to me.*

I try to shove the images away, but the shadows continue to gather and grow, slowly shaping themselves into the winged creatures built from nightmares. Already I can make out their massive shoulders, the claw-tipped nails of their skeletal fingers.

But when a branch cracks out in the jungle, somewhere to our right, the Dark Ones go still, as though listening for what made the sound. Rowan raises his blade, his eyes narrowed in alertness as he shifts uneasily, watching both the swirling shadows and the jungle beyond.

After a moment, the Dark Ones begin to billow and grow once more. Back to back, we track them as they circle us. I grip the dagger tightly in my sweat-damp fist and take shallow, anxious breaths as I watch the shadows finally begin to coalesce into dark, broad creatures.

Another crack sounds in the jungle—this time from the left.

Rowan glances at me, and the look on his face tells me what I've already realized—it would be impossible for a single creature to have moved that far so quickly. The Dark Ones seem to sense it too. Half-formed, they go still, and their metallic rustling changes—grows sharper. Then, without warning, the Dark Ones shrink, melting onto the ground and flowing like dark water back to the shadowy undersides of the leaves.

Rowan's expression mirrors my thoughts exactly—neither of us wants to meet whatever it is that can chase away the Dark Ones.

Without a word, Rowan takes me by the hand and picks a new path at random. Behind us, around us, the jungle crackles with life, but the sound isn't the steady pulse of before. The trees rustle more erratically and urgently as we break into a run. Behind us, the crackling rush of a tree falling pushes us to move faster.

At first I think we're putting distance between us and whatever's out there. But when the path empties out into a small clearing, I see we've reached a dead end. In front of us, a rocky precipice rises straight and sheer, blocking our path. Around us, the jungle shudders as the path we've just come down closes.

Rowan's eyes meet mine. His expression is tight with the knowledge I've already comprehended—whatever's out there wasn't chasing us. It was herding us.

"What do we do?" I whisper.

"You still have the dagger I gave you, aye?"

I glance over at him. "Yeah."

"Keep it out."

The jungle shudders again. Another crackling rush of trees falling just beyond out view. And then the foliage at the edge of the clearing shakes.

"Steady, lass," he tells me as two enormous creatures emerge from the still-silent jungle.

Of all the things I've seen since I've come to this world, of all the horrors I've witnessed, these creatures are the most horrible, the most terrifying yet. These beasts are more than twice as tall as any man, and they are like nothing I could have imagined.

Their long, claw-tipped arms and legs are corded with sinewy muscle that ripples and shifts as they move. Bloodred eyes set into their massive shoulders watch us as the beasts lumber into the clearing on long, powerfully muscled legs.

Their leathery skin is drawn tight over their misshapen bodies, and their whole torso seems to be nothing but a huge, gaping mouth ringed with rows of teeth. Those horrible jaws are already open in anticipation, cavernous voids built to consume. To devour.

And the smell of them. They make the entire clearing reek with the stomach-turning stench of bloated, rotten corpses and the bitterness of despair.

The beasts close in slowly, taking their time, as though they know we have no chance of retreat, nowhere to run. Next to me, Rowan shifts, balancing his attention on both of the monsters. I raise the dagger I'm holding too. Not that I have any hope of actually injuring one of these creatures, much less killing one, but if I'm going to die here, I won't die without a fight.

"Gwendolyn." Rowan's voice is tight, urgent. "If there is any sort of Fey magic you might consider working, now would be the time to be doing it." He glances at me, taking his attention away from the beasts only for a second. "A rescue, perhaps?"

A rescue? I look up at the sheer cliff face behind me—I doubt I can make something that big disappear. There's no way to climb it, and no way to get around these creatures. No way to escape.

Rowan sends me another impatient look, his sword at the ready as one of the beasts gnashes its horrible teeth and lets out a growl that sounds like the grinding of bones. Its long arms are tipped with massive clawed hands that swipe at him.

He swings his sword savagely to fend off the blow, but the

tip of the monster's claw catches his arm and shreds the sleeve of his coat. The rods of his arm glint beneath the gaping tear. "Anytime now, lass," he says, turning to ward off the second beast before it can lunge.

"What do you want me to do?" I ask, my voice rising in panic. The second beast is watching me with those bloodred eyes, but Rowan darts in front of me before it can attack.

"We both know what you did in the tunnel, Gwendolyn. Try something. *Anything*," he demands, his voice tight with more than impatience as he swivels to account for the other beast's location. "You're half bloody Fey, aren't you?"

"I—" The second beast lunges for me, but I stab at it with the dagger. Surprised, it backs away, shifting uneasily on its strong legs as it considers me with its burning eyes. "I don't know how." I clench my hands into tight fists. I'm still not sure what made the rock disappear in the tunnels. I have no idea what I finally did to get him out of that prison.

"Figure it out," he snaps, fending off another attack. "I have bet *everything* on you—my life, my friend. My crew."

"I *know*." My voice comes out angrier than I intended. "But it's not like I asked for this. It didn't come with a set of instructions."

"You don't need a set of bloody instructions, Gwendolyn. It's what you *are*. And if you don't stop running from it, we're not going to be making it out of this particular mess alive."

I take a shuddering breath as the truth of what he's saying hits me at full force. *He's right.* After all the horrors and mistakes, if we die here, at the hands of these monsters, it will be my fault. Because even with all I've seen, all I've done, there is a part of me that is still afraid to accept what I've come to know about myself. Because accepting it means letting go of the brittle belief that I could be a simple girl, a *normal* girl.

Because I'm not a normal girl—I've never been one. My mom knew that when she uprooted us time and time again. She knew that when she took a knife and sliced into my arm to try to protect me.

With the gaping, horrible maws of nightmarish beasts open before me and the deadly height of the cliff behind me, I have a choice. I can keep clinging to that fragile story of what I thought I was and I can die, devoured by those terrible mouths. Or I can admit that maybe I've always been something else—something more.

"Gwen," Rowan says, taking another swipe at the first beast when it gets too close.

My head snaps around, and my eyes meet his for a moment. It's the first time he's ever called me that. All along he's used the stiff formality of my whole name to keep me at arm's length. But for the space of a heartbeat, his expression is open and trusting . . . and hopeful.

"You can do this, lass. Get us out of here."

Then the moment is over, and he turns again to lunge at the monstrous Fey that have corralled us.

The time to be scared, the time to deny is over, unless of course, I want to die. Unless I want *him* to die with me.

I turn and press my hands against the rough surface of the cliff rising up behind us, tracing the rock tentatively with one finger, testing it. Nothing happens. Resolved, I lay my palm against it and I focus, just as I did when Pan asked me to. Just as I did when I felt the warmth flare beneath by palms near the edge of the trench. And as I did in the dark tunnel, when I wanted to destroy the bars that kept me from Rowan.

Closing my eyes, I concentrate on the erratic pulse of the rock beneath my hands. At first nothing happens, but I will not give up. I draw all my attention—everything I am—to the place where my skin presses against Neverland. The beasts growl, inching closer, but I do not let myself think, *It's not working*. The idea is there anyway, just below the surface. Taunting me. Threatening me. But I ignore it, and as I'm about to give up, the rock beneath my hand grows warm.

I force myself to hold steady as the warmth spreads through my fingertips, across my palms, and begins to creep up my arms, heating and burning as it climbs toward my chest. But when it reaches my elbows, the heat begins to sear me from within. I clench my teeth and force myself to ignore the pain, but when the heat reaches my shoulder, the burn flashes even hotter, and I wrench my hands away.

Immediately, my arms go cold, but the scar on my upper arm tingles and aches as I try to catch my breath. I was *so* close, but . . . "It's no good." Tears burn at my eyes.

They were wrong about me—*all* of them were wrong. I don't have this in me. Or if I do, it's not enough.

Rowan shouts in rage, and I turn in time to see him barely beating back one of the monsters. He's panting, his shoulders rising and falling with the effort of the fight, and I can see he's tired. Sweat has begun to bead on his brow, and his muscles are already drawn with the exertion. The beasts are toying with him, wearing him down, and at this rate, he won't last long.

He will die because of you—because he chose you and you failed him, a voice deep inside me taunts. *And then you will be alone, and you will die as well.*

I have to try again, but as I press my hands to the rock, I know deep down, where you know things without having to think about them, it will be useless.

Because you know what must be done, the voice whispers. *Because you know what your mother did to you.*

"No," I say, grabbing the scar on my arm, even as the terrible truth settles over me like a shroud.

What was it my mother told me after they found me in the woods—after she ordered me to forget what had happened out there?

The clearing, the monsters, even the sound of Rowan's exertion as he tries to battle the monsters falls away, and I can hear my mom's words clearly, echoing in the far recesses of my mind. *This will never happen again.*

And with them comes the memory of the sharp surprise of her fear and an even sharper pain. An *unbelievable* pain, because how could my mother have hurt me like that? I was just a child, and even as it was happening—even as the silver blade bit into my skin, I couldn't believe my mom was capable of hurting me like that. Even as the blood trickled down my numb arm, the younger me couldn't accept what she did.

I don't even need the Dark Ones now—the memories that have lain buried and suppressed for so long rise up like a wave and overtake me. The look on my mother's face when she collected me from the police station that night wasn't relief—it was terror. Not *for* me or for what had happened to me out there in the darkness. *No.* Even my five-year-old self understood she was afraid *of* me.

My breath rushes out of me at the memory of her blue-gray eyes nervous, fearful as the police explained where they'd found me and what I had told them. How long have I tried to forget the memory of that night? How long have I been trying to earn back her love—to earn a place in her life—by being the perfect daughter?

By doing what she commanded and forgetting. By always doing *everything* she asked of me.

Not five feet away, Rowan is being driven back against the rock by one of the beasts, and when it accomplishes its final victory over him, he'll be gone. And then it will turn on me, and any chance of saving Olivia, of getting back to my world, will be lost—all the human children in this world will be lost right along with me. All because I've been too afraid to do what needs to be done.

I remember now what my mother did that night when I was barely five years old, and I know how to fix it.

In this world, power requires sacrifice, Pan had once told me. The pain of his Queen carving into his skin had given him tremendous power. But my mother had done the opposite.

Pain. Sacrifice. Power. The words come together to form a terrible truth.

When we'd come home that night, my mom had started packing, but not before she took me into the kitchen and held ice to my arm. Not before she sharpened the point of a knife and opened my arm so she could place a sliver of metal beneath my skin. A rune, a protective spell against the voice

274

in the darkness that called to me. A defense against what I was. What I am.

Because she was afraid *of* me.

I look at the dagger in my hand and I don't let myself think about how it will feel. I look at the scar I've lived with for so long, and without any more hesitation, I press the sharp tip of the blade into my skin.

The angel smiled at the boy, her eyes hard and unforgiving. He knew that must mean something, though he could not think what it could be. There was a dull ache behind his eyes. There was something he should be thinking of, remembering. But he couldn't imagine— "And if I want to go back?" he asked. "There is only forward for you now," the angel said. She held out her hand again. . . .

CHAPTER 33

I DON'T FEEL THE PAIN AT FIRST. UNTIL THE blood wells from where the point of the knife has sliced into my skin, I don't feel anything at all. It's like a paper cut you don't notice until it starts to bleed—and sting.

Rowan says something to me, and I hear the shock in his voice, but I can't make out his words over the roaring in my ears. It's too late to turn back now, though. Too late to regret the blood trickling hot and sticky down my arm.

I grit my teeth against the pain and hope that I am right about what I'm doing. I pray the Dark Ones have not given me false memories and the visions aren't just another trap as I press the tip of the knife deeper into my arm, poking and prodding at the screaming wound until I think I'll pass out from the pain. Until the tip of my knife hits something solid that is not bone.

My skin is alive with white-hot pain. Still, I don't let myself stop. This pain is nothing compared to what I will suffer at the hands of those monsters. Nothing compared to what it would be to lose him now.

With a violent jerk, I use the tip of the dagger to pry the small, dark object from my skin. A thin, curved bit of metal rips free, leaving a jagged wound where the scar had once been, and something inside me breaks open—a painful shattering followed by a feeling of relief that almost brings me to my knees.

I don't have time to examine the strange sense of lightness I feel, but I look at the object dangling from the tip of my knife, and I know the Dark Ones didn't lie. The bloody metal glints in the afternoon light. It's a tiny rune my mother used to mute my power in the human world. Because she wanted to protect me . . . and to protect herself from me.

Unsettled and unsure, I tuck the bloody rune into a pocket and focus on what I need to do. Without hesitation now, I press my hands to the wall again. Blood has already left tracks down my arm, but I don't bother to wipe it away, just as I don't pay any attention to the burning ache from the still-bleeding wound. My blood courses hot and free through my veins, and I focus everything I have—everything I *am*—on the island. On the rock in front of me. On saving Rowan. And for the first time, I truly let myself believe in what I might do.

In what I might be.

Heat floods through my body, but this time, it's as welcoming and gentle as a summer breeze. Above us, the sharp report of cracking rock echoes. The monsters freeze, shifting uneasily as they search for the source of the noise.

"Christ, lass, what are you doing?" Rowan says hoarsely, and I can hear the wonder in his voice. And the fear.

I feel that fear too. I just don't let myself react to it. "I'm getting us out."

Keeping my hands pressed against the stone, I shift back a bit, allowing the cliff to move toward me. The whole wall rumbles with great, groaning creaks and thunderous crashes as the once-shear rock rearranges itself one bit at a time, creating a precipitous path up the face of the mountain.

The relief that courses through me nearly knocks me off my feet. "Come on," I tell Rowan as I step onto the first of the protruding rocks.

He hesitates only a moment before he begins backing his way to where I am. "You think it'll hold?" He eyes the newly formed steps uneasily.

"I don't think there's much choice." I climb to the next bit of rock. It seems solid enough, so I take another. And then another.

Behind us, the beasts begin to move again as they realize their prey is escaping.

The steps are steep—almost vertical. At times I have to claw at the rock for handholds to pull myself up, but we move quickly—Rowan following at my heels—and ascend at a steady pace.

"Faster, lass," Rowan urges.

I look down and see that our escape is not going to be easy—the monsters can climb too. So I move faster, ignoring the burning ache in my open wound, ignoring everything but the promise of safety above.

We're maybe halfway up the wall when I hear the rustling scrape that always sends ice through my veins. Before I can even warn Rowan, the dark spaces beneath the crevices in the rocks begin to move, seeping from their hiding places and creeping down, along the cliff. My heart races as I pick up my pace again, but the shadows are already gathering, sliding down the face of the rock like a dark waterfall, slinking steadily toward us.

When the still-unformed shadows reach us, there's nowhere to go. They blanket us with a layer of damp darkness that smells of decay as it slides along my skin and brushes softly at my face. I freeze, unable to keep climbing as long as they are touching me, unable to do anything but cling to the rock and wait for whatever will happen next.

But this time no memories assault me. I have no vision of a dark forest. This time, the darkness feels electric—raw and pure and almost exhilarating.

A voice whispering that sounds so very much like the one I hear inside me. This time it urges me on.

The shadows continue to flow over us, but they never form into the dark Fey. They never attack. They slide steadily down the face of the cliff, leaving us untouched.

When they reach the monstrous beasts, they are not so kind. In a matter of moments, the two creatures are overwhelmed by a blanket of shadow. With snarling growls, the beasts swat at the creeping darkness with their terrible claws, their mouths open to try to consume it. But the shadows never fully form. They swirl and creep, wrapping themselves around the beasts, taunting them. As the monsters try to pull the wisps of darkness away, they lose their balance and tumble one by one to the rocky floor of the clearing below.

"Go," Rowan urges again, and this time I don't hesitate.

I climb faster now, clinging desperately to the flinty rock whenever I lose my footing, and when I reach the top, I hoist myself over with my last bit of strength. Rowan is next, collapsing beside me, his chest heaving with the effort of his own climb. He rolls over and looks up at the sky, and then he looks over at me, his dark eyes steady and too perceptive.

And then, all at once, he's laughing, long and hard.

I join him, the overwhelming relief of making it to safety coursing through me and spilling out of me in halting, gasping laughter. But then, suddenly, I'm crying even as I laugh—hot tears of relief and amazement. And fear.

The place he found himself was not heaven, and still, it was also not hell. It was a cruel land filled with nothing but want. A place where boys ran and ruled and sated every desire at the point of the sword. The boy could not help but think that perhaps he had been to a place so much like it before. . . .

CHAPTER 34

WE DON'T LET OURSELVES RELAX FOR long. Neither of us trusts that we won't be attacked by some new horror. Rowan sits up and examines the gash in my arm. Without a word, he tears a piece of fabric from his shirt and binds the open wound for me, his dark eyes avoiding mine.

He doesn't ask me why I did it or what I cut from my arm, and that one kindness is more than I could have hoped for. Because even though I've admitted to myself what my mother did, I'm not ready to say the words out loud.

When he's done wrapping my arm, he offers me his hand and hoists me to my feet, and then we continue to make our way into the heart of the island, the center of Neverland.

The land at the top of the cliff isn't so thick with jungle growth. From here the terrain eases down into smaller hills, and as we walk, I hear the soft rush of flowing water in the

distance. In silent agreement, we follow the sound, and when we breach the top of a gentle rise, we look down to see a valley spread out below us.

Wordlessly, I follow Rowan down the sloping hill and into the valley's basin, but my heart sinks. We've arrived at the falls Pan first brought me to after he took me from Rowan's ship. It's another dead end.

When we finally reach the edge of the clear lake, I turn to Rowan and tell him what I've been worrying about ever since I saw the falls: "I don't know if I have enough energy right now to get us over those." My body aches, and I feel absolutely drained from the effort it took to move the last mountain.

"We're not going over." Rowan's eyes are sharp, assessing the space for danger. "We're here, lass. From here," he says, pointing to where the falls cascade over the stepped rock, "the water flows from that point, down and out to the sea, filling it constantly. This is the center. The heart."

"That can't be," I tell him, certain he's wrong.

He quirks a brow in my direction.

"He brought me here," I say, confused. "Pan, I mean. When he took me from your ship, this is the first place we came. He told me to call the island. Why would he do that if this is where he hid the Queen?"

"Cocky bastard," Rowan mutters, but there's a hint of admiration in his tone. "He always did enjoy showing off, lass, but he most likely brought you here to test you. If you'd have shown any indication that you sensed the Queen's presence, I'm thinking your stay at his fortress would have been a mite different than it was."

"Test me?" A feeling of unease creeps across my skin as I remember Pan pressing his hands over mine, tempting me to call Neverland my home. I *had* sensed something that day, but I'd felt stupid about trying to explain it to Pan. So I hadn't said anything.

He glances down at me. "He needed you to trust him, lass. It's what he does—seduces those who follow him with promises of pleasure and power, and then, when they give themselves to his keeping, he takes from them all he can. They sacrifice themselves to him and for him. It's what he would have done to you as well."

I rub my arms, suddenly chilled with how true and right Rowan's words feel. Didn't Pan himself tell me that power requires sacrifice? Isn't that what Fiona said as well—Pan allowed me to see what he wanted me to see? He told the tales he wanted me to believe, so I would trust him. Give myself willingly to him.

And it almost worked. When he rescued me from the ship, when he rescued Olivia from the End, I'd wanted to trust that I'd found a hero who could rescue me. I'd fallen right into his trap.

Turning away, I look out over the lake, around the valley, trying to focus on what's ahead of us and on what we still need to do. "You're sure the Queen's here somewhere?"

"When I was still one of his lads, Pan showed this place to me. Though it's possible it was a boast or a lie, I don't think it was. He wanted me to know what he'd done—he wanted me to understand his power over this world, because he wished me to follow him without question. But I do suppose there's only one way to find out." Rowan inclines his head in my direction, a challenge if I've ever seen one.

The valley around me feels different now. The first time I saw this place, the falls took my breath away. This was the place where I first believed I was truly in Neverland, but now, heavy shadows from the setting sun slant across the land. The water no longer throws up rainbows in its mist. It whispers, soft and deadly, of the secrets it hides.

I feel different too, though, and I don't think it's just the bit of metal I carved out of my own arm. It's more than that. It's about the way Rowan is looking at me right now, like he believes I am capable of doing what we must. And maybe also like he's afraid I am. He holds his face so careful, so still, but I can see his fear.

But his fear doesn't bother me. I feel differently about myself now—stronger, more sure. I'm unafraid now to examine even the darkest parts of my past, of what I am. And I'm unafraid to look to a new kind of future.

"If this works," I say softly, "will you come back with me?"

He startles, as though he didn't expect the question. From his expression, it looks as though it hurts him just to think about it. "There's nothing for me in that world any longer, lass," he says after a second.

"You don't want to go back?" But the tension in his face tells me the answer.

"I've dreamed of it, to be sure. Though I'm no longer certain, exactly, what it is I'd be returning to." He steps away from me, his gaze steady on the dark water. "Here, at least, I have purpose."

"But if you stay, you'll die," I whisper, shaken by the determination in his voice.

He gives a small nod, but there's no fear or pity or regret in his expression. Only resolve to do what he must.

I look at this boy before me—this boy who has lived through so much. He's killed and he's protected, but he's managed somehow, miraculously, to survive in this place. And I understand now that whatever happens, he doesn't expect to live through this—maybe he never has.

"You don't think this will work, do you?"

His gaze shifts away, uncomfortable. "We've come this far, haven't we?"

"But still, you're not convinced."

He doesn't respond, just frowns at me, those fathomless eyes of his refusing to look away.

Part of me is glad he doesn't lie. Somehow the starkness of the truth is easier to deal with. It forces me to consider my own actions, my own future. And it forces me to admit the decision I've already made.

Since being brought to this world, I've come to understand that everything I've ever learned about good and evil, about the choices we make and the choices we must live with, have been nothing more than convenient fictions invented by those who have never been confronted by the darkness and actually forced to choose. The choices Rowan has willingly made, the evils he has committed should give me every reason to fear him. He is, by his own admission, a murderer. A pirate. A man without anything left to lose.

But I don't fear him. Not anymore, and maybe, not ever

really. I trust him more than anyone else in this hellish world, because he's never spun fairy tales about good or evil. He has simply stood in the space between and not pretended the choice could be otherwise.

I take Rowan's face in my hands and make him look at me. It's been such a short time since we met, shorter since I came to understand who and what he is. I touch his cheek, tracing his scar with the pad of my thumb, memorizing every inch of his face. The sharp set of his jaw. The gold flecks in his eyes.

How could I have ever thought he had cruel eyes?

His eyes are not cruel now. They contain everything we are both too afraid to say. Every hope, every desire we both understand we can never have.

"Nothing good can come of this, lass." His voice is no more than a rasp, and it shakes with the same uncertainty I feel.

I know that, but he's standing there, so close, and looking so very far away, and I don't want to leave him in that place. "I don't care," I whisper, the words nothing more than a breath caught in my throat.

He studies me, his face too shadowed by the growing twilight for me to read the emotion there. "You're far braver than any wee slip of a girl has any right to be, you know."

"I don't feel brave." I feel nervous and scared and hopeful, all together in one overwhelming moment. "You're shaking," I say as he brushes my hair back from my eyes.

"Maybe," he whispers, his mouth against my forehead. "But it's been ages since I've felt as human as you make me feel. I've tried not to want you, but I can't bring myself to stay away."

"Then don't," I whisper.

His hands cup my cheeks, the hard steel on one side, the human warmth on the other. Both tremble as he leans forward until our faces are only a breath apart, and then he settles his lips against mine. They are warm and soft and taste of the spice of cloves and the saltiness of his sweat and of Rowan, and in a moment I'm lost.

He deepens the kiss, his lips pressing against mine in a soft slide of warmth, teasing me with the promise of something I feel like I will never reach. He shifts, wrapping his arms around me, pulling me closer into the heat of his body, and I cannot help but respond.

The unnerving softness of his skin, the lean muscle of his arms under my touch. I let my fingers ruffle the short dark hair at the nape of his neck as I kiss him back, pressing myself into him, as though this moment is the only moment. Because I know it is. I kiss him as though I could kiss away our fates. As though I could kiss away all the fear that riots inside me.

Before I'm even close to satisfied, he eases away, leaving me breathless and wanting. "We shouldn't tarry," he says, his voice as strained and unsteady as I feel.

We don't move away from each other, though. His body is still pressed against mine. He still cups my face gently with his hands, and my arms are still wrapped around his waist. Neither of us speaks as he pulls me closer against him again, and I let him, taking in all I can about this moment.

The future is impossible—I know that. So I settle for what I have—I memorize the steady beat of his heart and concentrate on the rhythmic rise and fall of his chest until the time comes that we can delay no longer.

In that world, the boy learned that boredom could be deadly. No one warned him, but he discovered it just the same. For hours the lads would sit or stand, arms in hand, blades ready in wait. And as they waited, every rustling sound, every shifting of the earth was the enemy. As they waited, their fear grew teeth. . . .

CHAPTER 35

A RE YOU READY, THEN?" ROWAN STEPS AWAY from me reluctantly.

The sun has already dipped behind the hills, leaving the air cooler, and without his body against mine, I feel more chilled than ever. "As I'll ever be."

He eyes me, expectant, but he doesn't rush me.

I settle myself on the ground near the clear pool. In the water, jewel-colored fish swim beneath the surface, and then my focus shifts and I catch a glimpse of my reflection. I look like a stranger. My face is smudged and my short hair is a wild tangle, but my eyes are steady and strong. The girl staring back at me isn't the Gwen from before. Even if she doesn't understand everything she's been through, the girl staring back at me is someone new. Someone I want a chance to know.

When I'm ready, I press my hands to the ground beneath me, feeling the sharp points of the rocky soil. I press with all my weight and all my focus, until my palms ache with the effort. Until the gash in my arm screams in protest. I focus on the way the land beneath me moves, pulsing in its steady, ever-present beat.

Show me. I direct every ounce of energy I have left into the ground, into the island beneath me. *Show me your Queen so I can free her. Show me so you can be free,* I tell Neverland, but the land beneath my palms pulses steadily, unaware—or maybe just indifferent.

Undeterred, I claw my fingers into the ground until the silty soil of Neverland scrapes beneath my ragged fingernails. My temper spikes hot and acidic in my veins, burning through me with all the anger from all the years I've spent feeling powerless and impotent. All those years being dragged from place to place with my mother, who kept this from me, who never gave me a say. All those towns and all those schools where I never fit. I am *supposed* to fit here.

"Show me," I demand, heat beginning to pulse through my arms. "Give me my Queen," I whisper.

The heat in my hands grows, spreads, as I feel the island shudder beneath me, and as something deep inside me answers. The ground shakes in response. Beneath my palms, the soft green ground cover begins to transform, each tiny blade of grass going stiff and still, rippling as it hardens into glasslike shards. The transformation spreads like a wave, climbing over the ground, right up to the edge of the water.

The ground quakes violently, and Rowan pulls me up and into the protection of his arms. "What have you done, lass?"

I look up at him and see again the fear in his eyes. But I'm not afraid. I wanted this. I commanded it. And now I'll see it through to the end.

I lick my parched lips. "We'll find out soon enough, I guess." All around us, the landscape turns hard and brittle as the ground continues to rumble and shake, and Neverland transforms itself in answer to my call.

The pool beneath the falls starts to churn and bubble, like it's boiling. One by one, the jeweled bodies of the fish rise to the surface, motionless, the once-brilliant colors of their scales fading into a glossy black, like the light within them has gone forever dark. They look like strange floating pebbles now, and are so thick and plentiful that it almost looks like we could walk across the surface of them.

Then, all at once, everything falls completely silent. The land goes absolutely motionless beneath our feet. The plants don't shift and change, and the surface of the water goes as still as glass.

Rowan releases me enough to draw his sword from its sheath. We wait for what will come next, holding our breath against hope, but nothing happens.

"Well, that was—"

An earsplitting crack shatters the eerie silence and drowns out the rest of what Rowan says. His arm tightens around me as the hilly land echoes with the reverberations of the noise, but otherwise, the world is still completely motionless and quiet.

Afraid to move, we both search for some indication of what caused the sound, but at first nothing seems different. Then I see what is happening.

"The falls," I whisper.

They aren't coursing as they once did. Instead, the water level is steadily dropping, exposing jagged steps in the rock as it drains away. As the last bit of water trickles down, it reveals a dark crack splitting the mountain in two. As we watch, the fissure steadily grows, traveling down the center of the rock, like the dark lines traveled across the skin of the boy on the ship.

The island rumbles again as the rock behind the falls begins to move apart, cleaving into two halves and exposing a dark crevasse. The remaining water of the falls drains into the yawning hole in the mountain, and the water left in the clear pool beneath the falls is also draining away, running back into the place where the island split itself apart.

Rowan's arms are still tight and protective around me as we watch, until all that's left is the dark, muddy bed of the lake and a wide, deep wound in the land.

I stare at the gaping fissure, horrified and awed by what I've managed to do. "Do you think that's it?"

"There's only one way to be certain." He releases me and offers his hand. "If you're ready?"

I'm not. I thought I was, but just looking at the dark gash in the rock makes my skin prickle in warning. Still, this is what we have come here for. This is what I demanded, and if Neverland answered my call, we need to see what it's trying to show us.

I take his offered hand, and Rowan leads the way out into the mucky basin of the falls. We avoid the gaping crack that runs down its middle as we make our way across it, toward where water had once cascaded down the mountain. Toward the place where the island has opened itself to us.

The ground of the lake bed is soft, but the brittle bodies of fish crackle beneath our booted feet when we step on them, popping and snapping as we go. Each tiny body I destroy seems like another threat, and another reminder of what we stand to lose.

When we reach the other side, the bare, wet cliffs loom above us as the dark split in the rock dares us to enter. Water still drips from the edges of the dark stone in an uneven rhythm

"It could be a trap," I say as I peer into the dark cave.

"This whole bloody world's a trap." Rowan never takes his eyes from the newly formed opening before us. "We're going to be needing some light, I think."

It takes him only a moment to find a branch thick enough and strong enough to serve as a torch. He takes his shirt off from beneath his coat and wraps it around the branch. With the tip of his metal finger, he manages to get enough of a spark on one of the drier surfaces to light the makeshift torch. Then he looks at me, nervous anticipation glinting in his eyes. He doesn't like this any more than I do, but he wants it to be true just as much.

"Let's be getting on with it, shall we?"

I give him a tight nod and follow his lead into the gaping jaws of the cavern.

Once we're inside, the air is immediately cooler. We hesitate, both of us waiting and listening for the unmistakable sound of the Dark Ones. But the cavern is silent. There is no scent of moldering leaves, no rustling of far-off wind. The air is thick and wet around us, but it is not dangerous—not yet, at least.

This is no normal tunnel, though—the walls are not the smoothly hewed stone of Pan's fortress. The walls here are all sharp edges and jutting corners that tell of the violence that created them. We don't speak as we walk, but my hand slides into his as we make our way deeper into the heart of the island.

Deeper into the mountain, the tunnel grows even narrower. It's all unexpected switchbacks and hairpin turns that make me feel like we're going in circles, spiraling farther and farther into the heart of Neverland. My skin prickles with the certainty that at any moment the rock will once again begin to vibrate and rumble, crushing us beneath its weight. But the island remains disconcertingly quiet. The rock around us remains cold and dead.

Finally the tunnel opens, flaring out to reveal a large room-like cavern that is a dead end. The ceiling is higher here, and it glows like a miniature night sky. Rowan notices the strange starlike lights at the same time I do and raises the torch higher so we can make out what's causing the effect. Dark crystals embedded into the rock glow like tiny false stars, but they aren't randomly scattered. There is a pattern to them, like tiny constellations.

Familiar constellations. The crystals in the ceiling form lines and angles that remind me of the runes on my mother's stones. The runes carved into Pan's skin.

"This is it," I whisper, afraid to disrupt the silence around us by speaking too loudly.

Rowan's face is all grim concentration as he raises the

torch from one side of the room to another, searching for some sign that I'm right. "It's a dead end, Gwendolyn. There's nothing here save some bits of rock and more dampness."

My heart sinks, because he's right—this *is* a dead end. I don't know what I expected to find, but there is nothing in this chamber but the glittering constellations above us and the silent rock surrounding us. Still, I can hear the sound of water rushing somewhere not so far off, and air is moving through the passage. It can't be a *complete* dead-end.

"Look at the ceiling. This is it." I can't shake the sense that the Queen is here . . . somewhere.

I let go of Rowan's hand and step away from him, beyond the light of his torch and to the smooth walls of the cavern. These walls aren't damp, and when I press my hands to them, they feel almost warm. If I focus, I can feel the heartbeat of the island racing at a dizzying speed, faster than I've ever felt it before. But it's softer than I've ever felt it too, as though it's buried somewhere deep below.

Show me. I channel the demand—not the request—through myself, into the rock. Rowan stands near me again, the heat of his torch warming my face as I concentrate on speaking to, listening to the world beneath my hands.

As I'm listening, my heart beating in time to the distant pulse of Neverland, I hear a noise in the darkness of the cavern behind me. A sharp plinking sound, like a penny striking a table, and the echo of the sound rings in the silence.

"What was that?" Rowan whispers, holding his flame aloft.

I don't let myself look. I don't let myself do anything but focus on the feel of the stone beneath my hand, on my desire to see the Queen. I allow myself to let go of all my fear, all my misgivings, and to *want*.

To free her.

To free all of us, because if we can do this, I can go home—I can get Olivia home. If I can do this, I can make everything right.

But a voice inside me whispers, *Not everything*.

The heat building beneath my hands falters, and for a moment all I feel is the coolness of the rock and the certainty that I can't save him—No matter what I do, I won't be able to save the boy beside me.

I shove that thought out of my head. I won't let myself be distracted. Not even for Rowan.

Plink. The sound comes again, and again it echoes. *Plink, plink*.

"It's the ceiling," Rowan tells me. He holds up the torch again, and in its flickering light, I see what he means. The glittering crystals in the ceiling are falling one by one, a solid, steady shower of stone. "Get back," he says, pushing me against the wall as more fall.

Rowan covers me with his body as the noises steadily increase, rising in speed and volume, but still I concentrate on my task, calling to the world. Asking Neverland to heed my desire. As the crystals fall like dying stars, they throw debris into the air around us. I can smell the metallic, almost mineral scent of the dust they kick up from the floor when they land. I can taste it—the heart of Neverland coats my tongue with its bitter taste.

Then the falling crystals slow until, finally, the cavern is quiet. Nothing else tumbles from the ceiling, and after a long moment we right ourselves and shake the dust from our hair.

"What was that?" I look up at the ceiling, thankful it hasn't collapsed completely, but it's pockmarked now and no longer flickers with diamondlike shards.

I start to step toward the center of the room, trying to figure out if anything else has happened, but my foot falters when the ground beneath it crumbles away. Where once there was flat, solid rock, the ground is now carved out into a deep crater. The floor is gone, and in its place a narrow path winds down, spiraling into the center, and in the center of that crater someone or something is huddled, a clumped mass of dirty rags that seems to be moving.

I step back as something within the pile of rags moves again. It can't possibly be the Queen. There is no way this crumpled bit of blackened fabric is what we need to save ourselves and this world.

"Bring the torch." I turn to Rowan, but before he can reach me, the world explodes in light.

Sometimes, though not often, he had dreams, unlike the other lads who slept deeply, like the dead. On those nights, he could not raise himself from the horrors held in his sleeping hours, though he wailed piteously in them. But when he woke, he could not remember the things he had forgotten. . . .

CHAPTER 36

I SQUINT AGAINST THE BRIGHTNESS THAT saturates the cavern, until my eyes adjust to the unnatural glow lighting the space. When I can finally see again, I notice that a figure stands in the center of the crater—a woman.

I know at once I'm in the presence of the Queen. Like Fiona, she is tall and slender, with long, graceful limbs and skin that glows like alabaster. Like Fiona, her face is both beautiful and terrible to behold. Her eyes are alert and, while they are the same deep, glossy black of Fiona's, the irises glow as though they're ringed in fire.

Her voice, when she finally speaks, is also similar to Fiona's, but where Fiona's voice had the threatening buzz of a hive of bees, the Queen's voice is purely feral, wild and almost unintelligible.

The world around us throbs—once, twice—then the steady, heartbeat of the island begins again.

I thought Neverland had been teeming with life before, but I'd been wrong. Now even the air seems alive, brushing against my cold skin like an electric current. Like the world itself is welcoming the Queen back.

Unbidden, a pulse of excitement and anticipation races through me.

The Queen tips her head back and inhales deeply, rolling her neck on her narrow shoulders, stretching and reveling in her new freedom. Behind her a flash appears, like a flame leaping from the ground, and when the light eases, Fiona stands there. Then another flaming column of light, and another of Fiona's brethren appears as well.

Rowan steps forward to protect me, and the movement catches the Queen's attention. She turns her terrible, beautiful face to him, her glossy black eyes narrowed in hate. Her lips pull back, exposing her wickedly sharp teeth, and she lets out a chilling hiss of warning. But before she can strike, she notices me.

Every muscle in the Queen's body goes completely, unnaturally still. For a moment, it looks as though she is a statue carved from alabaster, but then the moment passes, and her expression flashes with such hate, I take an instinctive step back.

"Abomination," the Queen snarls at me. Then she whips her head around as fast as a snake striking, and steps toward Fiona. "How did *this* come to be in my presence?" she hisses.

Abomination? I think, my chest tight. I don't know what I expected when we unearthed the Queen, but this is not it.

Fiona bows low. "She was necessary, my Queen," Fiona

explains, more humble than I have ever seen her. If I'm not mistaken, she might even be shaking.

The power in the cavern swells, pulses, until it feels as though a thousand needles are stabbing at me. "And is she still necessary?" the Queen hisses, her voice a dangerously unleashed buzz I feel as much as hear.

Fiona looks up then, a satisfied smile curving at her mouth. "No, my Queen. She is not."

Rowan takes my hand and begins backing away from the two of them as the Queen turns to me.

This is not how I'd expected her to react. After all, if Fiona is right, I'm her son's daughter—her own blood. "I don't understand. . . ." I whisper. "We freed you."

The Queen turns back to me in a single fluid movement that exposes her as the predator that she is. "Did you?" she asks, cocking her head at an unnatural angle as her glossy eyes burn into me.

"Aye, she did. In fact, she's risked everything to save you," Rowan adds, moving closer to me, as though intending to protect me if the Queen decides to strike.

The Queen's eyes flicker to him before coming back to stare at me with unconcealed distaste. "Has she?" the Queen asks, and then her eyes narrow. "Or has she something else in mind. Has she come to do her sire's bidding?"

"I don't even know my father," I tell her truthfully. "And besides, if Fiona's right, he's your son. Your blood." Which makes me her blood too.

The Queen's lips pull back into a snarl. "But he was not only of our blood," she snaps viciously. "Why do you think we cast him out of this world? Why do you think we abandoned him to his fate? The Dark King was his sire."

I blink, confused. "But you killed the Dark King," I say, remembering the story that Pan had told me.

"Yes," the Queen hisses, looking far too pleased with herself. "We did. Because his devotion to us was naught but an act. He promised we would rule this world as one, but we soon enough learned that the Dark King never intended to rule by our side. Once he knew he had a son, he betrayed us. And so, we brought down his reign and made his court our slaves," the Queen says, smiling that awful smile.

"Why not just kill the child as well?" Rowan asks, pushing me back. He's trying to distract her, to divert the Queen's attention from me.

But the Queen doesn't fall for it. Her cold dark eyes are still on me. "Because the True Child held our own power as well." The fiery glow in her dark eyes flares as she considers me. "But we could not risk the Dark King's court using our own True Child against us. And so we left him in the world of men, where he was no danger to our rule."

"The Dark Ones did rise against you, though," Rowan charges, more desperate now as he pushes me back, away from the Queen and her wicked smile.

Her face flashes with fury, horrible and beautiful all at once. "They shall pay for that, as shall the one who led them," she growls. "But you shall not be here to witness our final victory."

Then the Queen turns to Fiona. "Go and prepare the others. We shall finish them, as you should have long ago. Then there is much work to do."

Fiona hesitates only for a moment before she and the other Fey disappear in a flash of blinding light. It is only us and the Queen now. Instantly Rowan straightens, his hand already on his blade.

"For ages we have been a prisoner in our own world. For so long we have dreamed of this moment, and now it is here. Once we finish with you, my people shall wipe your kind from our world like the vermin they are. And when we have made our world whole again, we shall turn ourselves on yours."

The prickling sensation sears across my skin in warning as the cavern starts to shake.

"We need to get out of here," I tell Rowan as chunks of the ceiling begin to fall, but Rowan doesn't move. He's still staring at the Queen in fury. "We *really* need to go," I repeat, nodding toward the corner of the cavern.

There, at the edges of the Queen's light, shadows are gathering. We are too deep in the ground, and the darkness beyond her glow is too deep, too absolute here. I don't know what the Queen's revelation about my father means for me, but if the Dark Ones feel anything like she does, if they still want to kill us, it will be too easy here, cornered as we are.

"Go?" the Queen says, cocking her head at an awkward angle. "Oh, we think not, Young One."

Already I can detect the faint sent of mold and rot. Rowan seems to finally have realized what's happening. His hand grabs mine and pulls me back, farther into the cavern, away from the Queen and her threats. Away from the Dark Ones.

Behind the Queen, the shadows have started to climb up

the walls, slinking and creeping until they are as tall and wide as a man. But the Queen doesn't notice until the sound of the rushing wind starts to rustle and echo through the cavern.

When she realizes what is happening, her mouth twists into a snarl. "No!" she roars, and the cavern trembles and vibrates with the volume and tenor of her voice.

Behind her, though, the Dark One is fully formed. Its inky black wings unfurl and beat in a steady rhythm that causes a gust of wind to course through the cavern, whipping my hair and clothes.

It isn't alone. All along the cavern walls, more shadows creep and bleed into one another, gathering and swelling. The whole cave is saturated with the smell of them—the dampness of rot, the swirling shuffle of wind rustling. Soon the darkness is rising, climbing up to our knees, up farther then, our waists.

The Queen's eyes meet mine, and there is a look of such pure hate and rage in them that I gasp. *"You,"* she snarls, pointing at me. "You have done this." Her eyes are wild. "You dare try to rise against us?" She lets out a long, threatening hiss. Suddenly Rowan's arms fall away from me.

Startled, I turn and see that the steel hand Fiona had gifted Rowan with so long ago is at his throat—it looks like he's trying to choke himself. The steel fingers grip, squeezing until the skin under them is red and his face had gone ashen. His other hand is tight on the steel wrist, trying to pull away, but the hand won't release its grip.

The vicious glee that has curved the Queen's terrible mouth tells me she is the one doing this. She has taken the steel fist that is now so much a part of him, and she has turned it against him. I try to help him pull the hand away, but even I can feel how impossible a task it is. The metal fist is too strong, and the hand is too tight around his throat.

He shakes his head, grimacing against the strain of trying to save himself, but his face has gone deathly pale, and the edges of his lips are beginning to turn an unhealthy shade of blue. His eyes are starting to get an unfocused look about them that has me moving before I've realized what I've decided to do.

I press my hands into the wall of the cavern so firmly, I swear my nails are carving out pieces of Neverland's heart. I feel for the pulse of the world beneath my fingers. It's erratic now, a jangling rhythm that feels as unsteady and unmoored as I do. I close my eyes and I *demand*.

When the walls of the cavern begin to vibrate beneath my palms, the Queen's eyes go wide in surprise. I can't stop my own vicious smile as she stares at me. As the caverns start to shake and stones fall from the ceiling. The world quakes at *my* demand, and I feel its pulse singing beneath my hands. Its pulse matches my own—wild and erratic. Answering to *me*. I focus all my pain, all my rage into the rock under my fingertips, and I demand Neverland heed my call.

It happens quickly. The ceiling of the cavern cracks with a deafening sound, and rock pours down over our heads. Rowan is there in an instant, sheltering me with his own body, and I can't be sure if I see a flash of light or if I only imagine it before the cavern collapses around us.

• • •

In the silence after the dust settles, I can feel Rowan's weight heavy on top of me, his chest rising and falling with unsteady breaths. "Are you alive?" I whisper, knowing the answer but needing to hear it from his lips.

"Aye, lass," he says with a groan. "But I'm not sure for how long." Then I hear his dark, wheezing chuckle tickling at my ear. "You brought the whole bleedin' place down about our ears."

I shift a bit so his weight isn't crushing me quite so much. "She was killing you," I whisper into the darkness, stating the obvious. It's the only explanation I can manage. "We have to get out of here," I say.

He's silent for a long, tense moment, as though he's still waiting for some other explanation. But I don't offer anything more.

It takes us a while to free ourselves from the heaviest of the rubble. The cavern is barely the size of a small room now, but there's still some air moving through it, so even though we can't see past our own noses, we know there must be a way out—if we can just find it.

Rowan makes another torch, and we find the source of the air not much longer after that. With a little effort, we move enough of the boulders away to work free and crawl through the small opening to find ourselves in another cavern.

It's dark here as well, but though we listen and wait, there is no rustling. No smell of old leaves. "Do you think she made it out of there?"

The torchlight flickers over the sharp lines of his face. He looks even more drawn, even more worn-down than before.

"Aye. The Fey have a way of getting out of tight spots when they need to." Frustration flattens his mouth.

"Then we have to go back to the fortress," I say, the dreadful certainty of it like a stone in my stomach. "We have to warn the others."

His eyes are pools of fury and pain when they meet mine. "If it's not already too late."

In that new world, the boy was always happiest right before. When his blood ran cold, when his senses went dull to anything but the moment in front of him. The moment when chance would, by some horrible arithmetic, select the one who could not outrun death. Only then did he feel himself something more than a sack of skin and bone and endless breath. . . .

CHAPTER 37

THE TUNNEL EVENTUALLY ENDS AT A PLACE where a small river rushes along underground. A narrow ledge clings to the side of the cavern wall.

"I know this place," Rowan says, his otherwise exhausted face brightening in relief.

"You do?"

"We're just below the fortress." He searches the roof of the tunnel. "If we follow this, it will take us to one of the older parts of Pan's fortress."

Hope sparks in my chest. "Can you get us back there?"

"Aye." He scrubs a hand through his rumpled hair. "Though I'm not sure what good it will do."

"If we can get them out before . . ." But I can't finish. Before what? Before the Queen takes back her land? Before she kills us all?

"We can try," he says, taking me by the hand and twining

his fingers with mine to stop the futility of my thoughts.

We inch along the narrow ledge with the river rushing beneath us, until we reach a point where another tunnel breaks off and leads back and away from the water. We move faster then, and soon we make it to the place in the fortress where the different tunnels come together. From the sound of the noises echoing in the distance, we're too late. The attack has already begun.

By the time we make it to the Great Hall, the entire space is bathed in an eerie silence. The floor is littered with fallen boys. I don't know if they are Pan's or Rowan's, but it doesn't matter anymore. None of them move. Each of their small bodies is mottled with dark lines, like cracked porcelain, and wherever they've landed, parts of them have broken away, shattered.

I take a shuddering breath as I comprehend the destruction and the loss. Above, the door near the ceiling stands open, but no light shines from within it. I don't think Olivia would be up there, alone in the dark, anyway. She'd be with Pan. I can only hope Fiona and the Queen haven't already found them.

"We should split up. I need to find Olivia, and you need find any of your crew who might be left." He starts to interrupt, but I keep going. "We can't do all of that together, not if we have any hope of getting out of here. After that . . ." Well, I can't think that far ahead.

Rowan frowns. "I don't think that's such a good idea, lass."

I pull my hand out of his. "I'm not helpless, Rowan. I can bring the whole damn place down if I have to. I'm going to check the gardens," I tell him before he can argue. It's where I found Olivia last time, and it's the only other place I know she might be.

"And then what?" he asks, his jaw clenching in frustration.

"I don't know." His expression is tight, and I know he feels the same fear, the same pull toward hopelessness that I do. "But I'm not just going to stand here and wait for the Queen to find us. Are you?"

He runs his metal hand through his hair in clear frustration, but then his shoulders slump in surrender. "No." To my relief, amusement tugs at the corners of his mouth. "Do what you must, but don't be long. I'll meet you back at where the tunnels split off." His fingers brush against my cheek. "If I don't arrive, don't be waiting for me. Follow the second from the right, until it reaches the river. From there you should be able to find your way well enough out of this place."

I give him a sure nod and turn to go, but he snags my hand and pulls me back.

"Try not to die, aye?" And then his mouth is on mine, fierce and demanding and so full of wanting that my knees go weak.

He pulls away before I've had nearly enough, and with a roguish grin, he's off.

I hesitate only a second to gather my wits before I run as well, taking off through the passage to the far right—the one that leads to the gardens and, I hope, to Olivia. I make my way quickly, my breath coming hard as I run for the enormous cavern where I last left her, hoping with each step that she will be there. Hoping that I find her before Fiona or the Queen does.

When the tunnel opens itself into the gardens, I stop short. All around me, the once-blooming maze of flowers and trees are unbearably alive. If I thought they were beautiful before, it was nothing compared to what I'm seeing now. Their leaves are more lush, their colors more riotous. And they seem so much more menacing than they did before.

But I hear singing. The soft notes of a familiar voice carry to me over the silence of the space, and I won't be stopped.

"Olivia," I whisper, relief flooding through me.

I pick my way slowly through the overgrown brambles. The vines make way when they can, lumbering aside with unsteady progress, but mostly I have to climb over or through them. When I finally reach the center of the gardens, I'm scratched and bleeding in more than one place.

Olivia is sitting on a pile of fur near a small stream of water, alone in the center of a small clearing. She's seemingly unaware of the danger she's in. Her fingertips are stained dark from the blood drawn by the thorns of the dangerous-looking blooms she's still weaving into garlands.

"Olivia?"

She looks up at the sound of my voice, but when she finds me standing at the edge of the clearing, her expression doesn't change.

"Come on, Olivia. We have to go." I approach her slowly, because I don't want to startle her, my hand out, beckoning.

Her brows draw together, but she doesn't move.

At least she doesn't run.

"Olivia? It's me, remember?" I coax softly. "Gwen. Your friend?" I take another step into the clearing and then another.

She looks so different. Her once soft green eyes look hard and uncertain. They almost seem to glow from within, and her hair hangs in ragged disarray, an unruly halo. She looks as wild and untamed as the island itself, and if I didn't know she *was* human, I would never have believed *I'm* the one with the Fey blood.

I take a couple more steps into the clearing. "You need to come with me now. We need to get away from here." I hold out my hand like I would to a skittish animal.

But she doesn't show any sign of moving. She just tugs at one of her long ragged locks as she studies me with wary eyes—and even with the wildness, I know my Olivia—the *real* Olivia—is still in there, somewhere beneath the surface.

"Gwen," she says slowly, cautiously.

"That's right." I take another slow, cautious step. "I'm Gwen. And you're Olivia, and we need to get out of here."

But her eyes are narrowed. "No." She stands, circling away from me, and there's a wariness to the way she moves.

"It's not safe, Liv," I say, trying another appeal. "You don't understand how dangerous it is here."

"Pan will protect me." Her voice is steady, entreating, like she wants or needs me to believe.

I follow her progress, circling closer so I keep the water to her back, to block her escape. "If we don't get out of here, we are both going to die."

She shakes her head. "I'm not leaving."

But she isn't the only one who can be stubborn. I step closer, determined to reach her. I hope that maybe my touch might bring her back to herself, but a rustling from the brush to my left has me pulling up short.

"You heard her, Gwendolyn. Olivia doesn't want to leave." Pan's voice is a low, dangerous song, every bit as tempting as it always was. Every bit as deadly. As he steps into the clearing, those crystalline eyes of his are as turbulent as the sea. "Olivia wishes to stay here with me." A deadly smile curves his lips.

"You can't have her." I try to put myself between Pan and Olivia, but Olivia is faster. She easily sidesteps around me and runs to Pan's side.

"I'm staying with *him*. You have no idea what danger we're in—the danger you put us in—Pan is the only one who can stop it."

I stop short at her words. "The danger *I* put you in?"

"Yes, Gwendolyn," Pan says darkly. "You released the Queen, did you not?"

My stomach sinks. He knows what I've done, and he understands just how dangerous things have become for all of us. "I wanted to get us home," I say. "You weren't going to take me."

"Yet here you remain," he says darkly. "Did you truly believe the Queen would take you back? Fiona used you, and you were too stupid to see it, " he practically spits.

For a heartbeat, I feel the truth in his words. He's right. I freed the Queen and put us all in terrible danger. . . . But then the absurdity of that thought startles me, and I shake away my own cloying sense of guilt and focus.

I look at Olivia, who is clinging to Pan. "You can't listen to him, Liv. He's the reason we were brought here. You think he wants you?" I ask when her mouth turns down defiantly. "You're nothing to him. He wanted me all along. You were just an innocent bystander."

"You're wrong." Her voice is as stubborn and unyielding as it has ever been. It is the voice that convinced my mom to let her come to London, the voice that convinced me we really were friends. Even though the words are all wrong, that stubbornness gives me hope—Olivia is still there somewhere, below the madness of Neverland.

"I'm afraid she's not, pet." With a quick motion, Pan locks an arm around Olivia and holds his dagger to her throat. "You see, Olivia, I've been searching for one like Gwendolyn for some time now. I'm sorry, my dear, but lovely as you might be, you're nothing compared to what she can offer me."

Confusion and hurt rocket through Olivia's expression. "Let her go," I growl through clenched teeth.

His blue eyes appraise me with a nauseating combination of excitement and anticipation. "No, I don't think I will. Your dear friend provided the incentive for you to leave Rowan's ship, and I think she'll provide just the incentive I require for you to see things my way." He smiles then, a carefree boyish grin that makes my blood run cold. "I won't allow the Queen to win, Gwendolyn. Not after all I've done to make this world my own.

"Have you any idea what it is to discover the only mother you've ever known hates you for what you are?" He smiles then. "The Queen thought I was weak and insignificant. She believed man to be less than Fey, but it was *I* who defeated her. I, a mere human, who remade this world for my own plea-sure. . . . Do you truly believe I've come so close to finally being able to destroy her only to let *you* stand in my way?

"I will not allow all I've done to be undone, and I won't

312

allow you to get away from me again, Gwendolyn." He presses the knife until it dents the tender skin at the base of Olivia's throat. "It would be such a waste if I had to kill this girl just to make you understand reason."

"Please." I close my eyes, trying to think. Trying to find a way out of this. "Please, just let her go."

"Not until you surrender to me completely," he taunts. "Not until you vow to sacrifice your power and your life to me. Once you do, I will finally be able to finish what I started ages ago. Once the Queen has fallen, I will control the boundaries between our worlds, and only then will your dear Olivia have any chance of returning."

I consider it—*really* consider it. I know what's at stake, just as I know that even as we speak, the Fey are already taking back their world. When that happens, every human in Neverland is doomed. "What about the rest? Your boys and Rowan's crew?"

Pan chuckles, a dark dangerous sound that is more derision than mirth. "What few who remain may have their choice."

I take a step back, away from him, my mind racing with possibilities—none of them good.

But as I'm still struggling with my decision, a rustling comes from the deadened brush, and two ragged-looking boys emerge. They're dragging Rowan between them—his face is bruised and bleeding, and a dark stain is spreading across the front of his drab-colored coat.

"No—" I step toward him, but Pan steps between us, Olivia still in his grasp.

"Ah, Rowan. How delightful of you to join us," Pan drawls.

"Gwendolyn was just deciding how much she values the life of her friend."

Rowan coughs, blood dripping from his mouth. "Too late, Pan," he says in slow, halting words. "You've lost."

Pan smiles. "No, my dear boy, I don't think I have."

"Any minute now the Queen will be coming for you." Rowan tries to struggle, but the boys hold him tight.

"True enough," Pan says, "but by then Gwendolyn will have made her choice. Because she knows I am her only hope of stopping the Queen. Of saving her *dear friend.*"

Rowan practically growls, his breaths coming in difficult bursts. "Villain," he rasps.

"No, boy. You're quite mistaken. Have you not heard the story? I'm the hero of this piece—the victor," Pan says. "It was I who conquered the Queen of this world. I who ruled over the Fey, Light and Dark alike."

"You who murdered the helpless," Rowan chokes out, his face contorted with hate.

"Well, yes, that was unavoidable," Pan tells him pleasantly. "Though that ridiculous story did help." Pan looks at me, his eyes alight with amusement. "Imagine my surprise when that first boy gave himself willingly to me, all because he mistook this world for something out of a storybook. As entertaining as it always had been to listen to their screams, it was so much *easier* to just play along."

At first I don' t understand the meaning of his words. And then all of the things Rowan told me about him, about this world, come back to me. "You're not really Peter Pan?" I say, finally comprehending.

"Of course I am," he says pleasantly, his eyes flickering with amusement. "Ask any of my boys."

"Nothing but lies," Rowan says, barely able to get the words out between his painfully gasping breaths. "The boys never see through them."

"But *you* saw through them, didn't you?" Pan asks, his voice sharp. "When you first arrived, you were like all the others—broken, lost, wanting to believe in a place where you could forget every miserable part of yourself. Like the rest, you *wanted* to believe I was who I said. You were much too old for fairy tales, Rowan. You should have known better." His expression goes murderous. "And I should have killed you when I had the chance. Luckily, fate has given me an opportunity to right that particular mistake."

The walls of the fortress tremble, sending bits of debris and chunks of the crystal ceiling careening to the floor. Pan turns to me. "I'm afraid our time runs short, my dear." He presses the knife against Olivia's throat, and she closes her eyes, her face contorted in fear, in pain. "*Do* you care for your friend enough to save her?"

Olivia whimpers, her eyes flying open. For a moment I think it's *my* Olivia peering through those green depths.

"Do you care enough to save them all?" Pan tempts. "Give yourself over to me, and I will defeat the monster you have unleashed."

"I . . ." I can't say the words. Even though I know it is the only choice, the only way to get Olivia home, to save Rowan and the others from the danger we've unleashed—I've unleashed.

"Or perhaps you need more of an incentive?" Pan's beautiful features brighten in anticipation as he gives a tight nod to the boys holding Rowan. At his signal, one of them pulls Rowan's head back at a painful-looking angle and the other raises a knife to his throat.

"No!" I shout loudly enough that the boys look to Pan.

"It's your choice, Gwendolyn. You will die in this world one way or another, but you can decide who must die with you. Give yourself to me, and perhaps the ones you profess to love will have a chance. Perhaps I will be merciful."

"Don't," Rowan says, panting, his voice weak. His eyes blaze with fear, with fury. With pain.

Olivia still struggles in Pan's arms, and she, too, pleads with me.

"You know what I want from you." Pan's voice is low, a seductive purr. "You've seen with your own eyes how gentle I can be, how good I can make the taking for you. You could save them, Gwendolyn. You have only to give me what I want."

He's right. With Fiona and the Queen coming for us, no one will survive. Still . . . "You have to swear they'll be safe. You have to promise to take them back to our world."

"Do I, now?" Pan laughs, his eyes shining with amusement. "I don't think you are in any position to negotiate, my dear."

From my waistband, I draw the dagger Rowan gave me. Before Pan understands what I'm doing, I have it at my own throat. "I think I am," I say, pressing the tip of the blade against my skin. A sharp jerk upward, and it will be over. "Promise me their safety—swear it—or I'll spill my own blood here and now, and you will *never* have my power. Without me, you will be left to the mercy of the Queen—whatever mercy she has in her."

The corner of Pan's mouth curves up in amusement. "She *is* remarkable, Captain," Pan murmurs. "Fey or not, she would have been a treat, but with her fire, her own spark—what power her spirit will give me."

"Don't, Gwendolyn." Rowan's voice comes to me, the pain in it cutting through my fear. "You can't just give him your power. Not without giving him your life as well."

The look of anticipation on Pan's face tells me Rowan isn't lying. But I can't listen to Rowan's pleas. I saw the bodies in the Great Hall, and I know what the Fey are capable of—what Fiona and her Queen will do to all of them. What she may still do to the world I was taken from if she succeeds. I'm not strong enough on my own to defeat her, but my power combined with Pan's . . . It might be enough.

"Promise you will see them safe," I say, knowing even as I demand it, it is a fool's bargain. It doesn't matter what Pan promises. He is the prince of lies, the king of a thousand deceptions. And he is the only chance my friends have. "Let them go—a show of good faith—and I'll come to you willingly."

"Will you, then?" He laughs as he releases Olivia, and I nearly collapse from the relief of seeing her safe from his knife.

"Olivia?" She's not running from Pan as I expected. She stays by him, her hand on his arm.

Pan laughs at my confusion, an amused chuckle that runs along my skin as it echoes through the cavern. "Brilliant little actress, isn't she?" He pulls her into his arms and gives her an uncomfortably intense kiss.

317

"Olivia?" I don't understand at first, but then a terrible truth settles upon me. She was never in any danger from Pan.

"I told you I wouldn't leave him." She pins me with an empty, emotionless look, her eyes glassy and faraway.

Pan's beautiful, cold eyes are laughing at me. This whole scene has been nothing but a game for him, and he's enjoyed every moment of toying with me. In a blink, he's bounded across the space that separates us and has me restrained in his arms.

I fight to keep from struggling against his hold, to keep my voice level. "We had a deal, Pan. Let him go too."

"So we did," he whispers into my ear. His breath is warm on my neck as he buries his nose in my hair. "Run, Rowan," he says, his face still close to my neck. At the snap of his fingers, the boys release Rowan, who falls to the ground with a ragged groan. "Leave while you can, boy. You haven't much time before I'm done here."

But Rowan can barely move. He's lost so much blood and is too weak. "I'm not leaving without her," he pants as he struggles to his knees.

I want to scream for him to run, but the strangest feeling has come over me. I can't move. I can barely think.

Pan's shadow peels itself up from the floor and stands before me, its dark hand extending toward me. When it brushes my face with the tip of its finger, every molecule of my body wants to rush toward it.

"It's too late, Rowan," I hear Pan say, but even though he's still close to my ear, his voice sounds very faraway. I feel everything that was once Gwendolyn Allister pulling away from my body, flooding toward the call of the dark shadow, rushing toward Pan's outstretched hands.

No! I scream inwardly. It is too fast, too soon. Without a good-bye, without any sort of warning. I can't fight it, though. I can't struggle against the pull. *Let it be enough,* I think as the darkness begins to cloud my vision.

After, the boy never thought of those he killed. He did not recall their nameless faces and never dwelled on the capriciousness of chance. For when he fell—and fall, one day he would—he did not expect that world to remember him. Until one day he stood over a small body that dripped death from its head like a cracked egg and saw another face instead. One he should have never forgotten. . . .

CHAPTER 38

AS PAN DRINKS IN MY LIFE, I CAN STILL FEEL the pull of my flesh. But I'm not completely in my body, not really. I don't think I'm dead, but I don't feel quite alive, either. I simply feel apart, like I'm still floating just above my flesh. Above everything, watching it all with a strange detachment through blurred vision.

Across the clearing, I can just make out Rowan. His body is broken and battered, but he's still struggling to get to me.

Above Pan and me, a shadow suddenly appears. Already, my vision is beginning to cloud and go dark, which is why I think at first I'm seeing things. Because it can't be Fiona who is standing there. It can't be that treacherous Fey who is taking Pan by the scruff of his neck.

Pan jerks at Fiona's touch and releases me from his hold. I hit the ground hard, but I don't shatter. I don't come completely back to myself either, though.

"Rowan?" Fiona's voice buzzes, dangerously close. She doesn't release Pan from her grasp.

Rowan can't answer. A cough shudders through him, and his body slumps again to the ground, too weak to go on.

"Was this your work?" Fiona growls at Pan. Before he can answer, Fiona shakes him.

But Pan's eyes are unfocused, almost drunk on whatever power he'd taken from me. Fiona shakes him again before placing her hand against Pan's chest. Her face remains calm as she hisses for him to answer her, and when he does not respond, her fingers pierce his skin and he screams with pain.

Disgusted, she tosses Pan's limp body aside.

My vision is still dark around the edges when Fiona scoops Rowan up and brings him to where I lie.

"It is time," she whispers in that strange humming voice. "You have hesitated long enough." She helps him up to his knees, supporting him as they loom over me. And I see why I don't feel whole—Fiona has the thread of my life wrapped around her fist. When Fiona tugs on the trailing stream of light, I want to move toward her—and when she offers it to him, toward Rowan.

"Now, Rowan. It must be *now*," Fiona buzzes from somewhere very close. But I can't see her. My vision is darker now, closer to the end.

All I can see is Rowan above me, his dark eyes flat with pain, looking more lost than I've ever seen him.

Do it, I think. Because it doesn't even feel like a betrayal. *Do it.*

He leans his forehead against mine. It's cool, clammy. *Do*

it. Hurry. He needs to take whatever it is I can give him. He needs to go on.

"Hurry, Rowan," the Fey buzzes. "My Queen is free. Pan has been defeated. You need not die as well. If only you will take her."

"I can't—" I feel his breath on my skin, hear the weakness in his voice. "Won't—"

Fiona hisses, her voice dangerously low. "Do you think I gave you your place in my world to have you waste it on this pathetic excuse for a halfling? Take her Rowan, or I will kill her just the same."

"Kill us . . . both. . . ." I hear him say from far off. Vaguely, I feel the weight of his body slump on top of me.

I'm slipping, though. If a soul had fingers, mine are trying to grab at my frail body, reaching clumsily to stay with myself, but it isn't working. I don't have enough spirit in my hollowed-out body to keep my eyes open any longer, and I know, after everything I've been through, I've finally reached the end.

There are words. So many words I've never said. Words I thought I would have time for. But it's too late. My soul slides away from my body, the last fragile wisps of it leaving behind the pain and despair until I'm almost nothing more than light.

And then I no longer feel Rowan's weight holding me to this world.

Fiona has my life wrapped around her fist, and every bit of who I once was wants to flee from my body, toward that light.

But before I can, before my soul slides away completely, a shadow appears over Fiona's shoulder. A dark form whose eyes burn with hatred.

And Fiona screams.

That night the boy dreamed of hell—of fire and brimstone and a face he should never have forgotten. And in the morning it was as though he were waking from an endless dream. . . .

CHAPTER 39

JUST AS THE WORLD BEGINS TO SLIDE AWAY into a field of stars, a great roaring brings me back, slamming me into my aching body with a violence that leaves me shaken and rattled from the pain. Next to me, Fiona lies headless, her blood staining the ground. Near her, Rowan lies unconscious, his hand still holding a blade coated with the Fey's strange dark blood.

"No," I croak, my voice barely working. It takes an incredible effort to hoist myself up enough to move toward Rowan's still form. He could've taken everything from me. He could have saved himself, but he didn't. He used the last of his strength to save me.

"Don't leave me," I whisper, brushing back his hair. His face is so pale. His lips tinged with blue. My hand cups his face, and I press a kiss to his lips. "No," I whisper again, my throat tight and aching.

His eyes blink, but he's very, very far away. His face is almost colorless and his skin is growing ever cooler to the touch.

Little by little my strength is beginning to return, though. Little by little I become more conscious of everything around me. Pan's still body is slumped to the ground nearby, his skin covered in a maze of dark lines, like a shattered plate.

Olivia stumbles to Pan, a sleepwalker just beginning to surface from a dream, but when she takes his hand, his body is so fragile, so brittle, it shatters, crumbling beneath her touch. A strangled scream escapes her lips as she draws back in horror.

I should feel the same horror, the same revulsion, but I'm still too much in shock to feel anything at all at the sight of the headless Fey on the ground nearby. For a moment, I can almost begin to feel relief, but the moment doesn't last long.

All around me, the world turns a brilliant white, and I recognize the power strumming through the air that signals the presence of the Queen.

She comes and floats over us, her face strangely beautiful in its fury. "He has killed one of our own," she rages, her voice a terrible screech of fury. "He shall pay with his life." She raises her hands as though to strike him down.

"No," I say, covering him with my own body, as he once protected me. I steel myself for what is coming. For the terrible shattering pain that is sure to be my end.

But a screeching wail echoes in the air, and that blow never comes.

I look up, squinting against the brightness of the Queen's

glow, and I see what has caused that terrible noise—Olivia is behind the Queen. Her hair is a tangled mass around the blank fury in her face.

"Olivia?" I whisper.

She turns to me, but she doesn't see me. Her gaze is glassy and unknowing. With an almost hysterical laugh, she pulls the dagger from the Queen—Pan's dagger. It gleams dark silver in the Queen's light, tipped with the Queen's own blackish blood.

The Queen stumbles, her light wavering, her skin crawling with the dark lines of her unmaking. "No," she screeches, clutching at herself. Pain contorts her beautiful face as she turns on Olivia. A dangerous current crackles through the air in the wake of her fury and pain.

With a motion as quick and deadly as a striking snake, the Queen takes Olivia by the throat, lifting her until her feet dangle in the air. Black lines creep across Olivia's skin from beneath the Queen's hand as Olivia writhes and struggles, her eyes wide with fear. The black lines continue to craw across her skin—up over her face, down her chest, creeping across the soft skin of her arms, until Olivia stops struggling and goes still.

"No!" I scream, torn between protecting Rowan and helping my friend. Olivia looks up at me, her eyes clear again, and they are filled with pain and confusion.

Before I can choose, I hear the rustling call of the Dark Ones. They begin to creep out from beneath the dead and brittle plants and begin to gather, swirling, marching themselves around us until they surround the Queen. Again they pull at her, but this time, she stumbles beneath their fingertips, releasing Olivia, who crumples to the floor.

The Queen falls to her knees, the dark blood still spreading from the wound Pan's dagger made in her back—the wound Olivia gave her. The Dark Ones continue to swirl, pulling at the Queen, until they cover her completely. And as she disappears beneath them, she shrieks again, an ear-splitting wail that causes the caverns around us to shake and tremble.

Huge chunks of the crystalline ceiling tumble down, crashing with violent explosions to the ground below. The world is quaking, rumbling, and alive by the time the dark wisps form themselves into the shapes of monsters and an army of living shadow stands before me.

The scuttling wind spins faster now, whirling violently in that familiar rustling, but in that rustling, I hear someone speaking to me.

"Please!" I scream, trying to block the sound. I'm not sure what I'm even asking for, but I sob out the word again and again as the Dark Ones swirl. Telling me their secrets, whispering my own truths back to me.

"Please," I continue to repeat. But my voice is now a feeble whisper, begging for things I don't understand, and then the darkness overwhelms me and I am tossed back— and the voice whispers to me again.

But it's not a single voice. No, this time the voice is a thousand dark voices, singing to me and urging me. And all at once, I'm back in those dark woods of my childhood, the coolness of the night calling to me. The voices calling to me. The trees stretching their fingers wide toward the sky, caging the stars in their hands. Creaking and moaning in the rushing air, like the trees are translating the wind.

I am immersed in too-familiar images. And I remember *everything* then—the strange pull I felt as the voice called to me. The oddest feeling that I needed to go to them, to be with them. *Again.* For it felt so familiar, that wanting, that calling. So I followed the voice, away from the lights of our house. Away from the safety of my mother. Into the darkness, where the forest smelled of damp leaves, and the night spoke in a language I could almost understand.

It wanted me, I realize, but not to kill me. There was nothing frightening or unsettling about the voices I heard in the forest of my childhood. Nothing terrible about the thick and living darkness that brushed against me. It wanted me because I was *part* of it. It wasn't the darkness that hurt me that night. It was everything that came after.

Everything I forgot.

The Dark Ones might have been hunting me then. They were definitely hunting me in my own world and here in Neverland, but now I understand they didn't want to harm me. They wanted to show me what I was—the heir of my father. The heir of both Dark and Light, perfectly balanced. Just like this world should be.

All at once, the swirling darkness spins around me, excited that I've understood them. Joyful their message is clear. Welcoming. Like every soft summer night I've spent sleeping under stars without my mom knowing.

When I went running into the woods that night, it was because this world called to me, pulled me. That was why my mom embedded the rune into my arm. To keep me hidden and also to stop me from realizing what I was. This is the truth the Dark Ones give me.

You belong to us, they croon. *You can save us and reclaim the world for our King. For our kind.*

Neverland is quiet beneath us. It no longer breathes. Its heart no longer beats. The largest of the Dark Ones moves toward me, and even though I no longer sense it as a threat, I throw myself over Rowan more securely. Its faceless head turns and, with a wave of its arm, it shows me what is happening to the world. The fortress all around us is crumbling. Pan was right: without the Queen to hold it together, Neverland is breaking apart.

Then it speaks in that unfamiliar tongue, rough and grating syllables that once sounded like nothing but the wind. But I can't forget what they've shown me, what they've whispered to me about who I am. About the choice I have before me. This time I understand what they say.

Pan hadn't lied. Neverland could truly be my home if I choose it. I could embrace all the Dark Ones have shown me, I could claim what they believe is rightfully mine. For I am both Light and Dark, heir of the Queen and the Dark King. I could balance the power here, reclaim the world and live within it.

But when I close my eyes, trying to think, all I see is the blue-gray gaze of my mother. When I open my eyes, I see Rowan's unsteady breath, and I know what my choice is. What it will always be. "I need to get them back," I plead.

I can feel the disappointment rolling from the dark creature, but its faceless head gives a jerk, a nod of assent. Two others come forward, and this time I have no fear of them. I back away as one lifts Rowan effortlessly in its arms. He's pale and unconscious now, and far too close to death.

"Take care of him," I plead.

I go to Olivia, kneeling beside her as another Dark One approaches. She looks up at me with a lazy half-lidded gaze, surprisingly calm and unaware of what has just happened or of the state she's currently in. Her face is covered in a maze of dark lines. Her arms look like cracked porcelain.

"I'm going to get you home, Liv," I tell her, brushing her hair back from her face.

Weakly, she opens her eyes and looks at me, and I see them go from the soft glassy forgetting of Neverland to the sharp awareness of my friend.

"Liv?" I say, taking her hand gently. Her skin feels fragile as spun glass, but her eyes are still Olivia's.

"Gwen?" she says, her voice thick with pain and confusion. "What happened?" Her eyes dart wildly around, from me to the monstrous dark Fey lurking above her and back again. Panicked. Frightened. Like she is just waking up, just beginning to remember.

She tries to pull her hand away from me, and I feel pieces of it flake away. So I let her go, and the moment I release her hand, I see her eyes start to go glassy again. All at once I understand. *It's me.* When I hugged her that first day, when I touched her out at the End . . . *I'm* what was causing those moments of clarity in her expression. Because of what I am.

"Liv," I say, grasping her hand again, refusing to let her go.

Her skin crumbles under my grasp, and she moans in agony. But her eyes are so clear, and I can see the memories flooding back as her expression darkens with horror. "What did she do to me?" she asks, her face contorting in agony.

"It doesn't matter," I tell her, my throat tight. "We're going back now. We'll fix it. You'll be fine."

Panicked, I look to the Dark One, who is waiting for my signal. It comes forward, but when the Fey tries to lift her, Olivia screams as part of her forearm shatters and crumbles away. The Dark One hesitates, and Olivia's eyes meet mine and there is a look of such horror, such complete fear, that my vision goes blurry with tears.

"Please, Liv. Let him at least try."

"I can't," she rasps.

"I know it might hurt at first, but we can fix this. We're going back and—"

She stops me by laying a hand on my arm. Her fingertips are so fragile, a couple of them crumble beneath the pressure of her grip. But her eyes—those are horribly clear and every bit the Olivia I've always known. "Please," she whispers. "I can't. Just go. Leave me. You have to get out of here."

A sobbing gasp erupts from my chest. "I can't do that, Liv. You saved me. Now stop being so damn stubborn, so I can save you back," I tell her, my voice choked by tears as I cling as gently as I can to her hand.

Her mouth tries to smile, but she's too fragile. Too brittle. When the corners of her lips start to crack, she shakes her head instead, a barely imperceptible motion. Her eyes begin to go dim, and when she speaks, her voice comes out stiff and halting, as though she can barely form the words. "Go," she says, determined. "Someone has to . . . tell my parents. . . .

Make sure they're okay . . ." Her eyes meet mine, filled with pain and so terribly clear. "Go!" she demands in a dry, brittle version of what once was her voice.

I do cry then. In this moment she is completely *my* Olivia—whole and real and just as stubborn as she's ever been.

But I can't accept this. I can't leave her to this world after everything that's happened.

"Let me go, Gwen," she whispers, her voice like a ragged husk. Her color has all but drained away, and when she speaks, bits of the corners of her mouth crumble, leaving only blackness behind.

I shake my head, even though I know she's right. There is no way to get her back. The Queen has done too much damage. But I can't leave her like this. . . .

"Go," she whispers, her eyes closing as she tries to pull her hand away from me, her skin crumbling beneath my touch.

I don't have a choice—if I try to keep ahold of her, I'll hurt her even more—so I let her hand go. "Olivia," I plead.

But a second after I release her hand, her eyes open again, and the sharpness that had once been there disappears. Her eyes take on that glassy, forgetful look, and when they do, her body relaxes—all panic, all fear, gone.

My body shakes with the sobs I cannot hold back. "I love you, Liv," I say through my tears. "Whatever happens, I always will." She blinks up at me, her eyes soft, and I know she doesn't recognize me. My Olivia is gone. But at least the girl who looks back at me isn't afraid.

The Dark Ones stir behind me, their wings rustling. The largest of them holds out its great clawed hand. I look once more at Olivia, searching for some other way, but the world around me is already crumbling to dust. Even now I sense the Dark One's impatience, so without any other choice but to stay and die, I take its hand. And I leave my friend and everything I thought I was behind.

He remembered everything, then. In that frightful moment, his fierce heart broke. . . .

CHAPTER 40

I WAKE TO THE ICY KISS OF SNOW ON MY CHEEK. My hair is damp, and my body aches from its awkward position on the cold ground. In the distance, the sounds of the city wash over me. Above, the stars hold a steady, unflinching vigil. All at once, the memory of what happened and my own bone-deep regret flood through me. And it's only the sound of a weak, rattling moan nearby that urges me to do something other than give in to the icy cold.

Hours later, when the wailing sirens have stopped and the doctors have decided that I will be okay, my mother finds me. She perches carefully on the edge of the narrow hospital bed, her usually wild red hair tied back in a braid and her face as drawn and tired as I've ever seen it. When she sees me stirring, she takes my hand in hers carefully, like I'll shatter if jostled too much.

"I thought I'd lost you." Her hands are cool and welcoming

as they feel my brow and brush the flopping hair back from my face. "I thought they'd finally won."

I want to say a million things. I want to apologize for all the times I thought she'd lost her mind. I want to rail and scream at her for what she did to me. In the end, what I've lost is too great, and all I can do is cry huge body-wracking sobs that shake me to my core and leave me feeling emptied out as she holds me tight. Even after the last of my gasping sobs have eased, it still takes a few minutes before I feel like I can speak without losing it again. "All those years, all those moves. You could have told me. You *should* have told me."

She brushes my hair back. "Your father thought we could protect you. And I thought you deserved a chance at normal—a chance not to let what you were determine everything."

"So my father really did leave to protect us? He really knew about me—what I was?"

"He arranged everything before he left us. He thought he could draw off the danger somehow if he wasn't around, but"—my mom's lips press together—"none of those loyal to him have heard from him in years."

All at once the immensity of my mother's loss—of both our losses—overwhelms me, and I start sobbing all over again.

It's much later when I finally find the words to tell her everything that happened—how we were taken, how I found a way back, what I left behind. And when my story is spun out, when there's nothing else for us to say, I take a deep breath and ask the question I've been wondering—and afraid to ask—since I awoke. "Did Rowan make it?"

Her expression is guarded. "He's had a couple of transfusions already, but they think he'll be okay . . . eventually."

I sit myself up in the narrow hospital bad. "I need to see him."

"You need to rest," my mom says, sounding more like a mother than she ever has before.

"I've got an entire lifetime to rest." Somehow the thought is not comforting. "I need to see him." I need to make sure he is real, whole. That I haven't lost him, too. "Please."

She gives me the look she usually reserves for blank canvases, but in the end she relents and gets the nurse to wheel me down to the ward where Rowan is being monitored.

"Do they know who he is?" I ask once the nurse leaves us alone.

"Papers have been arranged." My mom bites her lip, a sure sign she's uncomfortable. "Not many knew what your father was," she said. "But there were those who wanted to see his world united once again. Those who have helped to protect us over the years."

"The landlord?" I ask.

She gives a small nod. "Not all my commissions knew who we were. But things had gotten more dangerous."

I let out a shaking breath, understanding why. It must have been after Fiona learned how the Queen was being kept. I would have been hunted by Light and Dark alike, then.

Rowan's room is silent except for the rhythmic beep of the monitors and the soft shushing whir of his oxygen. He seems shrunken in the narrow bed. Without his ship around him, he looks incredibly ordinary and incredibly young. "When will he wake up?"

"He's been through a lot," my mom tells me. "You can't expect too much too soon."

For once I'm thankful to have the mother I do. I'm glad I didn't have to worry about thinking up a lie to explain him or what he is to me now. That will come later, with everyone else. "Would you give me a minute with him?"

I can tell she wants to argue, but she doesn't. Instead, she gives me a kiss on the forehead and tells me I have five minutes.

His breathing is shallow but steady, and I notice he looks better than when he was unconscious in the snow. He isn't exactly well, but he no longer has the bluish tinge to his skin that had me pulling myself out of my own despair and screaming for help.

I reach out and take his hand in mine, stroking the back of it as I watch him sleep amid the blinking monitors and maze of tubes. After a few minutes I start to pull away, but his grip tightens and his eyes flutter open.

"Gwendolyn?"

I lean in closer so he can see me. "How are you feeling?"

"Where am I?"

I'm not sure what to say, but a second later, he notices the fluorescent lights and the strange machines, and I don't have to explain. His gaze darts wildly about the room, trying to take everything in as he struggles to sit up.

"*Shhh*, you have to settle down before the nurse comes." I place my hands on his shoulders and try to steady him in the bed.

His eyes are still wild with panic. "Why?" he asks in a shaky voice, and I know he isn't asking about the nurse.

"You were dying, and you were the last person I could save."

He stops struggling then and slumps back against the pillow, looking away from me. "Better to have let me die."

"Don't"—I cup his face with my hands and force him to face me—"don't you *dare* say that. Not after all we've been through."

"I told you, lass—"

"I couldn't leave you," I cut in. "I couldn't leave you to die there. It wouldn't have helped anyone." Then I explain what happened—how the Queen was killed, how Pan died, how Neverland had started to fall apart.

He hesitates. "Olivia?"

"She saved me. Or maybe she just did it to avenge Pan, but we wouldn't be here without her. I couldn't save her, though." I shake my head, unsuccessful in my attempt to will away the image of my friend cracked like porcelain doll, her eyes glassy and far away.

He pulls my hand away from his face and places a kiss on the center of my palm before he intertwines my fingers. "I'm not part of this world anymore, Gwendolyn."

"You are now."

"I don't belong here. . . ." he protests, his eyes still warily taking in the blinking lights and plastic tubes that surround him.

"You survived in Neverland," I say with a teary sniff. "The twenty-first century is going to be easy."

His mouth flattens into an unhappy line, but he doesn't argue. Or agree.

"We'll figure it out. Together," I promise.

His brow creases, but he doesn't argue. "My arm?" he doesn't look at the empty spot under the covers where his arm should have been.

"I don't know."

My mom peeks into the room at that moment. "It's time."

"Do you know what they did with his arm?" I ask her.

He eyes glance between us, appraising our closeness. "I'm not sure."

"We'll find it," I assure him. "And then we'll figure out everything else."

"You need to let him rest," my mom says. I think she can sense how badly I want to kiss him. If she thinks her presence will be a deterrent, she's wrong. After all we've been through and all I lost, I refuse to wait another moment.

I lean forward and press my lips gently to his. It's not more than a peck, and he doesn't return it.

"Sleep well," I tell him, backing away. "I'll see you tomorrow."

I don't need to look at my mom to sense her questions, just like I don't need to look back at Rowan to feel the intensity of his gaze following me out.

It takes a couple of weeks, but we eventually get Rowan out of the hospital. Thanks to the documents our landlord arranged, he becomes a new person—at least on paper. Behind those dark eyes, though, he's the same as ever. Still, there are moments I can't help but worry he's left part of himself behind. That he'll never really forgive me for bringing him back.

For weeks he's mostly silent, watching his new world with

338

wary eyes. I don't blame him one bit. When I finally came to, I'd hoped that I had only lost days, maybe weeks. But I later discovered I'd lost more than a year to Neverland. There were moments in those first days when I was almost as unsettled by the subtle changes to my world as Rowan must have felt. I had a new president, but whole countries had changed and rearranged themselves in the time he was gone, including his own.

As we waited for Rowan to be released from the hospital, I read through the papers my mom and the landlord kept that documented our ordeal. It took less than four days for our kidnapping to go from the front page to the inside of the paper. After a few weeks, we were rarely mentioned at all. To everyone but the few who were close to her, Olivia had already been forgotten.

But I hadn't forgotten, and neither had Olivia's parents.

I once thought the Fey were cruel with their lives built from nothing more than wanting, but after I returned to my own world, I came to understand they're not alone. By our very nature, humans are heartless things. The Fey, at least can be excused—their world, after all, wasn't made from memory. We humans, however, select the memories that suit us to remember and forget the rest—the wars, the tragedies, the lost. Neverland might have helped with the forgetting, but it didn't create it. That we do well enough on our own.

But in the moments that followed, the boy felt himself alive. No longer did he feel as though he were in a waking dream. He began to collect the pieces of his fragile heart, and though some would always be missing, there were enough of who he once was to fight . . . to go on.

EPILOGUE

I T'S A BLUSTERY WINTER DAY WHEN WE BRAVE the drifting snow of a French cemetery. We find Rowan's brother deep within a field of crosses as white as the snow that drifts around them, and at the sight of Michael's name, Rowan crumples to his knees.

I follow him down more slowly, no longer feeling the blistering wind that bites at my cheeks, or the damp cold that creeps up my legs. I'm not sure he even knows I'm here.

He's been practically silent for weeks, and he's silent now as he stares at the barren stone, his face creased with regret and pain, his shoulders rising and falling with the effort not to cry out. His arm—the one that had once been so alive with Fey enchantment in Neverland—hangs stiff and heavy at his side.

We tried to talk him into wearing a different prosthetic, one that's lighter and more useful, but he wouldn't listen.

Once we returned it to him, he refused anything but the heavy piece of dead metal that had been his constant companion for so long. It seems so unfair—with all he'd already lost—for him to lose the magic of that as well. I catch him looking down at the lifeless fist occasionally, but I never know what to do for him. Just as I don't know what to do as we kneel before Michael's grave.

But I want some closure or relief for him—some small thing that will help him knit himself back together and feel whole again. I want it so badly that my chest aches with it.

As we kneel there—he near tears and I wanting so much to help—neither of us notices at first what is happening. It's only when one of his tears finally does break free and he reaches up to wipe it away with what should have been lifeless metal that we know anything has changed.

He looks at me, the wonder in his eyes pushing aside a bit of the grief.

"Did you . . . ?" he asks, his voice barely a whisper.

I lick my chapped lips and watch him open and close the metal fist. "I think I did."

He blinks, raising his arm and testing it, opening and closing the delicately wrought fingers one at a time. "Well, then." He looks over at me, the ghost of a grin twitching at the corners of his mouth, the bleakness in his eyes lifting just a bit.

He laces the fingers of his mechanical hand with mine, and then—his eyes never leaving mine—he raises both to place a gentle kiss on the inside of my wrist. I let him pull me to my feet then, and with the snow swirling around us and

341

our fingers still intertwined, we start back to the warmth of the waiting car.

That's when I think that, someday, it might just be okay. Here on the snow-swept field that holds the bodies of so many forgotten lives—a field that might have held his just as easily—I know he'll heal. I believe I'll find a way to forgive. And together we'll remember the lost.

ACKNOWLEDGMENTS

This story has been through a lot since it started back in 2011 as a NaNoWriMo project, so I have more than a few people to thank for it finally making its way into the world:

First and foremost, my heartfelt thanks to my agent, Kathleen Rushall. She loved this story from the beginning and has been its constant champion. I can't imagine having a better partner in this crazy business, and I'm grateful every day that she's in my corner.

My brilliant editor, Sara Sargent—thank you for loving this story enough to make it into a book. I've learned so much working with you, and this story is so much better for it. And many thanks to the entire team at Simon Pulse who got behind this book and made it everything that it is.

Along the way, many people read and gave comments on various versions of this book: Amanda Kin, Stephanie Foote, Hope Cook, and Danielle Ellison. Thank you for your keen insights and thoughtful critiques.

Thanks to all the writers that I've come to count as friends, and who have made this journey a little less lonely: Christina June, Olivia Hinebaugh, Helene Dunbar, Kristen Lippert-Martin, Joy Hensley, Jenny Adams Perinovic, Rachael Allen, Vivi Barnes, and the amazing writers who debuted with me as the Fall Fourteeners.

And I have to thank one writer in particular—Jennifer Echols was one of the first YA writers I met back in 2010 when I decided to try writing a book. At my first meeting of Birmingham's chapter of RWA, she went out of her way to make me feel like I belonged there and to encourage me to keep going in the face of rejection. Four years later, she was assigned a new editor—one who had a pirate book on her wish list—and Jennifer remembered that I'd been writing this one. It's because of her generosity that this book found the home it did. She's the kind of writer—and person—I want to be when I grow up, and you should all go read her books right now.

And last, but never least, to my family—my boys who make every day an adventure, and to J, who makes it all worthwhile.